Always You

A Second-Chance Romance

Zoe Dod

Copyright © 2022 Zoe Dod

All rights reserved

The characters and events portrayed in this book are fictitious. Any similarity to real persons, living or dead, is coincidental and not intended by the author.

No part of this book may be reproduced, or stored in a retrieval system, or transmitted in any form or by any means, electronic, mechanical, photocopying, recording, or otherwise, without express written permission of the publisher.

Print ISBN: 9798358303164

Editor: Claire Strombeck

To you the Reader, for picking up this book and taking a chance on a new author. Thank you from the bottom of my heart. I hope you enjoy Star and Damian's story as much as I did writing it.

Zoe xx

Always You

*Giving him up was the hardest
thing she's ever done.*

Chapter One

A gentle breath across her ear roused Star from her sleep. Having gone to bed what felt like only minutes earlier, her body and mind groaned at the interruption, pulling her back into the depths of sleep. A high-pitched giggle replaced the gentle breath. "Come on, Mummy! Wake up, it's time to get up!"

Growling, Star grabbed her self-appointed alarm clock, twisting the giggling, rabbit-suited youngster, until she was lying next to her on the bed. Star tickled her until she begged for mercy, and they both collapsed back onto the pillows, breathing hard, grinning at the ceiling.

"Someone is up early," Star said, trying to catch her breath, sleep long gone – as always, when you have a child.

"Nope, you're late!" came a reply from the doorway. "You've switched your alarm clock off three times. The last time I heard it go off, I sent Skylar in to get you up."

Sitting up, Star grabbed her phone and stared in horror at the screen. It was nearly seven, and she needed to get Skylar ready, dressed, and at Breakfast Club by seven-thirty, before she headed into the office. This morning was not the morning she could risk being late. She hadn't spent half the night updating her project to miss her timeslot with the boss.

"Oh shh— sugar!" Star said, catching herself before she swore. Throwing back the bedcovers, she swung her legs onto the floor, sending her housemate a grateful glance. "Come on, munchkin," she said, "it's time to shift, or we're going to be late."

Star watched as the little girl darted off the bed and headed for the door.

"Don't worry, Mummy," Skylar said, turning back, "Aunty Laura has said she'll take me to school with her this morning. That way, we can still have breakfast together."

Star sat for a moment, taking in a deep breath and sending up her thanks for such a wonderful friend. Today was the start of a big week. It was her time to shine, to prove she deserved this promotion. Having breakfast with her daughter, however, was one of the non-negotiable rules Star had set for herself as a parent. She might be a single-working mum, but mealtimes where possible were her and Skylar's connection time, especially breakfast. There was no excuse for not spending that time together. Working in the city was crazy enough, but Skylar was still Star's number one priority and had been from the moment the little girl had been placed in her arms.

Getting ready in record time, Star flew down the stairs to find Skylar and Laura waiting for her at the breakfast table. Skylar was dressed in her uniform, her hair done neatly. Laura grinned at her flustered friend as Star threw her a grateful glance. Laura and her husband, Tobias, were Star's lifeline. She would never have survived the past six years without her two best friends.

Their love and support had been a constant, and would be the one thing she'd miss when she and Skylar had the money to move into their own place. Now Laura and Tobias were expecting their first child, Star was aware of the urgency to move, and it was why she was hoping this new promotion would be the answer to all their prayers. It was the driving force for her all-nighter, during which she had added the finishing touches to the client presentation.

"Come and sit down before you fall down!" Laura said, offering a plate full of warm, buttery toast. Star dropped herself into the seat next to Skylar, and watched as her daughter finished her cereal. "You were up late," Laura added. "Toby said you were still going at three am."

Star choked on her toast, her heartrate increasing, "What was Toby doing up at three am?" She knew that Toby was travelling up to Manchester that morning to see an important client, and hoped she hadn't disturbed him.

"Cravings," Laura said with a grin, rubbing her stomach. "The one and only time Toby will get out of bed with no complaint. At twenty weeks, you'd have thought he'd be bored by now."

Star smiled, knowing how besotted Toby was with his pregnant wife. Toby had always loved his bed. Even when they were students together, he would often spend half his weekend wrapped in his duvet if he wasn't out partying.

It showed his devotion to Laura and their little bump that he would drag himself out of his pit for her and her cravings at three am.

Star bit into her toast and groaned in delight at the perfect mixture of toast and butter, before adding, "I called it a night at around four. I had some last-minute changes I wanted to make. I'm meeting with Lucas first thing, and then the team later this morning, to run through the presentation, ready for my meeting with Lucas and the Accounts Manager on Wednesday. If he likes it, we can arrange the sit-down with the client."

"I'm sure it will be amazing, knowing you." Laura said, placing her hand on Star's shoulder, before clearing away the breakfast things.

"How are you this morning, munchkin?" Star asked, turning to Skylar. "Did you sleep well?"

"Yes, Mummy," Skylar said, finishing her last mouthful. "Can we do my project tonight?"

Star's eyes opened, racking her brain for information about "a project". "Project?" she squeaked, shooting a look at Laura, with a vague recollection of a project Skylar's teacher had mentioned a couple of weeks ago, when Star had collected Skylar from school.

"Yes, you remember, silly," Skylar giggled, unaware of her mother's rising panic. "We have to build a Tudor House for our Great Fire of London project. All houses have to be in by Friday, so we can set fire to them in the playground and create our own great fire."

Skylar's enthusiasm for the project was palpable. Star couldn't believe she had forgotten all about it. To hide her lapse in memory, she smiled. "Of course we can. I'll get all the bits together after work and we can start when I get home this evening." Star's mind ran ahead, the Project Manager in her taking over. "If we cut out all the pieces tonight, we can glue them together tomorrow and then paint on Thursday night. How does that sound?"

"Perfect, Mummy, you're the best!" Skylar said, throwing her arms around Star's neck.

After giving Skylar an extra tight squeeze back, Star pulled away and rubbed her chin. "Brush your teeth and grab your bags for Aunty Laura. I put your PE kit by the front door last night, so don't forget it," she said before watching Skylar rush off to finish getting ready.

"This is why I always do breakfast!" Star

groaned once her daughter was out of earshot and thinking about the weekend that has just been and gone. Over the past few days, her brain had been full of work. "I need to get myself a 'Things to do – Homework List'," Star said, dropping her head onto the table in front of her with a gentle smack.

"Don't be too hard on yourself," Laura said with a laugh. "You're amazing. That little girl wants for nothing. We'll get the project done."

Star sighed. "You know what the mums are like in Skylar's class. Half of them are stay-at-home mums. The Tudor houses are going to be spectacular. I can't let Skylar down or have her model embarrass her, even if it is only going up in flames! It's the photos on the school's blog!" Star groaned even louder, the more she thought about the task.

"Skylar is six! I know Toby will be into it. He loves building things and making a mess."

They both laughed, as Laura was spot on – this was something Toby would love. They'd have to rein him in if he got involved. If not, Skylar would have built the entire City of London by Friday.

Star placed her head back on the table in

defeat. Laura was a Year 3 teacher at the school, so was more than aware of The Parents of the school. The competition was off the charts, and something that was often talked about around the dinner table. Last year, for Year 3's Romans' battle against the Year 4 Egyptians, one parent had kitted their child out in full Roman armour. The parents had spared no expense, but it had caused quite a ruckus among the other parents and children. Laura had spent most of the afternoon soothing children's broken hearts instead of preparing for war. They'd all wanted the same outfit as their classmate and were unhappy with their cardboard replicas. This year, Laura had promised they would create their outfits in school as part of their art course to prevent any further disruption.

Head still on the table, Star's phone pinged.

"Don't thank me yet, but that should help," Laura said with a wink, before moving away from the table.

Star opened her messages and stared down at the text containing a link to a YouTube clip on "How to Build a Tudor House". Her excitement grew as she clicked through to the link, taking in the description and templates.

Star left her seat and moved across the kitchen, throwing her arms around her best friend.

"What would I do without you? You've saved my skin, yet again," Star said, tears forming in her eyes.

"Don't be silly, you'll make the pregnant woman cry!" Laura said, hugging her back. "Besides, I'm a teacher. Of course I have an arsenal of useful YouTube clips and templates. I couldn't survive day-to-day if I didn't!" Stepping back, she added with a wink, "And don't be too grateful. It's quite a feat, but we should be able to cobble it together by Friday."

Skylar returned to the kitchen, and Star bent down to show Skylar the picture of the Tudor House Laura had just sent her. "What do you think? Can we superstars do this?"

Skylar's grin said it all, and Star's heart melted a little further. Laura stuck her hand in the middle, and they all piled theirs on top. "To the Tudor House!" Laura said before throwing their hands up in the air. The tension of ten minutes ago was gone; the project finally felt possible!

"Come on, munchkin, we need to get to school. Give Mummy a kiss and we'll see her tonight, ready for the big build," Laura said, her hand resting on top of Skylar's head.

"Bye, Mummy, see you tonight. Safe travels," Skylar said, running forwards and throwing her arms around Star. Star scooped her up, knowing this hug would keep her going for the rest of the day.

"You be good today and I'll see you tonight with all our necessary building materials." Star bent down and kissed her daughter's cheek, inhaling deeply before she let her go. Yes, that would get her through today. That, and a large quantity of caffeine.

Star waved Laura and Skylar off before grabbing her bag and heading for the car. With Laura taking Skylar to school, Star had been given the breather she'd needed this morning. If she could get a seat on the train, she could list the building materials they required for the house. Planning was everything. Sometimes she missed things – everyone did – but she just had to catch up. And on the positive side, at least it wasn't Thursday morning; she had three days to get this done. Thank goodness she'd pulled the all-nighter last night. She was not sure what she would have done if she still had that outstanding.

Chapter Two

Star got to the office with twenty minutes to spare. This gave her the time to grab a large, extra-strong coffee from the on-site cafe in the lobby and print out a copy of the report before heading up to Lucas's office. Star took a seat outside Lucas's office, her confidence growing with every minute she waited for him.

Yesterday's team meeting had gone well. The presentation and sample advertisements were all falling into place. The buzz coming off the team was positive and gave Star the confidence that they had nailed the client's brief. Hopefully Lucas and the Account Manager would feel the same way. She was looking forward to the next phase, which was taking their ideas back to the client. If she succeeded, then it would be full steam ahead and her new position would become permanent, along with the pay-rise that went with it. The client had been delighted so far. But this was the last hurdle, and not something she wanted to mess up. There was too much riding on the success of this project – not just her reputation, but her and Skylar's future. If everything went to plan, she and Skylar could finally afford to move out and get their own place.

Checking her email quickly, it did not surprise Star she was still missing Jackson's figures needed to complete the presentation. Her all-night session had been the result of one of her team members not pulling his weight. After yesterday's meeting, she'd pulled Jackson aside and told him the information he had provided had been substandard and only half complete. Star had requested the update by the end of yesterday, but nothing had arrived. Jackson had disappeared and hadn't answered his phone, which meant compiling the data had been down to her.

Star wasn't the only one sick of Jackson Brown's games; other team members were starting to complain about his inability to deliver anything in a timely fashion. Some had even approached her, as she was their manager, but Star was biding her time. Jackson's backstabbing and laziness were a persistent drain, but Star was determined he wouldn't win.

To do that, she must see this project delivered on time. Her meeting this morning with Lucas Hunt, the CEO was important. He'd added it to his calendar as a favour, and had promised to go through the presentation before she presented it to the Account Manager on Wednesday. Their long-standing friendship and his support of Star had been a bone of contention with Jackson, who continued to shout favouritism from the rooftops along with other more derogatory comments. Star knew Jackson would look to discredit her any way he could.

In reality, Lucas Hunt had been a part of Star's life since she was a university student. She had first met Lucas while dating his son, Damian. For over two years, she had been part of the Hunt family. Lucas always said he'd recognised her potential for marketing and advertising from the beginning, so even when things had ended with Damian, Lucas had followed Star's progress.

When Skylar came along, Lucas had arranged for an internship while Star continued with her studies to ensure she could support herself and her child. For that, she would forever be in Lucas's debt. When her life had felt like it was ending, Lucas and Mary, his wife, had thrown her a lifeline. It was not something she would ever forget.

Over the past six years, Lucas had offered immense encouragement, acting as an unofficial mentor. Although he stayed out of her career, leaving that to the correct channels, he offered advice and help from the side lines. Star was lucky; like Lucas, her direct managers had spotted Star's potential, and had put her on the company's fast-track programme.

Star needed to find a way of putting Jackson Brown in his place, but that could wait.

Star looked up as the buzzer at Pam's desk went off. Pam grinned and waved her into Lucas's office. "Good luck, Star, you've got this," she said.

Star grinned and moved towards the door. It was time to shine.

∞ ∞ ∞

Star's meeting with Lucas lasted half an hour. It was intense but highly productive. Lucas had been complimentary on the team's work and Star's position managing them. He'd suggested a few improvements, and Star had made notes, promising to have them updated and ready for Wednesday's big meeting. Thanking Lucas for taking the time to see her, she'd made her escape, high-fiving herself on the way out of the door.

"So?" Pam asked as Star passed her desk.

Star couldn't keep the grin off her face. "It went really well," Star whispered, looking around to make sure no one was listening in. "Lucas loved the presentation and was thrilled with the outcomes from the focus groups. We have some more feedback due in, but we are almost ready to go."

"Congratulations," Pam said, her eyes lighting up.

Pam Fletcher was in her early sixties, and her skin held laughter lines that told the story of her life, yet her hair was still a rich chocolate brown. She'd always laughed that no one would ever see her go grey. Pam was elegant, with a grandmotherly nature that enveloped those she cared about in a blanket of love. Star was lucky enough to be one of those on the receiving end.

Star had known Pam almost as long as she'd known Lucas. Pam was Lucas's PA and right-hand woman. For the past forty years, Pam had helped the company grow into the international conglomerate it was today. There wasn't anything or anyone Pam didn't know. Lucas's wife, Mary, always said with a laugh that Pam was his office wife, even though Pam had been happily married to Gerry for thirty years. Outside the office, their families were close, and it was a bond that had stood the test of time. Lucas Hunt and Mary were godparents to Pam and Gerry's children, while Pam was Damian's godmother.

"Thank you," Star said to Pam. "I better go and let the team know the good news. They'll all be on tender hooks."

Star headed back downstairs and gathered the team together. The new LiveIt sportswear line was cutting-edge, offering an alternative to the current brands on the market. Star was determined the campaign would meet all their client's needs and more.

The team spent the rest of the morning rechecking their research and looking at the various focus groups they had put in place should the client give the go-ahead. Jackson had been decidedly quiet, working diligently alongside his colleagues, taking notes and even contributing. He'd failed, and he clearly realised it. A point to Star.

∞∞∞

When Star arrived home, she took a moment to herself before getting out of the car. Today's presentation had gone better than expected. She'd shown everyone what she was capable of, and that their faith in her was justified. Tonight, she was back in her role of Mummy and, she chuckled to herself, "house builder".

The front door flew open, and Skylar dashed towards the car. Laura stood at the door, her arms folded, a grin on her face. Star could only imagine the conversation Laura had been having with Skylar for the past hour.

Skylar ran up to the car window, scanning the front seat. She shot Star a look of horror before Star shooed her back and stepped out of the car. Skylar moved in for a quick hug, before looking up hopefully at her. Star tapped her lips, as though not sure what she was being asked. Skylar's face dropped, but she said nothing, and stepped back in for another hug, trying to hide her disappointment. Star took Skylar's hand, leading her to the boot of the car. Skylar bounced on the balls of her feet, realisation dawning. The boot was full of supplies. Star knew she had bought more than she needed, but didn't want to make any further trips this week. Even if this house was going up in flames by the end of the week. One evening at the craft shop was more than enough, but a warmth spread through her chest as she watched Skylar rummaging through the bags, her eyes wide with pleasure.

"You are the best mummy in the whole wide world," she whispered before making a grab for one of the bags.

As Star watched the little girl glow with excitement, she thanked the universe that the local store had everything they'd needed for the project. The thought of disappointing Skylar was heart-wrenching. In her brief life, this little girl had already lost so much; Star would give her the world if she could.

Laura joined Star and Skylar at the car, the three of them carrying in their supplies, including the large bunch of flowers Star had bought for Laura. Skylar chatted nonstop, telling Star how she had told her teacher they were building their house this evening. Star groaned, which made Laura chuckle. Now Skylar's teacher would know how disorganised she was.

Once inside, Star took charge of Skylar, who was busy tipping the contents of each bag over the floor. Star picked up the remaining bags from the floor and explained that, before they built the Tudor House, she needed to get out of her work clothes. She set Skylar the task of clearing the kitchen table and laying out all the pieces in groups. As Star walked up the stairs, she sent the template to the house printer before heading to her bedroom.

Star sat on the edge of the bed, her body folding in on itself. Her late night and hectic day were catching up with her; even the many coffees she'd consumed were wearing off. She knew to linger would mean she'd fall asleep, and she couldn't do that to Skylar. After taking a deep breath, Star headed to her en suite and threw cold water on her face. She grabbed her most comfortable clothes and headed back downstairs, where she heard Skylar's chatter.

Laura had rescued the printout, and she and Skylar were already going through the instructions, laying out the template on top of the cardboard. Laura was watching and guiding Skylar as she cut out the pieces, as only a primary school teacher knew how.

Star sat down at the table, picking up a piece of the template. She still found it hard to believe how lucky she was to have such amazing friends who had stood by her all this time. It had been her decision to raise Skylar, and they had never questioned her choice. They had been there with her every step of the way, taking some of the night-time feeds when she was so punch-drunk she struggled to put one foot in front of the other. Loyal friends in every sense of the word.

"All done!" Star said as she finished the last cut of the template.

"Yay, Mummy, you're amazing," Skylar said, jumping off her chair and throwing her arms around Star's neck.

"Hey, what about me?" Laura said, holding up her cut-out for Skylar to see.

"You're super amazing, too, Aunty Laura," Skylar answered, switching her super hug to Laura, who squeezed her back hard.

Star looked at the clock. It was getting close to Skylar's bedtime, and she needed some time to regroup. "Right, I'll clean everything up," she said, turning to her daughter. "You, munchkin, need to get into your PJs …"

"Wash my face and clean my teeth!" Skylar chanted. She gave Laura one last squeeze before heading for the stairs.

Star pulled herself up and started stacking the cut cardboard before returning all the extra bits into the bags. Laura, in the meantime, returned with a recycle sack for the waste cardboard.

"You know, you could always see if your mum can have Skylar for the weekend," Laura said, scrutinising her friend. "You and I could hit the town before this baby bump gets too big? Let our hair down? I don't remember the last time you went out."

"Last week, remember. I went to the pub," Star said, giving her friend a cocky smile.

"That doesn't count. That was a client meeting," Laura said, crossing her arms. "I'm talking about going *out*. Where you are choosing to socialise. A time when you may meet someone."

Star fixed Laura with a challenging stare. "I don't have time to meet anyone, and I'm happy with the way my life is. I have you guys – what more can a girl want." Laura's look said it all, so Star added, "I know you worry, but I can't be bothered with adding more complexity to my life."

"Okay, but what about your needs, Star? You're a twenty-eight-year-old, beautiful woman who's in her prime. You need physical contact. I don't know how you do it. You haven't been with anyone since Damian as far as I'm aware. Don't you miss it?"

Star let out a laugh. "When would I have the time? I need this promotion if I'm ever to get out of your and Toby's hair. Once we have our own place, then I can 'try' finding a man. But I'm happy – really, I am. Skylar is everything I need."

"Toby and I love having you and Skylar here. You're family. The house wouldn't be the same without you. Skylar is going to be our little one's big sister, so you can't leave. We don't want you to move out. You know that!"

Star rested her hand on her friend's growing bump. "You, Toby, and the baby will want all the space you can. You won't want us underfoot."

Laura's mouth slackened. "Says who? This is a six-bedroom house, paid for outright by Toby's trust fund. We've lived together since our second year at university, and you know I always say it, but there wouldn't be a Toby and me if it weren't for you! Skylar joined our family. I'm looking forward to her helping me, the way we helped you when she was little. She's going to be an amazing big sister and, come on, admit it, there is more than enough room." Laura giggled. "Think of how many bodies we had lying around during our student heyday!"

They both looked around them and shuddered at the memory. Every weekend, bodies had littered the floor, students sleeping where they'd dropped after a night of partying and drinking.

"Toby and I have discussed this. We don't want you to move out because you feel you have to. We love having you here. Skylar is part of our lives, too. We love her; we love you."

Star rubbed at her eyes, swallowing hard at the lump that had formed in her throat. "Love you both, too," she said, pulling Laura into a bear hug.

Laura pulled back, resting her hand on Star's cheek. "You need to live, hon. This is not healthy. Life can't only be about work and Skylar. Star Roberts is a person with needs. Please talk to your mum – think of it as a favour to me." She stepped back, resting her hand on her stomach. "Think about me, too. This is going to be the last celebration I can partake in for the foreseeable future. Once I start to waddle, we won't be going very far. Not to mention after the baby arrives." She gave Star a pointed stare. "I've seen first-hand what that does to someone's social life."

Giving her friend a half-smile, Star nodded in agreement, then moved away to continue tidying the remaining pieces away. She knew Laura meant well, but the thought of adding another complication to her life filled her with horror. Looking up, Star caught Laura's glare. "Okay, I'll ask," she said, before the yell of "Ready" took her attention to upstairs.

Star motioned to the stairs as if proving her point.

"I'll get the hot chocolates ready for your return," Laura said.

"Marshmallows are in the cupboard. I bought a new packet," Star said over her shoulder as she headed up the stairs to Skylar.

Star dropped onto the sofa opposite her friend, and leant her head against its back, before closing her eyes. Taking a deep breath, the tension of the day slowly ebbed away. Opening her eyes, she grinned at Laura and grabbed a steaming cup of hot chocolate from the table, raising a toast towards the neatly piled cardboard. "To the Tudor House and The Great Fire of London Project!" she said, before tipping her cup towards Laura and adding, "and an amazing friend who helps me out whenever I need her."

Laura added her mug to the salute, clinking it against Star's before taking a sip and adding, "To reinforced cardboard! A parents' nightmare, a teacher's secret weapon!" Both women spluttered, before Laura continued, "And to my best friend, who needs to realise she's not in this alone!"

Star remained silent for a moment, staring at her hot chocolate. "I'll speak to Mum and Dad in the morning. Maybe they can take Skylar for a weekend. It would be nice to have a night out."

"Mine, or Toby's parents are always happy to babysit," Laura said. "They love Skylar. Plus, they are both desperate to come down and help plan out the nursery."

Star's belly knotted. Her own parents' lack of support and love for Skylar was renowned. Laura and Toby's parents had spent more time with Skylar than her own, which was not surprising, as Toby's father had been the one to arrange Skylar's adoption. Star had spent a lot of time with Ian Grant QC, as she navigated her way through the legal process of becoming a new parent.

"I'm sure my parents would be happy to

babysit," Star said unconvincingly. She had never fathomed how her mother could turn her back on her only grandchild, when Skylar was the only part of her dead daughter left.

"Don't worry, we'll sort something out," Laura said, having noticed her friend's shoulders dropping. "This is not what Lily wanted for you. She would not have wanted you to put your life on hold."

"Maybe not, but it wasn't what Lily wanted for herself either," Star said, trying hard not to snap at Laura. "Lily would love to be here raising her daughter. Being her mother. Loving her." She squeezed her eyes shut as memories of the short time her sister had had with Skylar flooded her brain. Even now, six years on, the pain was almost overwhelming.

"That is not what I'm saying," Laura said carefully. "You can have a life, child, and career. Even if you don't think you can. You just need to let us help."

Star wrapped her arms around herself, a deep chill settling in her bones. It always did when she thought about her sister. "She entrusted me, Laura." Star whispered. "They only had three weeks together. So I'll go to school plays, build cardboard houses, and be here for Skylar, in every way my sister can't. I'll be everything our own mum wasn't to Lily and me. Everything Lily would have been, because instead of Skylar having her mum, that beautiful little girl got me!"

Laura had sat forwards. "I know, hon, and life sucks! But you are not a poor substitute for your sister," she said, shaking her head. "You are an amazing mum and Skylar adores you." Laura's voice caught as the conversation headed down a path they usually tried to avoid. "That little girl loves you and wants for nothing. Stop being hard on yourself. No one is perfect." Before Star could interrupt, Laura raised her hand. "I'm not perfect. No one is. I'm about to be a mum, but it won't stop me. I will make mistakes, but I'll learn and I will love. That's one thing you've shown me – love gets you through even the darkest of times. Love surrounds Skylar, and Lily would be so proud of you."

Star rubbed her chest as the pressure built.

Laura shrugged and gave Star a watery smile. "Watching you try to live up to the ghost of your sister is more than I can take in my condition."

Star moved next to her friend, placing her arms around her.

"Laura's right," a voice said from the doorway.

Star jumped. She'd been unaware of Toby's arrival or that he had heard their discussion. Toby crossed the room, dropping a kiss on his wife's lips, before wiping her tears away with the pad of his thumb.

"Stop doubting yourself," he said, his attention returning to Star. "You've come home after a long night and a full day and started building a school project. How many parents do that!" Star's eyes widened. When had Skylar spoken to Toby? He smiled, as if reading her mind. "My little squidge told me while I was waiting at the station this morning. You, my friend, are her hero – not just her mum. She loves you with every ounce of her being. I just wish you'd stop comparing yourself to a ghost." Toby leant down, pulling Star into a hug, and whispered in her ear, "By the way, four am finishes are not healthy!"

Star felt her body relax once more and returned his hug. "I'm a tired, emotional wreck! But the presentation is done, which allowed me time to play with cardboard! I'm just waiting on one of the team members to deliver their part."

"I take it you mean Jackson. Is he still being an asshole?" Toby had perched himself on the sofa arm.

"He's made it quite clear he wants me to fail. But I'm not giving him the satisfaction. Today in our meeting he went very quiet after he realised his non-delivery yesterday hadn't stopped me."

Laura huffed. "You should speak to Lucas about him. He shouldn't get away with it."

"True. But if I go running to Lucas, then everything Jackson's been saying will appear to be true in the eyes of the team. I can deal with him, and I will. His review is coming up. What can he do? He's one man, and the rest of the team is coming round and seeing him for who he is. And I'm looking forward to my meeting on Wednesday with Lucas and the Account Manager. I think they'll be happy with what we've produced."

"We're proud of you," Laura said, patting her arm. "But as your best friend and housemate, I'm going to tell you that, after last night, you need a warm bath followed by bed, or you'll be falling asleep on Lucas Hunt's desk ..." Horror crossed Laura's face before she burst into giggles. "Oh god, that didn't sound right."

Laughing, Star stood up and headed for the door. "Thank you, Mr and Mrs Grant, for the hot chocolate and the pep-talk – it's just what I needed. I'm going to take your advice and call it a night. Thank you. Love you both."

Chapter Three

The following morning, Star sent a text message to her mother asking if she and her father could have Skylar for the weekend. The screen flashed, notifying her they had read the message, but there was no reply. Star stared at her phone, imagining the conversation her mother would be having with her father. "Who does she think she is?" ... "We're far too busy!" ... "I told her that child was her responsibility!" Star hoped she was wrong, but this argument had been on repeat for the past six years. Her mother's lack of interest no longer shocked Star. From day one, she had made her thoughts clear. Star was not sure why Laura thought that would have changed or her mother had suddenly grown maternal feelings.

Daphne Roberts could never have been mistaken for a nurturing mother. Image was everything to their mother, and Star and Lily had been perfect little dolls for her mother to parade around. But, what they'd received in material possessions, they'd lacked in a mother's love and tenderness. Luckily, Lily and Star always had each other to rely on, supporting each other in everything they did. As Star got older, she'd become convinced her mother had only had children to keep their father around.

James Sinclair had been married to a socialite and Daphne had been his "bit-on-the-side". He had been absent for much of Lily and Star's youth, with his actual family taking priority over his secret one. James had always made sure Daphne and his girls were well provided for, but Daphne had known the score. It meant that when James appeared, Daphne put him and his wishes above their children's, often leaving Lily and Star alone or with neighbours while they went gallivanting on romantic adventures. James had been Daphne's priority, something Star had come to terms with many years earlier. Her mother's rejection no longer burned the way it had when she was little. She had soon learned to hide her emotions when she'd been sitting alone or with the teacher as the other children's parents fussed over their children's work at school events. It was why Lily and Star had been so close. To their mother, Lily and Star had been an inconvenience; they'd cramped her style.

By the time Star reached the office, there was still no reply, so Star put her phone away and threw herself into the day ahead.

Star unpacked her bag, connected her laptop, and started checking her emails. As with most mornings, she was one of the first people in. Most staff headed to the on-site cafe in the lobby before coming up. To Star, these quiet moments were precious, allowing her to get through anything that had come in early, or needed her urgent attention before she got caught up in real-time issues. It did not surprise Star that she was still missing Jackson's contribution to the presentation, not that it mattered anymore. Star opened her folder on Jackson and made one more note against him. His annual review was going to be interesting.

The team arrived a short time later, and it was lunchtime before Star realised. Getting up, she motioned to her team that she was stepping out. The weather was warm for the end of March, and she wanted to get some air to blow away the cobwebs of the past couple of days.

Star burst out of the office onto the busy lunchtime street. Local office workers charged past on a mission. Stepping out of the rush, Star pulled her ringing phone out of her pocket, letting out a low groan as she identified the incoming caller.

"Hi, Mum," Star answered, trying to sound enthusiastic.

"Star, where are you? It's very noisy!" Her mum's impatient tone set the scene for what Star knew was going to be a difficult conversation

"I'm on my lunch break. Hold on." Star paused as she stepped into the nearby park, away from the traffic and hordes of people. Making her way over to an empty bench, she said, "Is that better?"

"I suppose so."

Star rolled her eyes and counted to ten before adding, "How's Dad?"

"You're father's fine. We got your text message."

"Okay …" Star decided against mentioning

she knew that.

"The answer is no," came her mother's curt reply. "We're going on a cruise in two weeks and will be really busy getting ready. You know how stressed your father gets, so I can't take on any more."

"Not even one night? You and Dad haven't seen Skylar in two months."

"I'm aware of how long it's been, but your father and I are not convenient babysitters for you to put upon," her mother replied.

"Convenient babysitters? Mum, I never ask you or Dad to have Skylar."

"I don't have to explain myself to you, young lady. The answer is no, and I won't be made to feel guilty about saying no."

Star gritted her teeth and once again found herself counting to ten. "Fine, I just thought you'd like to spend some time with your granddaughter, but I understand if you're both too busy. Anyway, Mum, I've got to go. I need to get some lunch before the end of my break." She needed to end the call as soon as possible.

"Star, before you go, remember it's Aunty Clara's birthday next week. Make sure you send her a nice bunch of flowers and a card." With that, the call ended as abruptly as it had begun, leaving Star staring at her phone.

Her appetite suddenly gone, Star headed back to the office, unsure as to why she'd even let Laura convince her to ask her mother. Nothing had changed; it had been the same six years ago when she'd first brought Skylar home from the hospital. Her mother and father had both made it clear that Skylar was Star's responsibility and hers alone. They'd felt at twenty-one she was too young to take on her sister's illegitimate child. Her mother had had the nerve to call Toby and Laura "enablers" when Toby had stepped in and said he was happy for Star and Skylar to remain living with them. Daphne Roberts thought it totally inappropriate that Star had taken a baby back to a student house, although she'd refused to let Star move back home. She'd even tried raising it with social services, but her friends had stopped partying at the house, tidied up their act, and offered Star support, so nothing further had come from it. Everyone had pulled together for their newest member, and Skylar had been surrounded by a loving and supportive network from the day she'd come home. A network which had not been built from blood, but from love, which Star had learned was more important. In turn, Star had taken a year-long sabbatical from university, and had cleaned and cooked for the house while looking after Skylar.

Walking back into the office, Star heard her name being called.

"Star, there you are!" Star came face to face with Lucas Hunt. "Are you all right? You look harassed."

Star couldn't help but laugh. Lucas always was straight-talking. Waving her phone, she said, "Yes, just my mother."

"Say no more," he said, patting her shoulder in solidarity. "I just wanted to check how the changes we discussed are coming along? You put forward a very convincing plan, young lady."

"They're fine – everything will be ready for tomorrow morning. Hopefully, once he sees the presentation, we can arrange for the Account Manager to get the client in early next week. I know they're desperate to start this phase of marketing as soon as possible to catch the new season."

Lucas nodded, then grimaced as he rubbed his chest, and it was Star's turn to frown. "Are you okay, Lucas?"

"Just some indigestion." He smiled, waving off her concern. "I ate a pie from the restaurant and obviously it was too stodgy for my old body," he said. "Don't you worry about me, I'll see you in the morning."

Lucas continued to the door and exited just as his driver pulled up outside. Star turned and carried on towards the lift, only to bump straight into Jackson.

"That looked all very cosy, chatting to 'Lucas'," Jackson said, making it known he'd heard Star had used Lucas Hunt's first name in her concern for him.

Star fumed at her slip. She knew yesterday's reprieve had obviously been too good to be true. The smirk on his face said everything. Soon he'd accuse her of sleeping her way to the top. Arriving back at their desks, she heard Jackson make a crack to some of the team about her "getting cosy with the boss". Most chose to ignore it, but some sniggered along with him. Star was getting sick of his games and his constant need to undermine her position. Walking up to his desk, Star hissed, "Instead of worrying so much about me, how about working on the figures you still need to give me for the presentation. Everyone else has pulled their weight, apart from you. I expect them on my desk by the end of the day." Star didn't wait for a reply. Between her mother and Jackson, today was turning into a nightmare.

Grabbing her phone, she sent a quick email to Laura, letting her know her mother was a no-go on the babysitting front, but promising she'd arrange a babysitter for an evening out. Star didn't want to put on Laura or Toby's parents any more than her friends; they had already done so much. She knew that Laura would be vocal in her thoughts on Daphne's lack of grandmotherly support, but Laura also knew she wouldn't be able to say too much as she wouldn't want to risk Skylar overhearing.

Putting aside her personal life, Star threw herself back into the project. She needed to ensure everything was done early, as she still had a Tudor House to construct today. She'd made a promise, and those promises were unbreakable, whatever else was going on in her life.

∞∞∞

The next morning, Star had an earlier start than usual. Skylar had been up with the sun to check on her Tudor House. The night before, Star, Laura, and Skylar had spent the evening gluing the structure together. Star had lost count of the number of times Skylar had replayed the YouTube video on her iPad; she almost knew the script word for word. By the time they'd called it a night, Star had to admit they had produced a fantastic project. Toby had had his ear chewed off for twenty minutes and had been shown every little detail of the house when he'd arrived home.

This morning when Star emerged from her bedroom, she'd found Skylar downstairs, evaluating the structure.

"What are you doing?" Star asked.

"I'm deciding on the paint," Skylar said without taking her eyes off the house. "I looked up the colours in my book, and I need black paint for the wood and window frames, and white for the walls, and we need a brown, red colour for the roof. Plus, it needs to look like tiles. I'm not sure how to do that."

Toby entered the kitchen behind Star and said, "Well I have just the thing, squidge."

Skylar's attention went straight from the

house to her uncle Toby. "What?" she asked.

"Skylar!" Star warned.

"Sorry, Uncle Toby, what is your idea? Please," Skylar said with wide eyes, and Toby laughed.

"Well, I was thinking, we have some coloured paper left over from your craft box. We could cut those up into tiles and then stick them on the roof. We have some brown paper and some red and orange. We could mix them up and see what it looks like."

"Oh yes, that's brilliant," Skylar said, hugging him.

"Okay, now that's sorted, go and get yourself ready for school, young lady, or we're going to be late," Star said, sending Toby a grateful glance. "Thank you," she said as Skylar left the room.

"No problem! I'll be home early tonight and I'm happy to take on roof duty, if it's still outstanding. I can't have you ladies having all the fun." With a cheeky wink, Toby grabbed his bag and headed out the front door.

Alone, Star stared at the structure that was fast becoming a full-on architectural project, a lump forming deep in her chest at the love directed at her daughter by her friends.

It was time to get ready, take Skylar to breakfast club, and then meet Lucas and the Account Manager, to go through the final presentation. Breakfast this morning was going to have to be at school, but Star knew she'd spent a lot of time with Skylar this week, so didn't feel quite so bad that they wouldn't be sitting down together for once. Today was *the* day.

∞∞∞

Star knew as soon as they pulled up at the school gates that something was wrong. Parents were everywhere, looking flustered and some even angry. Walking towards the entrance, Star was greeted by more parents and a flustered-looking Head Teacher.

"I'm sorry, there is nothing I can do. The school is flooded – it's not safe for the children and therefore we have to close for the day. I'm sorry for any inconvenience," Mrs Morris said.

Star glanced at her watch. She knew she was already pushing it to make her eight-thirty meeting with Lucas. Now she'd be lucky if she made it at all.

Skylar had run off to play with some of the other children she knew from breakfast club, oblivious to the turmoil Star was now facing.

"Ms Roberts, a quick word?" Mrs Morris asked, inching her way towards Star and away from the other parents. "Ms Roberts, Mrs Grant wanted me to tell you she'll be home soon. Due to her condition," Mrs Morris whispered, "she's not permitted to stay in school to assist with the clean-up. She said to tell you she'd be home within the hour and is happy to have Skylar for the day."

Star thanked Mrs Morris, who had obviously enjoyed sharing her cloak-and-dagger message, and collected Skylar from the climbing frame. Skylar was not disappointed to have a day off school, and asked if they could continue with her house project. Star only half-listened to Skylar's busy chatter as she fired off a quick message to Lucas and Pam explaining the situation, promising that she'd be in as soon as possible. It was seven-thirty, so if Laura was going to be home in an hour, she'd hopefully be able to make the office by nine-thirty at the latest. In the meantime, she and Skylar would be able to have the breakfast they had missed this morning.

When Star arrived home, she checked her phone, not surprised to see she hadn't received a reply. It was still early, and although Pam usually made it into the office for eight am, it wasn't unusual for her to get caught up with other issues first. The joy of being the Boss Man's PA, Pam always said.

To kill time and distract herself from the disaster of the morning, Star threw herself into breakfast with Skylar. Her daughter had requested fluffy pancakes, and Star had been only too happy to oblige. At eight-thirty, when the front door finally clicked, Star was a bundle of nerves.

∞∞∞

The train journey into the office was uneventful. It was half-empty, which allowed Star to get a seat and review the presentation for the last time. She checked her phone again and was surprised that there was still no call from Pam or even a message from Lucas. She hoped Lucas wasn't unhappy with this morning's events, he was usually pretty understanding when it came to all things Skylar and it was rare that Star's personal life ever interfered with her work life. But today was important, and this was not the professional image Star wanted to portray.

By the time she arrived at the office, she barely registered anyone or anything, heading straight to her desk and then to Lucas's office. She failed to notice the unusual quietness, and didn't stop to speak to any of the team who were speaking in hushed tones. Her focus was on apologising and starting her meeting as soon as possible.

Pam was not at her desk when Star arrived, although that was not unusual. The woman was a one-person machine when it came to the office. Lucas Hunt's door was closed, but she could hear voices inside. Star took a seat outside and waited. It was not long before the voices quietened and Lucas's door opened. One of the Board Members exited, his focus elsewhere as he failed to even acknowledge her presence. She wasn't the only one having a bad morning, Star thought. Standing up, Star headed towards the door and knocked before entering the room. Stepping into the room, Star's body froze, her breath faltering.

"Come in Ms Roberts and shut the door," came a voice Star hadn't heard in seven years.

∞∞∞

Star froze, adrenaline racing through her system. A tightness gripped her chest as the past seven years melted away.

Cold features stared across the desk at her. "You're late!" Damian's icy tone was a clear sign of his displeasure. "I hope you don't usually keep my father waiting this long."

"Yes, I'm sorry," Star felt her cheeks grow hot under the scrutiny. What was Damian doing here and where was Lucas? Damian had not set foot in the London office for over two years and hadn't been a permanent fixture for seven. In recent years when he had visited, Star had made herself scarce, visiting clients or taking holiday.

Concern had begun pooling deep in her stomach. "I'm sorry, there was a family emergency. I left—"

Damian waved his hand, dismissing Star's explanation, and gestured to the seat in front of him. Star sat, heart pounding, her laptop and presentation documents clutched tight like a shield in front of her.

"Where is Mr Hunt? Mr Hayes?" Star asked, her voice sounding strange, even to herself.

"I sent Mr Hayes back to his office. He had another account meeting to attend, and he didn't have time to sit around waiting for you. My father is in hospital," Damian stated, his focus now on his father's diary.

"Oh my god, is everything—" Star stopped as Damian's gaze clashed with hers. She suddenly saw the exhaustion in his eyes.

"He's been taken in for some tests," Damian said. "So, as you've probably gathered, my father is indisposed. Your meeting is now with me. Shall we begin?"

Caught once again in his dark stare, Star's breath hitched, the fine hairs on her arms and neck rising. Her confusion and discomfort were evident, yet Damian appeared calm and unaffected after all this time. Shaking herself, Star decided that if he could be professional, then so could she. She placed the client presentation on the desk in front of him, and returned to her seat, watching as he flipped through the folder.

Damian's once-boyish features were no more. His deep-set eyes had a new depth, a hardness that hadn't been there before. His full lips now held themselves in a grim line, outlined by the twelve o'clock shadow darkening his jaw. At his temples, flecks of grey had appeared against his almost black hair, not aging him, but adding distinction and maturity. His shoulders were broader than before, as if he'd spent many hours in the gym, and he projected an undeniable air of confidence. Damian Hunt was still the most attractive man Star had ever seen, but he was no longer the quick-to-laugh, easy-to-smile man she'd loved. The man in front of her today was a cold, hard stranger.

"If you've finished staring, maybe you could set up your presentation and we can begin this meeting!"

A dark flush spread over Star's cheeks. She dipped her chin, wishing the ground would swallow her up. Five years of professionalism, gone within two minutes of being in this man's presence.

Gripping her laptop, Star connected it to the electronic whiteboard. A sense of warmth flooded her body as Damian moved from his desk to the sofa behind her. The familiar scent of bergamot and cypress invaded her senses, transporting her back to a time she'd long ago buried. Shaking her head to clear her thoughts, she took a deep breath and reminded herself that she was proud of herself and the presentation her team had produced. She had every right to be here, despite what Jackson Brown might think. She'd graduated top of her class against all the odds. Lucas Hunt had hired her, because he thought she had potential. It was time to reconstruct her professional mask and face her nemesis, showing him she was no longer the woman he'd left behind, but his equal in the work place.

∞∞∞

Over two hours later, Damian had gone through the presentation with a fine-toothed comb, questioning her on every little detail.

Star stifled a sigh as a loud knock interrupted Damian's line of questioning. Pam entered the room. "Sorry, Damian," she said, "I've set up your appointment with the Board for midday. I thought you might want some time to go through everything before then." As Damian turned his back, Pam shot Star an apologetic look

Damian closed the presentation, which now contained all his scribbled notes and pointers, before handing it back to Star. "Make the changes we've discussed and we'll meet again in the morning at ten. Try not to be late." With that, Star was dismissed.

"I take it you didn't get my text message," Pam said.

As if on cue, Star's phone pinged in her pocket. Taking it out, she saw the message Pam had sent and remembered she had put it on a timed "Do Not Disturb" while she was on the train, as she'd known she'd soon be in her meeting with Lucas.

Groaning, Star shook her head. The shock and panic she had felt after walking into Lucas's office and finding Damian standing there was coming home to roost. If only she'd waited for Pam to return to her desk rather than barrelling into the room without thinking. A lesson learned for the future.

In Star's defence, she did feel the meeting had gone well. Damian had been complimentary about most of the proposals they were putting forward, especially after seeing the initial focus group feedback. She'd answered all of his questions, even with her head feeling like it had been stuffed full of cotton wool. The suggestions he had made were relevant and thought-provoking. At one point, it had felt like they were back at university again, sharing and debating ideas. The pain Star had felt as those memories had risen to the surface was real. She thought she'd buried her feelings for Damian long ago, along with her sister. Now they were back and rearing their ugly head. This was not something that could happen; she had her promotion and Skylar to think about. Her history with Damian could not stand in the way. She would have to show him like she'd shown everyone else she was more than capable.

Heading back to her desk, Star found herself surrounded by members of the team. She fielded as many questions as she could, letting the team know that the meeting had been a success, although not with the Account Manager as she'd hoped. The team were on board to make the necessary changes, although it was impossible to ignore Jackson smirking in the corner. A sense of doom sat heavily on her stomach, well aware her lateness had been the reason the Account Manager had not been present and the project wasn't moving forwards today. Shaking herself off, she plastered a smile on her face, hiding from the world the chaos raging inside her head and body. She could do this.

Chapter Four

An excited squeal greeted Star when she arrived home. "Mummy!" Arms circled her waist, and a head mashed into her stomach. The stress of the day and Damian's reappearance were temporarily pushed to one side while Star enjoyed the love and comfort of her daughter. For Star, everything was once again all right in the world.

Bending down, she returned Skylar's hug, before conspiratorially handing her a large box of chocolates and whispering in her ear, "These are for Aunty Laura, as a thank you for looking after you today."

Excited to be given the task at hand, Skylar ran back into the kitchen towards Laura, who was taking the latest batch of cookies out of the oven.

Following the delicious aroma, Star joined her daughter and best friend in the kitchen, snatching one of the cookies already cooling on the rack.

"Mummy, you'll ruin your dinner!" Skylar said, before turning back to Laura and proudly handing over the box of chocolates. "Look what we've got you. Mummy said they're a thank you for having me."

"Thank you, Skylar, that's very kind of you," Laura said as she bent down and hugged the little girl. "We've had lots of fun today, haven't we, squidge? Why don't you show Mummy the house while I put these on the cooling rack. You've done such a great job of painting it."

Chest puffed out at all the praise, Skylar led Star into the conservatory where the Tudor House was drying near the open window. The house had been painted white with black beams. Star was amazed at how neat everything was.

Taking Star's hand, Skylar pulled her closer. "Aunty Laura showed me how to stay inside the lines. We did the white first, and then outlined the black beams with a black sharpie so

I knew where to paint."

"Well, I think it looks amazing. You and Aunty Laura have done a great job."

"Aunty Laura said if we put it by the window, then it will be dry in time for Uncle Toby to help me with the roof when he gets home."

"You'll have to see how tired Uncle Toby is when he gets in," Star said, thinking her friends had already done more than enough for Skylar's project and bracing herself to find the energy to complete the roof herself if she needed to.

"Oh no, Mummy, Uncle Toby already called Aunty Laura and spoke to me. He told me he's been looking forward to it all day."

"Well, you go and get washed up ready for dinner. I'll help Aunty Laura, and then we can get you ready for bed and you can sit and work with Uncle Toby when he gets in."

Skylar dashed back through the kitchen and headed up stairs.

Star leant against the doorframe, watching Laura clear the baking dishes. "Thank you. You saved my bacon this morning."

"No problem, hon, it's what friends do. How did it go, by the way?" Laura asked.

"The meeting was interesting." Star paused, before adding, "Damian's back."

Laura dropped the baking tray into the sink with a clang and spun to face Star. "What do you mean Damian's back? You've been in the house twenty minutes and this is the first time I'm hearing about it. What about a text message? Wasn't your meeting this morning?"

Star dropped down onto one of the kitchen chairs, her head hung low. "It's taken me all day to really accept this morning happened."

"Oh, honey, talk to me. Why is he back? It's been what - seven years?" Laura said moving towards Star.

Before Star could reply, Skylar entered the room, her hands and face now clean.

Shooting Laura a look, Star got up and headed to the fridge, pulling out the salad and quiche she'd made the day before. Understanding Damian was not someone Star would want to discuss in front of her daughter, Laura changed the subject, but sent Star a look that told her this conversation was far from over. Star deflected, pulling Skylar back into discussing her day, rather than letting her mind drift to earlier events.

Toby walked in as they finished dinner, greeting his wife with a PG-rated kiss. Skylar never batted an eyelid when they showed their love for each other; it was part of everyday life. Star smiled to herself – at least her daughter knew what a loving relationship should look like.

A lump formed in her throat as she watched her friends. Star had had that kind of love, but had given it up for a different kind of love. A love she would not change for the world, one that sat next to her, chatting nonstop about everything that had gone on today.

"Mummy, you're not listening!" Skylar looked at her mum, brow furrowed.

"Sorry, honey, I was day-dreaming. What did you say, munchkin?" she said.

Instead of letting Skylar repeat her question, Laura stepped in, suggesting Skylar go and get into her pyjamas while Uncle Toby ate his dinner. Not needing any further encouragement, Skylar sprinted for the stairs.

Before Star could say anything, Laura spoke: "Damian Hunt is back." It was Toby's turn to drop his knife, while choking on a mouthful of salad.

"A warning next time, please," he said, shooting his wife a look. "Damian's what? When? How?"

Star shrugged. "He was in Lucas's office this morning. I walked in totally unaware I was no longer meeting Lucas, only to come face to face with Damian."

"What do you mean Lucas wasn't there and Damian was. Lucas wouldn't do that to you. He knows your history," Toby said.

A heavy weight sat in Star's stomach as she thought more about Lucas. Toby and Laura were right: he wouldn't have just dropped this on her; he'd been as excited about presenting to the Account Manager as she was. Whatever was going on must be serious for Damian to have come all the way from the US to be here. Her thoughts returned to the day before, when Lucas had clutched his chest. Star had been so shocked with the turn of events, she hadn't had time earlier to analyse the situation. Not that she would have called Lucas with Damian around. However close they were, Lucas was still her boss, and if she needed to know something, he would have contacted her.

"Apparently Lucas is in hospital," Star said, before recounting her meeting with Damian to her friends. She just hoped Damian's visit was a fleeting one and that he would return to the US so she could put her heart back in her chest.

Before Tobias and Laura could question her further, Skylar reappeared in her PJs, ready to begin the final part of their three-day project. Who would have thought this week would be as eventful as it had been. First an emergency project, a presentation that could kickstart her career, and now Damian. Next week couldn't be as crazy as this one. Surely.

∞∞∞

Star awoke hot and trembling, desire pulsing through her body. Groaning loudly into her pillow, Star was unsure how she was going to face Damian today. Just the thought of where her mind had taken her overnight caused a rush of heat to her cheeks. Damn her seven years of celibacy, and damn Damian. Not once in that time had she felt so empty, so raw. Her stomach contracted, and another rush of heat flooded her body. Star and Damian's sex life had been passionate and loving. But last night, it hadn't been memories of their time together that had heated her blood; instead her imagination had taken her on a whole new adventure, one starring the new, more mature Damian. It was those thoughts, the crystal-clear images her imagination had conjured up, that had her body hot and wanting.

Star switched the shower setting to cold before stepping in. She needed to get her head, and heart under control, or the next couple of hours would be torture.

Before going to bed the night before, Star had sent a message to Lucas, wishing him a speedy recovery and sending him her and Skylar's best wishes. She'd not heard back, but hadn't expected to, knowing Mary she'd probably confiscated his phone to ensure he rested.

The school was officially open again, so, after breakfast, Star and Skylar took one final look at the Tudor house, which Star had to admit was pretty amazing. The journey included a running commentary from Skylar on the class preparation for tomorrow's Great Fire of London re-enactment. Star thanked Skylar silently for her much-needed distraction, although she failed to shift the heavy weight that had settled in her stomach every time she thought about work.

As soon as they arrived at the school gates, Skylar took off, excited to be back with her friends. Star headed to the station earlier than usual, trying to look on the positive side. School was open, so she could concentrate on her job and not worry about Skylar until this evening. She wasn't having to rely on her friends as emergency babysitters, off-loading her daughter in order for her to go to work. Instead, she just had to get through this morning, and face Damian again with last night's erotic nightmares still fresh in her mind.

∞∞∞

Star arrived at the office early, putting out a plate of Skylar and Laura's cookies for the team. They were always appreciative of Star and Skylar's baking and the plate would no doubt be empty before mid-morning. Star had grown up cooking with Lily, so it had felt natural to continue that tradition with her daughter. At least once a week, they'd bake and Star would share the goodies with the team – a perfect way to keep her figure and build a good relationship with her colleagues.

As expected, the cookies soon disappeared. But the team chatter did little to settle Star's nerves. Pulling the team into a meeting room, Star set about organising the next focus groups, and working through the team's list of outstanding jobs. Jackson was late as usual, but Star decided she needed to cut him out of their deadlines. The team was functioning well without him and his attitude. She didn't need the hassle of relying on him, and today, especially, she didn't need his attitude on top of everything else. She'd decided last night to deal with Jackson when Lucas returned. His lack of respect was beginning to grate on her nerves and Star had the impression that the rest of the team was getting as annoyed with him as she was.

Once the team's next steps list was agreed, Star added it to the client presentation and headed up to Damian's office. It was just before ten; she was determined not to be late. The team meeting had done its job, acting as a distraction to the turmoil that raged inside her, but a sick heaviness had begun to settle in her stomach the closer she got to the door. Lucky for her, telepathy wasn't one of Damian's many skills, so he wouldn't be aware of her erotic dreams. The thought made her cheeks flush; only she was privy to that knowledge.

Pam looked up from her desk as Star approached. "Morning, Star, he won't be long. He had an emergency meeting this morning."

Star smiled and took a deep breath. "Skylar made some cookies for you and drew you another picture," she said, placing the container of cookies and a drawing of Pam's dog on her desk.

Pam picked up the picture and studied it lovingly. "Send that gorgeous girl a big hug from me. She's caught Jessie's likeness beautifully," she said, before grabbing some blu-tac and sticking the picture to her filing cabinet for everyone to see. Pam nodded at the cookies. "Perfect to go with my cup of tea."

Pam was a soft touch, never forgetting Skylar's birthday. Pam had adult children, but, as she said, they were high flyers, and children were low on their priority list. Pam decided she would "borrow" Skylar and, whenever she felt grandmotherly urges, she'd treat Skylar as her own. The pair had developed quite a bond over the years.

Behind Star, the office door clicked, signalling the end of Damian's current meeting. Turning, Star froze as Jackson emerged from Damian's office. Her shock must have been visible, as a smirk appeared on his face. "Have a good meeting," he whispered as he passed her, his swagger doing little to settle Star's butterflies.

An impending sense of doom enveloped Star. Pam, sensing something was wrong, placed a hand on her arm. Jackson's meeting with Damian couldn't be a good thing. Both had it out for her, one out of jealousy and one by her own making. As if summoned, Damian appeared in the doorway, his dark eyes locking on her instantly. Star felt the colour once again rise in her cheeks, the intensity of his stare burning into her soul. Raking his hand through his dark hair, he motioned for her to follow him before closing the door behind them. It didn't take long for Star to realise how tired Damian looked.

"How's your dad doing?" she asked.

Rubbing his face, Damian looked up. "It looks like he's had a minor heart attack. They're taking him into surgery later today."

"Oh my god, Damian. Should you be here? How's Mary doing?" Star said, her hand flying to her mouth.

"You know Dad. He's more worried about the business. I'll head over this afternoon before he's taken down. We'll know more by the end of the day." Damian paused, his face hardening. "I'd appreciate if you kept this to yourself. Dad doesn't need to be the centre of office gossip until the proper announcements can be made."

Star braced herself before answering, "Thank you for telling me. Your mum and dad mean a lot to me, and of course I wouldn't dream of saying anything." Star felt lost. Lucas and Mary were like family, but Damian didn't need to know that.

Obviously sensing her distress, Damian added, "I'm not sure what's gone on over the past seven years, but not once has your name been mentioned. Last night, however, Mum made it very clear how close you are to them both." A look of hurt flashed across his face before a mask of indifference returned.

It was true – since Damian had left, she had remained in contact with his parents. They had helped her when her life had gone to hell and back. They'd been there when Lily had been taken ill, and when Skylar had come into her life. Lucas had supported her when she'd needed a job. She'd repaid him by working hard to ensure she lived up to the faith he'd put in her. Damian didn't know any of this. He didn't know anything past her betrayal. To Damian, she'd betrayed him seven years ago, and now he clearly thought his parents had betrayed him, too.

Star decided to get them back on track. They were treading on dangerous ground and not one she was emotionally ready to tackle yet. Her nerves were already frayed from Damian's reappearance; she didn't need to be raking up the past, certainly not in the office.

Taking a deep breath, Star broke the silence. "I'm sorry if my presence offends you, Damian, but we still have a project to approve."

Star wished she'd kept quiet, as Damian's demeanour changed. "Do you want to explain to me why one of your team arrived in my office this morning and told me how incapable you are? That you are taking the ideas of others and selling them as your own? Basically implying that you're little more than a pretty face who has slept her way to the top?"

A vice-like grip encased her chest as Star stared at Damian. She'd known Jackson had been up to something when he'd appeared out of Damian's office, but she could never have imagined he'd go this far. She was unsure why he hated her so much – and it was hate, because this was way above jealousy. What could she say? Damian didn't know her anymore. Lucas would have known it was a pile of horse manure, but he wasn't here. This was her battle.

"Nothing, no defence?" Damian continued. "Is what he said true?"

"No!" Star finally managed to say. "It's far from the truth. You can ask any one of my team, other than Jackson, and you'll hear the truth." Still in shock, Star raised a shaking hand to push her hair back from her face. Damian watched the movement, his eyes never leaving her face.

"I'll have to follow up with your team, and inform HR. These kind of accusations can't be brushed over."

This was not what Star needed – not on top of the presentation deadline for the client,

Lucas's illness, and her potential promotion. She didn't need a black mark against her. But she understood. She should have dealt with Jackson a long time ago; instead she'd let his poison fester and now she was going to pay for it.

"I understand," she said. "The team will be happy to speak to whomever they need to." Star was impressed with the fact her voice didn't wobble with the tears that were currently clogging up her throat. "Shall we address the reason for this meeting and revisit the presentation?"

Star would have missed the flash of respect in Damian's glance had she blinked, but it had definitely been there. Star was hit with wave of clarity. Damian had given her the heads-up: he was letting her know that someone was gunning for her and that she needed to be prepared. Well, if it was war Jackson wanted, then that was what he would get.

Damian left Jackson's accusations to one side and the rest of their meeting went without a hitch. By the time they'd finished, he was happy for Star to rearrange a meeting with the Account Manager and get the final mock-ups sent to print. If they were happy, then the client could be contacted.

∞∞∞

Star headed back to her desk. She ignored a smirking Jackson, instead praising the team and letting them know that they were good to go. She made a call to the Account Manager, and they agreed to set up the next client meeting for as soon as they got a date back from the printers. Damian's sign-off seemed to be enough for them. The team's excitement helped to settle Star's agitation. Everyone had worked hard on this project and deserved to enjoy their success. They'd had multiple client meetings, but this was a chance for the team to shine, to show them what they were proposing. Star wasn't prepared to let one rotten egg ruin that for everyone.

Jackson sat staring at everyone around him, his expression switching from smirk to sulk as time went on. That afternoon, he was called away. Star could only assume that Damian had approached HR. Jackson had no doubt been called to give his official complaint to them.

Despite everyone's cheer, the office was

starting to close in around her. Star knew she needed to get out and take a break before something happened. Getting up from her desk, she let the team know she was taking an early lunch and headed out of the office, stumbling to the nearby park. She collapsed on a bench and wiped angrily at the first tears that fell, doubling over as a silent scream exploded from her lips. Why? Why was this happening? She had evidence to disprove Jackson's claims; she had collected documentation to highlight his incompetence and substandard work, but she knew mud had a tendency of sticking. Why did this have to happen now, when everything was starting to go right for her? It wasn't like she hadn't fought hard to get where she was. She'd raised a child, studied part-time while working to put food on the table, and then Jackson came along and tried to discredit her, for what?

A soothing hand rested on her back. Star jerked up, staring into Pam's concerned eyes.

"Damian told me what happened this morning. Once the team told me you'd gone for an early lunch, I decided to track you down." Pam pulled Star in for a hug before saying, "Don't let that thug get you down – he's not worth your tears!"

"It's not that, Pam. I'm angry at myself for not shutting his pettiness down months ago. What kind of manager am I, if I can't control one of my team?" Star said, her voice tight with tears.

"A good one," Pam said firmly. "You gave him the benefit of the doubt. The rest of your team love you – they love working for you, with you. Don't let one rotten apple spoil the rest. You are brilliant at what you do. Lucas would not have supported you if he didn't think you had the makings of a superstar. Jackson Brown would not have dared try and pull this rubbish had Lucas been here." Sadness tinged Pam's voice.

Star returned Pam's hug, knowing how much Lucas's condition would be affecting her.

"Rotten apple or not, I'm not exactly Damian's favourite person. Our history is not a pretty picture, Pam. You of all people know that."

"Piffle. Damian is old enough to know his own mind, and he won't be fooled by some upstart! As for you and him, it's been seven years. Both of you need to look to the future and leave the past exactly where it is, in the past!"

"At this rate, I may not have a future," Star said.

"Star Roberts, do I hear pity in your voice? After all you've been through, you're just going to roll over? Where's your backbone?" Something in Star's expression must have stopped Pam, because instead of pushing further, Pam nudged Star with her shoulder and said, "What are you going to do about Jackson Brown?"

"I'm going to fight!" Star said, looking at her. "I was never not going to. You're right, I am having a pity party." Wiping her eyes, Star grinned at Pam. "I wasn't expecting company."

"That's my girl!" Pam said, standing up and holding out her hand to Star.

"I have emails that show he hasn't been pulling his weight. I'm not sure what he thought he was going to gain, but I'm ready for him," Star said.

"Great, so this is what we're going to do," Pam said linking her arm through Star's. "We are going to the coffee shop down the road. I'm going to shout you a Frappuccino, and while I'm buying, you're going to fix your makeup and come out fighting."

A hour later, when Star returned to the office, Jackson was still nowhere to be seen. But several members of the team looked up sheepishly from their desk. It was only when Sandra approached Star with a piece of paper that Star realized she'd obviously missed something in her absence. Taking the paper from Sandra, she quickly scanned the printed email. It was from Jackson, addressed to the team. He was accusing her of having an affair with Lucas Hunt and stealing the team's ideas.

"Sorry, Star, but I wanted to bring this to your attention. I want you to know we don't believe a word of what he has said. You're a wonderful manager and great at what you do. He's just bitter and jealous."

"Thank you for bringing this to my attention. Do you mind if I keep this? Even better, could you send me a copy?" Star said, her shoulders straightening. Jackson had started a war she wasn't about to let him win. He'd bad-mouthed her friend and their boss in his vendetta against her and that was not okay. Star would have laughed if it weren't so serious. In his bitterness, Jackson didn't realise the damage he'd done to himself in the process.

"Of course. Let me know if there is anything I can do," Sandra said before scurrying back to her desk.

Several other voices from the team joined Sandra's, making Star feel confident in what she was about to do.

On receiving the email from Sandra, Star forwarded it straight to HR, copying in Damian, along with every piece of evidence she had collected over the months. She had an electronic trail documenting incomplete and substandard work, alongside a few complaints from other team members. If Jackson wanted to fight dirty, then so could she.

∞∞∞

Jackson didn't return to his desk for the rest of the day. Star and the team carried on as normal, although she felt eyes watching her from every corner. Good news always travels fast; gossip even faster. Ignoring the elephant in the room, Star threw herself into preparing for the client meeting. The Account Manager had come back to say that the client was ready whenever they were, and would be happy to meet with the team early next week. Star updated the team and kept herself busy, booking the meeting room and organising for the catering company to supply lunch. By the end of the day, she'd heard nothing from HR and Jackson was still a no-show.

By the end of the day, Star's nerves were frayed, and she had a headache forming behind her eyes. She knew the information she had sent covered her on most aspects, but she was afraid of the mud Jackson would sling and the damage he would do to her reputation.

Laura had a staff meeting after school, so Star headed off to pick up Skylar from after-school club. She grabbed some fresh produce from the supermarket on her way home. Star needed a distraction and was determined not to let the day's events cloud her evening with Skylar. As with baking, Skylar loved helping in the kitchen, so with the Tudor House now complete, this would be their evening together. Star also owed Toby and Laura a home-cooked meal as a thank you for all the help and support they'd given her this week.

Skylar had been working on alliterations in class so named all the vegetables before telling stories based on each character. By the time Laura came home, both Star and Skylar were in fits of giggles and the kitchen looked like a bomb site.

"Wow, it looks like you two have had fun!" Laura said, walking into the kitchen, "Whatever is cooking smells delicious."

A grinning Skylar pointed to the oven and announced how they had made a vegetable bake with Colin Carrot, Percy Pepper, and Oli Onion, as well as a roux sauce with Chelsea Cheese and Margo Milk, before falling into peals of laughter again.

"Well, I'm sorry I missed it," Laura said, laughing, the infectious giggles of Skylar becoming more than she could withstand.

"Mummy was sad when she picked me up, so I cheered her up," came the innocent reply.

Startled at Skylar's words, Star went over and dropped a kiss on top of her head. "Thank you, angel, it worked." Sometimes, she forgot how perceptive Skylar was.

Laura raised a questioning eyebrow but said nothing.

"Hey, Skylar, want to read to me while Mummy cleans up this mess? I'm most definitely not on cleaning duty this evening!" Laura said.

"Dinner will be ready in half an hour. Get washed and grab your book," Star called after her daughter, who had made a dash for the door. "And make sure Aunty Laura puts her feet up while you read her a lovely story."

They could hear the water going as Skylar washed her hands, so Star turned to Laura.

"More issues with Damian?" Laura asked, her concern obvious.

"No, not Damian. I'll fill you in later when Skylar is in bed. It was Jackson today." Star gestured to the mess just as Skylar burst back into the room. "I'd better clean up this mess before Uncle Toby walks in and has a nervous breakdown," she said indicating the large notice that was still attached to the wall in the kitchen from their student days.

Rule number 1 was "NO Mess to be left on any kitchen sides". The notice had been purchased by Laura and Star when they first moved into the house. Toby had bought the house with part of his enormous trust fund and had rented out all six of its bedrooms to fellow students. After one week of living with six, Laura and Star had reached the end of their tether when they'd come home late after a study session and there hadn't been one clean pan or plate in the house. Even the microwave had needed a health warning. The girls had taken it on themselves to organise the four boys, including Toby, to clean the kitchen after every use. It had taken six months, but eight years on, the kitchen rules remained, even though there were now only the four of them living in the house.

Star cleaned while Laura and Skylar read. Toby turned up halfway through and they all sat down for dinner together. Skylar regaled them with her Great Fire of London project, Toby updated everyone on office gossip, and Laura told Skylar about the classroom project that she'd probably be doing next year. Star brushed over her day, admitting it had been long. She did pass on the good news that the Account Manager had signed off on her project and it was full-steam ahead.

By the time Skylar was tucked in bed, Star was exhausted, the day finally catching up with her. Walking into the living room, Laura and Toby were waiting for her. She recounted the day's events, saying, "I just wish I knew what his problem was – it seems more than jealousy."

∞∞∞

After a fitful night, Star managed to deliver Skylar and her Tudor House to her classroom. The playground had been packed with parents dropping off their children, so, to protect the house, Star had taken it directly to Skylar's classroom and passed it over to her teacher. The teacher was as excited as Skylar, their heads close together as they studied and discussed the cardboard building. Star was sure her teacher had preparation to do before school started, but the time and effort she gave her daughter warmed her heart, even more so when her teacher said she was happy for Skylar to stay with her to help her set up.

Star made it to the train station in plenty of time. As the train drew closer to London, a sick feeling began deep in the pit of her stomach, and by the time it arrived she wished she'd skipped breakfast. Leaving the station, her phone pinged with a voice mail from the office.

The message was from one of the HR team asking if she could come and see them as soon as she arrived at the office. Her heart thundered in her chest as she made the short walk from the station to the office.

HR was in the basement of the building. Star supposed it was for times like this – fewer prying eyes watching your every move. By the time the lift opened, Star felt like she was carrying a boulder on her chest. A smiling member of HR greeted her as she arrived and directed her into one of their nearby offices, offering her a tea or coffee. Star declined, the simple thought threatening to evacuate her breakfast.

"Sorry to keep you, Star," Gerry, the head of HR, said as he entered the office. His smile did nothing to calm Star's racing heart. She took a deep breath and tried to return his smile, but she was sure it looked more like a grimace.

Gerry took the seat opposite Star and opened the file he was carrying. Star instantly recognised the emails and documentation she had sent the previous day.

"Just to let you know, Jackson Brown is upstairs with one of my colleagues clearing out his desk," Gerry said, finally looking at Star. "We reviewed your documentation, and spoke to Mr

Hunt and Mr Brown at length yesterday. As you are aware, Mr Hunt had to leave to spend time with his father yesterday afternoon, but I was able to catch up with him last night." Star felt a pang of guilt. In all the drama of yesterday, she had forgotten Lucas was heading into surgery.

"Do you know how Mr Hunt's surgery went?" Star said.

"By all accounts, his surgery went well." Gerry smiled kindly. "I want to add, following our investigation, the email that Mr Brown sent was unprofessional and inappropriate and constituted gross misconduct. He was unable to substantiate any of his claims. As a result, Mr Brown resigned his position this morning, effective immediately. He is currently being escorted from the premises." Gerry looked at Star and closed the file in front of him. "It was decided that we would bring you down here to prevent any further disruption. I do hope you understand, and that you can put this nasty business behind you. Your team speaks very highly of you, as does Mr Hunt Senior. We would hate to lose you, Ms Roberts."

Star's throat clogged with tears, making it difficult to swallow, let alone speak, so she simply nodded. This past week had been too much. Closing her eyes, she sagged in her chair. With Damian's return, Lucas's health, and then Jackson's betrayal, Star felt like she'd fought a battle. "Thank you, Gerry," Star said, and tried to sit up straighter. "I appreciate all you've done." Gerry gave her a nod of approval. "Am I clear to go back to my desk now?"

Checking the clock, Gerry nodded. Star knew the floor would be alive with gossip, and that she was going to be the centre of it. Jackson wouldn't go quietly; he'd make sure he put the knife in somehow. She'd just have to wait and see what came at her. Resigning before they fired him was a clever move, but at least his departure meant she no longer had to deal with him.

Star returned to her floor. Sandra was the first to approach her, soon followed by the rest of the team, who offered their unwavering support. Star had to sit down, overwhelmed by the backing of those around her.

By lunchtime, the initial interest had worn off. Star didn't hear anything from Damian, although she was sure that he would have been made aware of the situation. She assumed he was with his mother and father, and besides, he didn't owe her anything. Pam sent her an email, letting her know she was there should she need her. The only caveat – it was Star's turn to buy the coffee, which made Star smile.

By five pm, Star was ready for the week to end. The weekend was her time with Skylar. This weekend, the weather was supposed to be better with spring well on its way. Star had promised Skylar they could take her new bike to the park, and maybe meet up with a couple of her classmates and their parents. Star was planning the park visit when she stepped out of the lift and collided with a hard, powerful body. Large hands closed around her arms, steadying her. Electricity sparked through every cell his hands touched. Her head shot back, her eyes clashing with Damian's dark defiant ones. Star tried to step away, but found herself locked in place, her body suddenly too warm. Heat flooded her cheeks as a look of arrogance passed over Damian's features, leaving Star mortified.

"Sorry ..." Star stammered, making another attempt to step away. This time, Damian let her go, causing her to stumble. He caught her arm again, steadying her, but this time let go instantly, although the impression of his hand remained, burned into her skin. How, after seven years, could this man have such an impact on her body? Her mind wandered to the erotic dreams that had plagued her sleep all week, and more heat flooded her body. She needed to get out of here before she made a fool of herself.

Stepping to one side, Damian let her pass. His companion said something and she thought she heard Damian reply, but she didn't hang around to listen. She needed to escape, to put as much distance as she could between her and Damian Hunt. She needed to spend this weekend getting her raging hormones under control. She'd made a choice seven years ago, but her body, it seemed, hadn't got the memo.

Chapter Five

When Star arrived at the station, the shutters were down. A swarm of angry passengers surrounded a harassed-looking Underground worker, who was trying to pacify them. A notice was pinned to the shutters stating the line was closed and would be for the next couple of hours. So much for getting home early for a relaxing evening.

Star fired off a quick message to Laura, letting her know what was happening and apologising once again. Laura sent her an immediate reply telling her not to worry about Skylar and to get home safely.

There was not a taxi in sight, although what did Star expect for a Friday evening? Everyone was in the same boat; all office workers wanted to get home. Friday night was renowned for being the quietest night in the City for revellers. Weekdays were for socialising, weekends were for family.

After ten minutes of pointless searching, Star decided to head back to the office. At least her time wouldn't be wasted. She could call a taxi and finish some work while waiting. By the time she reached her desk, the majority of staff had left for the evening. Star collapsed into her chair and pulled up the number of a local taxi firm. When she finally got through, she was told there was about a three-hour wait for taxis. There had been an accident on the Underground, and as a result, the service had been seriously disrupted, with everyone booking taxis now, it seemed. Star got the same message from every firm she tried.

Star was convinced this week had a vendetta against her, so she decided to use the time to make a start on the team's appraisals. Uninterrupted time was precious, and what she got done now, would mean less work later. Caught up in her work, Star lost track of the time. The cleaners had been and gone, working round her to get their job done. The sun was finally setting, the office silent apart from the hum of her computer and the buzz of the overhead lights. The ding of the elevator let Star know that someone had entered the floor. Thinking it was one of the cleaners, Star remained focused on her phone, redialling the last taxi company.

"Still here?" Star jumped at the sound of Damian's voice. "Spending the night here, doesn't win you any brownie points, you know, especially if no one knows you're doing it."

Ending the call, Star spun her chair to face him.

"It's not by choice," she snapped. "My train line is down and there isn't a single taxi in London available. I decided to get on with some work while I wait." Star stopped herself when she realised Damian was smiling and holding up his hands in surrender. She'd been baited. "Sorry …" she muttered.

"No harm done. I'm heading home. If you want a lift, Marcus should be here in five minutes, and he can drop you where you need to go."

Helpful Damian had Star's nerves on edge. Who was she to turn down a lift, especially tonight … She wanted to be home to tuck Skylar into bed. Marcus could drop her off at her car;

it wouldn't be the first time. Lucas had come to her rescue on a number of occasions in the past when there had been problems with the train.

"Thank you," she said, gathering up her belongings.

Damian's phone buzzed to indicate Marcus's arrival. An awkward silence stretched between them as they headed down in the elevator. They both wished the reception staff a good weekend, automatically talking over each other, then stopping. Star's heart was pounding by the time she reached the car. Always the gentleman, Damian jumped in front of her and opened the door.

"Thank you," she said. A memory of their time together flashed before her eyes ... Damian making a sweeping bow as he had held open the door to a waiting limousine, looking striking in his full dinner suit. She'd been in a full evening gown, one he'd purchased for her. He'd explained she was his guest and on a student loan, so she shouldn't have to waste her money on frivolous items because he wanted the pleasure of her company. She had been a first year, when Damian had been in his fourth year at university. That evening, she'd truly realised who she was dating. It was the night she'd first met Lucas and Mary Hunt, and most of the board of Hunt and Hunt Advertising Group. Star had known who Damian was, but after that evening, she finally understood what was expected of him, his legacy. They'd discussed it, but his future had always been just that – words. It was why, just two years later, she had had to walk away from him. She'd had to let him go.

"Evening, Miss Roberts," Marcus said, snapping Star out of her memories. "Usual drop off?"

"Yes, please, Marcus. It's very kind of you," Star said, a flush reaching her cheeks as Damian got into the car next to her, his muscular thigh brushing up against her leg, sending jolts of pleasure straight to her core.

Star shifted further to the other end of the back seat.

"Not the first time?" Damian asked.

"What?" She was startled out of her trance.

"Not the first time Marcus has dropped you off at home?"

"Oh, no, there was an issue with the trains last year, and your dad offered me a lift to my car." An awkward silence floated between them. "How is your dad doing?" Star eventually broke the deadlock and looked at Damian.

"The operation was successful, but he won't be allowed home for at least six to eight days. He's currently hooked up to a lot of machines. I spent most of the day with him. I was heading into the office when I bumped into you earlier." Damian sighed. "He's very protective of you." A hint of bitterness edged into Damian's tone.

Star chose to ignore Damian's final statement, just saying, "I'm glad the operation went well. He's in the best place. How's your mum holding up?"

"She's trying to be brave, but I can see she's terrified. Dad is her life. This has really shaken them both. I think she's aged overnight. She doesn't want to leave his side."

"Oh Damian, I'm sorry." Star turned to face Damian, placing a hand on his arm before she could stop herself. His eyes flew to where she touched him. Pulling her hand away, Star looked out of the window, rubbing her fingers together. "Please tell him we're all thinking of him." Her palm was tingling from the contact. What had she been thinking?

"The Board aren't happy," Damian said. Star turned her attention back to him. "They want him out. Too old, stress, poor health, blah, blah, blah." The bitterness in his tone shocked Star. "They're worried about the share price once the news gets out about his heart attack."

"But your dad is the majority shareholder. They can't just get rid of him, can they?"

"There has been an ongoing power struggle for a while – it's why I'm here. Dad made me promise to keep the vultures at bay while he recovers."

Damian's sudden reappearance made sense. And so did the shadow of exhaustion hanging over him. It was more than jet lag; it was a war he was waging.

"Let me know if there is anything I can do."

Damian looked sick as it dawned on him what he'd just offloaded.

Understanding his fear, Star inclined her head towards him. "It's okay, Damian, I won't say a word."

He visibly relaxed, although there was still tension present in his shoulders.

"Here we go, Miss Roberts," Marcus said as

he pulled into the station carpark. Opening her bag, Star dug around for her car keys. Groaning loudly, she realized she'd thrown them in her desk drawer that morning after the Jackson incident.

Her hand came out empty.

"No keys?" Damian asked.

"Nope, they're in my desk drawer, although I have a spare set at home." Star sighed.

"Marcus, can you drop Miss Robert at her home, please."

Star reeled off the address and she felt Damian stiffen beside her. Of course he'd recognise the address; she'd lived there most of the time they'd been together. He'd practically lived there with her, except when he went on business trips. Marcus pulled out of the carpark and drove the ten minutes to the house.

Star directed him onto the driveway just as the front door was flung open.

∞ ∞ ∞

"Mummy!" Skylar charged out of the house towards the car, her excitement clear. Getting out of the car, Star bent down and opened her arms, grinning as Skylar barrelled into her. Star ignored the man behind her and the questions he probably had; she wasn't ready for the inquisition. The little person in front of her was her highest priority and always would be. Damian Hunt could take a long walk through the woods for all she cared.

"I'm so sorry I'm late," Star said.

"My house burned so well," Skylar started, before her eyes looked past Star, her attention locked on the man who Star knew had stepped up behind her. Skylar straightened up and tilted her head, holding her hand out, in a very un-six-year-old gesture. *I have Lucas to thank for this*, Star thought.

"I'm Skylar, pleased to meet you. Are you a friend of my mummy's? Mummy, why are you in Uncle Lucas's car?" Leaning round Damian, Skylar waved at Marcus who was still in the driver's seat. Star didn't need to turn round to know that Marcus would be waving back.

Star wished she had a camera to hand. The look on Damian's face was priceless, but her heart stuttered the moment he took Skylar's tiny hand in his much larger one. A small smile appeared at the corner of his mouth. "I'm pleased to meet you too, Skylar. I'm Damian, and Uncle Lucas is my father. That's why I've got his car."

"Do you work with Mummy? Mummy works very hard. She studies all the time when she's not playing with me," Skylar said, looking up at Star.

"Your mummy is a very clever lady and she does work very hard. She's working on a very important project at the moment."

Star felt the heat rise in her cheeks, What was Damian doing?

He turned to study her, and in that moment Star realised how much she wanted Damian to see her, and how hard she'd worked.

Skylar pulled on Damian's hand, drawing him towards a house he hadn't entered in seven years. Damian followed, helpless to deny the excitement only a six-year-old could muster. "Come on, Mummy. Aunty Laura and I have made a cake. We can celebrate how hard you have worked."

Laura appeared at the door, her face set in a frown, which didn't quite work with the smear of flour gracing her cheek.

"Damian, what an unexpected …"she said,

raising her eyebrows at Star.

"Surprise?" he finished for her, shooting Star a pointed look. "It seems like it's a day of surprises." Damian turned back to Laura. "How are you Laura? You're looking well."

Grinning, she stepped forwards and pulled Damian in for a hug. "Good to see you, Damian, it's been too long," she said. "I'm twenty weeks pregnant and a lot better than I was, had you asked me a few weeks ago."

Damian gave his congratulations as he followed Skylar and Laura into the kitchen, Skylar's hand still clasped in his. Star's heart sank. This was too cosy; too many memories were flooding her system. Her brain was too tired to handle this shift in events. The fun times they'd all had, the parties, the love they'd shared. Now he was winning her daughter over. She knew questions would come, and she wasn't ready to answer them yet. It's not like Skylar was a secret.

"Sorry about the mess – we were just finishing up our baking project."

"I see you still have the list of rules," Damian acknowledged the list on the walls.

"Uncle Toby is very strict about the

kitchen rules," Skylar said.

Damian made no comment, although Star swore his jaw tighten at Toby's name.

"I remember your mummy and Aunty Laura insisting on the kitchen rules," Damian said to Skylar.

"You knew Mummy before?" Skylar asked, and Star's heart skipped a beat.

"I did – I knew your mummy a long time ago." Star watched as her daughter's face took on a look of intrigue, and groaned internally. She knew she was never going to hear the end of this. Skylar was fascinated with the past.

Star released her breath in a silent hiss, needing to change the subject before it ventured into territory best left untouched.

"So where is this cake you were telling us about? We don't want to hold Damian up – he was kind enough to give me a lift home, but it's late and he needs to get home himself." Star knew she was waffling, but couldn't help it.

Skylar pulled Damian further into the room and pointed to the cake on the table.

"Wow, that looks delicious," Damian said, crouching down to Skylar's height, "Am I allowed some?"

Spinning to face Laura, Skylar gave her a pleading look.

"Of course. It's your cake, Skylar," Laura said, moving forwards, having grabbed the carving knife off the sideboard. "Why don't you get some plates?"

Skylar finally let go of Damian's hand and ran to the cupboard, counting out the plates carefully, before returning them to Laura.

Damian took an enthusiastic bite. "This is delicious! You are a fantastic baker! How old did you say you were?"

Beaming with pride, Skylar said, "I'm six."

Damian froze, his gaze finding Star's across the kitchen. It was a look that demanded answers. "Well, I can't believe someone of six can make such delicious cake," he said, sending Skylar a thousand-watt smile.

"I also bake cookies," she said.

Damian gave Skylar a quizzical look. "You didn't happen to bake some cookies for Pam, did you?"

Skylar grinned. "I did. Did you have one?"

"Well, she told me that they were made by a very special young lady and I had to convince her to share, but she did let me have one."

Star's heart sank as she watched Damian ensnare her daughter's heart.

"Mummy, can we make some cookies for Damian? Pleeease!"

Damian turned to Star and gave her the same look.

Raising an eyebrow at Damian, Star smiled at Skylar and nodded. "But, you have to read all the amounts and use the scales."

Skylar nodded and threw her arms around Damian's legs. Like mother, like daughter, this man was a magnet. In less than thirty minutes, Skylar was infatuated, just like Star had been nine years ago.

The audible click of the front door announced a new arrival. "Uncle Toby!" Skylar yelled, rushing from Damian, out of the kitchen and into the hallway. A second later, a laughing Toby was dragged into the kitchen by the hand, his eyes fully on Skylar. "Uncle Toby, meet Damian. He knew Mummy lots of years ago and he's Uncle Lucas's son."

Damian had frozen at the sight of the new arrival, while Toby kept his attention on Skylar, sweeping her into his arms and tickling her. "I know Damian too, squidge," he said finally returning the squirming bundle to the floor and raising his eyes. "Good to see you again, Damian."

Holding out his hand to Damian, they both froze, before Toby dropped his hand. Ignoring Damian's rudeness, he went to Laura and pulled her in for a quick hug.

Damian scowled and Skylar laughed. "They're always lovey dovey," she said before skipping off.

An awkward silence descended on the kitchen now Skylar had left.

"One friend not good enough, Toby. You had to swap?" The venom in Damians' voice was unmistakable.

Toby flashed Star an angry look. "This is on you. Laura, let's go. We're not getting into this here." Laura sent Star an apologetic look, but followed Toby from the room.

"Thank you for the lift home, but I think it's time you left," Star said.

"Six. Wow, you didn't waste much time. I know she's not mine, but as she called him 'Uncle Toby', I'm taking it she's not his either." It wasn't so much a question as an accusation.

The venom in Damian's tone was like a punch to the gut. Star staggered back under the pressure. "Get out!" she spat. She didn't owe him an explanation, and she was too tired to fight.

Damian headed past her to the door. "Maybe I never knew you at all!" Not waiting for a response, Damian left without looking back.

Star sank onto the kitchen chair, deflated. Skylar entered the kitchen her favourite doll in hand. Her face fell when she realised Damian had left. Pulling her daughter into her arms, Star said, "Sorry, sweetie, Damian had to go. You know Uncle Lucas isn't well. He needed to go and visit him in the hospital."

Keeping her head buried so Skylar couldn't see her glistening eyes, Star promised her daughter they would make cookies over the weekend and she'd deliver them to Damian on Monday. Pulling herself together, she went in search of Toby and Laura. She had some serious grovelling to do.

Chapter Six

Putting the disaster of Friday evening behind her, Star stayed out of the house all day Saturday, determined to give Toby and Laura some space. Toby was unhappy with what had occurred on Friday night and Star couldn't blame him. He'd been insulted in his own home, by her ex-boyfriend, over drama she'd pulled him into seven years previously. Laura had sided with Toby, which wasn't surprising. She'd been horrified by Star's plan all those years ago, and had been disgusted at Toby for the part he'd played in it.

Toby and Laura had been Star's best friends for so many years, so when she'd asked Toby for his help, although he'd had his reservations, he'd agreed. Now he was facing the consequences, but without telling Damian the whole thing had been a lie, Star was stuck. She was certain, however, that the past needed to be left where it was, as nothing had changed and raking it up would only lead to more pain. Toby would have to live with it. There was no reason he would have to see Damian again while Damian was in the UK. Star certainly wouldn't be forgetting her keys or taking lifts from a tall, dark and handsome man, who was by all accounts a complete stranger.

The weekend was over in a flash. Toby had come round on Sunday, after Skylar and Star had cooked everyone a large roast dinner with all the trimmings, topped off with apple crumble and custard. Laura, however, was a different matter. She wanted Star to confess to Damian what she'd done seven years ago and clear the air. Star agreed to think about it, but had backed away from that particular argument, hoping her friend would drop it over time, or Damian would simply disappear back to the US office and the need would be moot.

Monday morning came around too quickly and the sick feeling reappeared. The project was going well, but every step forwards she'd made with Damian last week had evaporated on Friday night. Unsure how she was going to explain Skylar if Damian asked, or Toby and his relationship with Laura, Star decided to just stay out of Damian's way. The client was due in this week, so she had the perfect excuse to be too busy if he did ask to see her. Star even toyed with the idea of asking Pam to run interference. Who was she kidding? Damian probably never wanted to set eyes on her again, and for some reason that left her feeling empty inside. She realised how much she'd been keeping her eyes open for him last week when she knew he was back. She really was in trouble.

The next two days went by without incident. Preparation for the client meeting was in full flow, the team more engaged now that Jackson had left. Apparently no one had heard from him since his departure, although Star was not sure if anyone would want to admit being associated with him after everything that had gone down. Instead of worrying, she decided to focus her thoughts and effort on the results which were in from the latest focus group. Star had organised for a few members of the team to have a sit-down and go through them, inserting the latest data into the presentation.

"Star, there's something wrong with the focus group data." Sandra came bundling out of the meeting room towards her desk.

"What do you mean?" Star put down the printout she was looking at.

"These results are for the marketing campaign we scrapped, or, should I say, the client rejected. It doesn't match what we've just received."

Star pulled up the data on her own screen, and sure enough the data was for a test that had been side-lined weeks before.

"Get on to the moderating team and find out what's happened. This can't be right." Star looked at the data in front of her, a sinking feeling in the pit of her stomach telling her that this probably wasn't wrong and someone had authorised the wrong campaign. How was she going to explain this to the client, to the company? The time and effort of running an incorrect campaign – someone's head was going to roll, and at the end of the day, the buck stopped with her.

Sandra eventually came back, looking even more flushed than before. "It looks like the campaigns were switched. Paul can see the original request we sent in, but someone called and cancelled that. It looks like a second request was then entered in its place."

"Do they have a name? Who requested the switch?" Star asked, starting to feel hot under the collar.

Sandra looked embarrassed. "Apparently it's your name against the switch."

Star stared at Sandra. "It has my name against it? That's not possible. I haven't spoken to anyone at the market research centre."

"I'm just saying what he told me. Why don't you give him a call?" Sandra said, biting her lip.

Two hours later, Star was no closer to getting the answers she needed than she had been at the start. Paul was adamant that it was Star's name against the log, but he himself had been on holiday, so couldn't verify or deny whether it was correct or not. Star began to despair; this could mean her job. The client was not going to be happy picking up the bill for a campaign they had already rejected, and Hunt and Hunt were going to be upset paying for something that was both unauthorised and useless.

Paul promised to go away and dig deeper. Luckily, Star had built up a good working relationship with him over the years, having been the liaison between the production teams and focus groups during her intern days. He told Star to sit tight, which didn't help; the client was due in tomorrow, expecting all the focus group results ... and now this. She was going to look stupid and unprofessional, and she was going to have to confess to Damian and the Account Manager in order to do some damage limitation. She'd successfully avoided Damian for the past two days. Could she please get off this rollercoaster!

The team was in overdrive, checking and rechecking documents. The final proofs had been delivered for the correct campaign, so that was a relief. The problem now was she had no focus group data to go with it. Star put in a call to Pam and asked if Damian was available. Unfortunately for her, he was, so Star bit the bullet and headed into the lion's den.

Damian looked up from his desk, his eyes grazing over her before coming to rest on her face. Star took a seat, while Damian sat back expectantly.

"We have an issue." Star said, her hands clasped tightly in her lap. Damian didn't say anything, so Star took a deep breath and continued. "The wrong advertising campaign was authorised with the focus group."

Damian remained silent, although moved forwards so his elbows were resting on the desk.

Star waited for him to say something, but Damian continued to look at her. Star felt her cheeks redden at his scrutiny. "Say something," she said in the end, unable to take anymore today.

"What do you want me to say, Miss Roberts. I'm waiting for an explanation as to how the wrong campaign was authorised? What does that mean for this project? And what is being done about it?"

Calm Damian was not someone Star felt she could deal with.

"I'm simply here to escalate what has happened, as is company protocol."

"And what would that be?" Damian wasn't giving up.

"This morning, the final feedback arrived, and the team realised the wrong campaign had been run with the focus group. This campaign was side-lined by the client in favour of another one we put forward. According to the Market Research Manager, in charge of our focus group, I made the call and changed the tests over. I know for a fact I didn't do this, but it's my name on the switch."

"So what did the manager say? Was it you he spoke to?"

"No, he was on holiday. He's currently chasing the person who was in charge while he was away to see if they have any recollection of the switch. However, it doesn't solve the problem we have, as the client is in tomorrow and expecting to see the data." God only knew what Damian was currently thinking of her; she certainly wasn't coming across as the cool, calm businesswoman she had worked so hard to be.

"If you didn't make the change, then I suggest we focus on who might have made the switch and why? Who could have had access to the focus group tests? Whose idea was the original test – could they have switched it? Is there anyone who may wish to discredit you?"

Star looked at Damian, her jaw hanging open. Was he really giving her suggestions on how to clear her name and place doubt on the evidence?

"Don't look so shocked, this isn't the first time something like this has happened." Star closed her mouth and sat up straighter. "As for the client tomorrow, there has been a delay in the test results. You have plenty of other data and material to go through with them. Speak to Market Research Manager and get the other test rerun through the focus group as quickly as possible. You'll need to go back to the client as soon as possible once those results come in."

Star's phone started to ring, cutting Damian off. She motioned to Damian that it was Paul. Answering on speaker, Star let Paul know that she was with Damian and he was on speaker.

"Hi Star, Damian. Okay, this is what I've uncovered. It looks like it wasn't you who called up, but apparently someone on your behalf. I spoke to Tessa. She remembers a guy ringing up. Apparently she questioned why he didn't want his name put against it, but he said he was an intern and was just doing what his boss asked. I know you don't have any interns working with you, Star, so what's going on?"

The colour drained from Star's face. It all made sense now, only it had backfired on him as he'd already gone. "Did Tessa have a name?" she said.

"A Simon something. He had a strong Yorkshire accent if that helps. I did find something else out, though. The focus group you wanted run, it has been done – it was just filed under another project. I've sent the results over to the team."

Star and Damian thanked Paul and let him go. Star collapsed back into her chair.

"Someone really has it in for you. Who is Simon? That's not a name I recognise from the project."

"There isn't a Simon working on the project, and as a new manager, I don't have interns under my care. I can surmise who was masquerading as Simon, as he tried to stitch me up. The campaign the client shelved was his idea; the one they chose to adopt was mine. He fought hard to get his campaign reinstated. What better way than to make me look incompetent and then have proof to back it up. The fact both groups were run is even more proof he wanted to appear to be the golden boy in all of this."

Damian sat back surveying Star. "You think this was Jackson?"

"Don't you?" Star shot back.

"It has merit, but I didn't think he was smart enough to try to pull something like this. He wasn't very smart when he came to see me. His accusations held no weight when he could only give me a brief, simplistic view of the project, unlike your detailed one. He was easy to see through."

Star shot Damian a look. He'd known all along that Jackson was lying, yet she'd spent the day wondering if she was going to have a job by the end of it. Star's heart began pumping hard as she felt her temper rise.

"Great, you left me hanging all day knowing his accusations were false!"

"I followed protocol," Damian said.

"Protocol! This is my life. I have a child to support. I need this job. It isn't a game to me."

"This company isn't a game to me either. This is my family's life and livelihood! What he was doing needed to be dealt with. With the evidence you sent, you hadn't been doing that, which on its own is damaging and today has shown why! Your lack of strength as a manager has put this company's reputation in jeopardy. It's not just about being great at creating ideas – any team member can do that. It's about standing up when the going gets tough, and that goes double when the people are friends or peers!"

Star sat back, her voice tight when she said, "You're right, I'm sorry. I should have dealt with Jackson months ago, but I thought it would calm down and it was just the initial sting of me being promoted over him. It's only recently it's got totally out of hand."

"It's dealt with, and he's gone. Luckily his plan has worked in your favour, as the focus group results have been found. Now you need to get out there and get this ready for the client. No more mistakes, Star, or your career will be on the line."

∞ ∞ ∞

The next morning, Star waited in reception for the client to arrive. Her team had set up the boardroom last night. She'd spent the evening going over everything in minute detail, and had rechecked everything again when she got in early this morning. She'd mailed the latest presentation to Damian late and he'd responded almost instantly. He'd been happy with the changes and positive about the results that had come out of the focus group study. This gave her added confidence that today's meeting should go well.

Just before ten, Star's heart began to pound and she felt someone's eyes on her. Looking round, she saw Damian striding across reception towards her.

"Damian," she said, horrified at how breathless she sounded, "is everything okay?"

"Fine, I'm here to meet and greet." The colour must have drained from Star's face because he was quick to add, "That's all. The client is yours, but as acting CEO I'm set to greet all clients who come to the office. Don't panic. I won't be sitting through your presentation,." The corner of his mouth twitched as he saw her discomfort.

Taking a deep breath, Star smiled, although it didn't reach her eyes. She'd presented to this client, what felt like hundreds of times over the past eighteen months, but the thought of Damian watching made her feel sick. The effect he still had on her body was purely physical, but she didn't need the distraction; her heartrate was already elevated! The swishing of the doors signalled the client's arrival and allowed her to make a quick escape. Walking forwards, she greeted Matthew Morris and his team with a handshake.

"Mr Morris, welcome. It's great to see you again." Star plastered a smile on her face, although it was not difficult, as Matthew Morris and his team was one of the easiest clients she'd worked with. "May I introduce you to Damian Hunt."

"Star, how many times do I have to tell you, it's Matthew," he said with a laugh. "Damian, how are you?" Matthew looked around, before asking, "Where is your father? I was expecting to see him this morning. I didn't know you were gracing the London office with your presence."

Star realised Matthew and Damian had history together. Not waiting for Damian to reply, Matthew said, "Star, I was one of Damian's first clients when he joined the firm, right until the New York office snatched him away."

Flashbacks hit Star as she now

remembered all the conversations she'd had with Damian about Matthew's sporting firm. Amazed she hadn't put two and two together before, she simply smiled.

"Well," Matthew continued, "not that I need him now I have you. And I must say, Damian, this lady is an absolute gem. She just seems to get what we need. You need to make sure you keep her, or the competition is going to snap her up."

Star glanced at Damian. He was smiling, although tension seemed to have appeared around his jaw. Matthew continued his friendly banter all the way to the boardroom, where refreshments had been laid out.

It wasn't long before Damian made his excuses and left. Star was glad to see the back of him. She didn't need the additional worry; her nerves were already frayed, without him adding to it. Two hours later, however, Matthew Morris and his team were celebrating. They loved the presentation and the results from the focus groups had been better than they'd hoped. It was full steam ahead: they wanted the new marketing campaign to be out before Christmas to catch the festive season fitness market. Star could not help but cheer inside. She'd done it!

"This could skyrocket the company to the next level," Matthew said to Star as she walked him out of the building. "Remember, Star, if you ever want to leave the stuffy coats here, then there is always a place for you at our table."

"Thank you, Matthew, that's very kind of you. I'm glad we were able to meet the needs of your company, but this really was a team effort," Star replied, her heart still racing with adrenaline.

"Good leadership, though, Star, that's what makes a good team," Matthew said, and Star's mind wandered to the previous day. She hadn't been such a great leader then. But like with everything, you had to learn, and she really had. She'd never let anyone take advantage of her again.

After saying goodbye, Star headed up to see Pam to let her know that the presentation had gone well. The Account Manager who'd been in the meeting was over the moon, no doubt seeing pound signs being added to his bonus. Pam wasn't at her desk, but Damian's door was open. Knocking gently, she waited for an invitation to enter.

"Come in."

Damian's voice caused her stomach to contract and a warm flush spread over her body.

Damian looked up, his dark eyes studying her as she entered, his face a mask. "How did it go?"

"Good, really good. Matthew was impressed – they want the project to go full steam ahead for Christmas."

"Congratulations," Damian said, sounding less than impressed.

"Okay," Star said preparing to leave, even though her body begged for her to stay, "I just wanted to say thank you for your input and with the Jackson issue. You were right."

"Where's Skylar's Dad?" Damian threw out as Star reached the door.

"What?" Star turned, her face having lost every ounce of colour.

"Well, she's obviously not Toby's daughter, as she called him Uncle Toby, and she's not mine. Who knocked you up and abandoned you?"

"I'm not sure it's any of your business," Star shot back.

"Maybe not, but you jumped out of my bed straight into Toby's, and then within the year you obviously had a child. I'm just wondering if I ever knew you. Seeing you flirting this morning with Matthew Morris—"

Star had heard enough. "Excuse me! Flirting with Matthew Morris! How dare you? He's my client and old enough to be my father. What crawled up your ass this morning? Some incorrect assumption that I was flirting with Matthew. You know him – he's friendly and he's left this building singing our praises. That should be all you're interested in." Star's temper was beginning to flare, but she didn't stop to think about why she was so angry, or why Damian was.

"He's married," Damian interjected, his own colour rising, getting up from his desk.

"I know – his wife came to dinner with us all at one of the early meetings. I sat next to her all night talking about our daughters," Star spat, sick of the accusations, not sure where they were coming from. Every muscle in her body was tense at the prospect that people could think this of her – that Damian could think this of her. Walking to the door, Star stumbled as Damian slammed it shut, pinning her against the inside of the office with his body.

"Do not walk away from me!" Damian's lips slammed down on hers, and Star gasped, allowing Damian to deepen the kiss. Shocked by the turn of events, she relaxed into the kiss, her body melting against Damian's. His initial anger dispersed; the kiss changed as he reclaimed her lips with a passion that took her breath away. Taking control, Star pushed him away. Drawing her swollen lip between her teeth, Star raised a hand to Damian's chest and pushed. His eyes had darkened as they'd always done in moments of passion, his breathing uneven. Shaking her head, Star slipped out from under his arm and pulled on the door handle. Damian stepped back, allowing her to make her escape.

∞∞∞

Hitting the elevator button, it seemed forever before the doors opened doing nothing to help calm her racing heart. Damian still stood in his doorway watching her, his eyes locking with hers as soon as she looked up. Holding his gaze until the doors closed, she expelled a breath in a slow, steady hiss. What the hell had just happened? Damian had kissed her! Yes, it had been in anger, but he'd still kissed her. Pressing the back of her hand to her lips, she shook her head. No, this could not be happening.

Star headed back to her desk, before slumping in her chair. A steady stream of well-wishers made their way past, congratulating her on the success of the morning. The high she should have been feeling was lost to something more powerful, but Star hoped they'd think her flushed cheeks were due to their congratulations, not to the fact she'd been pressed up against the door by Damian Hunt.

Just the thought of Damian's powerful body pressed against hers, his arousal hardening against her stomach, was causing electricity to spark through her body. Biting her lip to stop herself groaning out loud, Star decided it was time for some fresh air. It had been far too long since she'd had any physical contact. That was the reason her body had responded so desperately to his affection. Star clearly needed to start dating again … Maybe she should take Laura up on one of her blind dates. A seven-year dry spell was probably too much in most people's books. Her body's reaction was to be expected.

Star grabbed her purse, and headed outside, hoping the crisp April air would calm her down. The coffeeshop was only around the corner, so Star took a detour through her favourite park, needing a form of escape to pull her thoughts together.

"Star ..." Star froze at the sound of Damian's voice, "stop please."

Star stopped, unsure why her body had stopped listening to her head about half an hour before. "What do you want, Damian?"

"I just wanted to check you are all right," he said.

"As you can see, I'm fine. What did you expect?" Star held her hands up and motioned down her body. "It was a kiss, Damian, it's not like we haven't done that before." She stopped herself from saying anymore as a group of businessmen walked by.

Damian's gaze had locked onto her hands.

"True, but it was unprofessional of me," Damian apologised, his gaze returning to hers.

"Forget it – I will," Star said turning to leave.

A hand landed on her arm, pulling her back round to face him.

"You said 'will', not 'have'," Damian said.

"Will, have, what's the difference? You're right, it shouldn't have happened, and it's not going to happen again. You're here to stand in for your father, and then you'll be heading back to New York. I'm here with my daughter, trying to carve out a future for us. End of. Don't apologise, don't repeat it, and we'll be good." It took all of Star's energy to shrug off his hand and walk away.

"Who was he?" Damian called out after her.

"No one you knew," Star said, turning back round but keeping her distance.

It wasn't a lie. Skylar's father was no one Damian knew, no one she really knew either. He'd been Lily's secret boyfriend – someone Star had met once when her sister had told him about her pregnancy. He was not someone who'd made a favourable impression; he had stood by doing and saying nothing when his father had thrown him and Lily out of his house. Damian didn't need to know that. Skylar was her daughter, and if it meant Damian Hunt stayed out of her way because of her, then good. Not wanting to read into the expression on Damian's face, Star turned and headed back to the office, an intense pain emanating from her heart.

Chapter Seven

The rest of the day went by without incident. Pam sent Star a congratulatory message and Star texted Mary to let her know that the client meeting had been a success, and to let Lucas know if she felt it was appropriate. Star knew Damian would update him, but she wanted to share her success with them herself. Star let the team go home an hour early, as a bonus for the late nights and early mornings they'd all put in. She busied herself finishing up all the necessary paperwork. The team had done her and themselves proud. In the eyes of the others, they had made a success of their project. She, the newest manager, hadn't fallen flat on her face as some had hoped, but instead risen to the challenge. For the first time in a long time, Star let herself feel that maybe her luck was changing. Was this where life started to get easier?

∞∞∞

Star walked through the school gates, pleased she would be the one picking up Skylar this evening. After everything that had happened over the past week, she needed some normality, and Skylar would bring that to her. Entering the school hall where the after-school club was held, Star stood and watched as Skylar interacted with her friends. All the children had smiles on their faces, and one of the helpers was laughing at something one of the girls had said. Looking up, Skylar caught sight of Star and nudged her friend. Both girls came running over, Skylar pulling the other girl by the hand.

"Mummy," Skylar said, launching herself into her arms, "come and meet my new friend, Olivia." The little girl who'd followed Skylar came forwards a little more cautiously. "Olivia is new today, Mummy, and I was made her buddy. I've helped her and shown her where everything is.

Can she come round to play?"

Skylar's enthusiasm brought a smile to Star's face.

"Welcome, Olivia." The little girl looked on shyly as Star greeted her. "Of course Olivia can come round for a play-date, but I'd need to organise that with her mummy."

Olivia's face dropped.

"Oh, Olivia doesn't have a mummy, like I don't have a daddy. She only has a daddy," Skylar chirped up.

Star smiled at the little girl, who'd obviously captured her daughter's heart. "Well I'll have to speak to her daddy then." Olivia's face picked up; a look of relief clear. Star got it; she wondered how many parents didn't invite her round because she only had a daddy. Star had found that on a number of occasions, Skylar wasn't invited one-on-one because Star was a single parent, as if it were contagious. Some people didn't seem to want to look past the situation to the child. Star had removed as many small-minded people from their lives as she could, but it still hurt when Skylar was excluded.

"I'll go and speak to Mrs Linford. I'll leave my name and number for Olivia's dad and ask him to ring me to see if we can arrange a get-together."

The two girls ran off hand in hand, smiling and whispering. Star grinned, watching Skylar with her new friend. Most of Skylar's friends didn't have to go to breakfast or after-school club as their mums didn't have to work, so it was nice that she would now have a friend to keep her company, and Olivia seemed like a sweet girl.

Mrs Linford looked up as Star approached and smiled. "Good evening, Ms Roberts. I would like to say what a beautiful young lady you have raised. She has been, as always, an absolute dream. Today she's been so kind and caring where Olivia is concerned. She's taken her under her wing and really looked after her." Mrs Linford was obviously very proud of Skylar, which made Star feel equally as proud.

"Thank you, that's lovely to hear. It's actually the reason I've popped over. Skylar wants me to arrange a playdate with Olivia, and I was wondering if you could pass my number on to her dad when he comes to collect her."

"Of course, that's no problem." Mrs Linford said grinning, "If you want to write your details down, I can pass them on. Hopefully he will be open to the girls getting together. It's always hard when they are the new child in the school." Grabbing her notepad, Mrs Linford indicated for Star to write down her name and number. "I'll pop that in her school bag and let him know it's there when he collects her."

Star gathered together all Skylar's belongings before she headed off in search of Skylar and her new friend. She found them playing in the new playhouse. Star let Skylar have time to say goodbye to Olivia before eventually coaxing her out of the school and into the car.

"Olivia is really nice, Mummy," Skylar said, after filling her in on all the things they'd done together. Skylar told Star how her teacher had asked Skylar to be Olivia's buddy. She'd obviously taken the job very seriously, introducing her to all her friends and making sure she sat next to her at lunch. "Olivia's mummy left when she was a baby, and so she now only has a daddy."

"Oh dear," Star said, unsure what to say to her daughter, without knowing all the facts. She didn't want to make a comment that could be passed back to Olivia and then her dad. Star knew all about the rumour mills and gossip.

"Yes, she just has a daddy. I told her that's okay, as I only have a mummy."

Star's heart stuttered. It was very rare that Skylar mentioned not having a daddy. She had Toby, who had always stepped in and acted as a father figure, having been there since Skylar was born. She'd initially called him Dada, not knowing the difference, but they'd gently corrected her until she could say Uncle Toby. Skylar had of course asked about her father, and Star had been as honest as she could without hurting the little girl. She'd told her that her mummy had loved him very much, but they'd had an argument before mummy knew she was pregnant. Then Lily had got sick and it was too late. The truth hadn't been quite the fairy tale she'd painted, but the truth would have hurt Skylar and Star would do anything to protect her from that. When it had become clear Lily wasn't going to recover, Star had promised she would love and cherish Skylar, raising her as her own. Star had promised Lily she would always be a part of their lives, and she would keep her sister's memory alive, even when she couldn't be with them.

This was partly why Damian had been

the last man in Star's life. Star had made a decision the day her sister had died that she would devote her life to the baby who had been left with no one. Star's mother and father had disagreed adamantly, telling Star she should put Lily's child up for adoption. Daphne Roberts had been devastated when Star's relationship with Damian had ended, telling Star she was ruining her life for her sister's mistake.

Star's half brother and sister were cold towards her and her mother, and she couldn't blame them. After their mother's death, their father's "other" life had become public knowledge, which was embarrassing for everyone involved. But Daphne loved it. She was now the society woman she'd always wanted to be and had the man she'd chased after for thirty years doting on her. Their relationship was a strange one, but they seemed to get along.

∞∞∞

Skylar was still talking about her new friend Olivia when they walked through the front door. Star hoped Olivia's dad got in touch, otherwise

Skylar was going to be very disappointed. After unloading the car with the food she'd bought, Star set Skylar up at the table to do her homework while she set about preparing dinner.

In between stirring the curry, Star helped Skylar with her homework. Skylar was a bright little girl, and she loved numbers like Lily had, although she struggled more with her reading.

"I read this one today with Mrs Linford," Skylar grumbled, taking out her new story book and looking at the cover in disgust. "Do I have to read it again?"

"Well, I haven't heard it," Star said. "I also need to hear your version." Skylar's face lit up and she opened the book.

Star turned back to the stove and carried on stirring the curry. Skylar preferred to make up a story rather than read the actual words on the page. Skylar's teacher had called Star in and discussed the issue, as she was falling behind her peers. She'd recommended Star let Skylar tell her version of the story and then read the story the author had written. It took more time, but the battle to read was less intense, as they got to discuss the pros and cons of each story.

"Once upon a time ..." Skylar started.

It was not long before Skylar was engrossed in her storytelling. With the curry simmering, and the naan bread rising, Star sat down and followed along, looking at the pictures. This was a story where Skylar and Olivia went on an adventure into space. Skylar's characters always had amazing adventures and Star liked to encourage her imagination. When Skylar ran out of pictures, she announced "The end!", and Star gave her a round of applause.

"Wow, Skylar and Olivia had some interesting adventures in space."

"Yes, better than the actual author's silly story," Skylar said, pulling a face.

Laura had given Star several tips for helping with her reading, so Star decided to implement one now. "Your story was so great, but we still need to read what the actual author wrote so we can compare. How about you read a sentence and I read a sentence?" Not looking convinced, Skylar pulled another face, but shrugged. She'd had this argument with her mother many times, and she knew she wasn't going to win. Plus, every other sentence was better than all sentences.

Together, they worked their way through

the book. Laura came in halfway through and praised Skylar for her reading, before going to get changed. Encouraged, Skylar took over all the sentences. Mrs Linford had obviously worked hard to help Skylar earlier in the day because, by the time she was finished, Skylar was really proud of herself. She put her book away and handed Star her reading log for her to write in. Star made sure she put down a smiley face and a positive comment, reading it back to Skylar so she could hear the praise. Star let Skylar head off to play before dinner, just as Laura returned, in her sweats, dropping herself into the chair opposite.

Star popped the kettle on, making Laura a herbal tea. Laura had stopped drinking tea and coffee when the morning sickness had hit and had never restarted. Star still couldn't get over this, as Laura had spent many of her formative years living on caffeine. At university, Laura's day couldn't start without at least two large coffees.

"Thank you, you're an angel," Laura said, cradling her mug and sighing.

"Long day?"

"Yes, the little ones were having a lively day and then we had a staff meeting to discuss new literacy standards." Laura groaned into her mug. "But less about me and more about you. What happened? How did your client meeting go?"

With everything that had happened, Star had almost forgotten that the big meeting had been the start of her day. "Perfect," Star said. "They loved the presentation, were over the moon with the results from the focus group studies, and have commissioned us to get this campaign out at the start of the Christmas season."

"Amazing!" said Laura. "I'm so proud of you."

"I didn't think I could do it and I have. When Lucas first told me he was giving me this client, I thought he was mad. Then with all the Jackson fiasco, I thought I'd blown it, but it's all come together."

"And only because you've put all the hours and hard work in." Laura walked to the fridge and pulled out a bottle of alcohol-free bubbly. "It's time to celebrate," she said, unscrewing the lid and getting two champagne glasses out of the cupboard. "So what did Damian say?"

Star choked on her bubbles, and began

coughing furiously. Laura laughed, patting her on the back. "So he was pleased, then!"

"No, he kissed me," Star spluttered, not quite having got her breath back.

"He what? Did you just say he kissed you?"

Star nodded, a warm flush creeping up her cheeks. "One minute we were arguing, the next he was kissing me."

Laura looked shocked but her eyes held a glint of excitement. "Where did this happen?"

Star could no-longer look her friend in the eye, "In his office, up against the door," she mumbled.

"That sounds kind of hot," Laura said, fanning herself. She'd always been a staunch Damian supporter. "I think you better tell me everything," she said. For the next twenty minutes, Star recounted her morning, and then her meeting with Damian and the kiss.

"So how did it feel?"

Trust Laura to get to the crux of the story … Star blushed at her friend's question but remained silent.

"That good, huh?" Laura said, looking at her friend sympathetically.

"It felt like coming home," Star said

quietly.

"Oh, hon, he always was your home. That was why I never understood why you did what you did."

"I had to let him go – you know that. I couldn't hold him back." Tears filled Star's eyes, the loss and longing too strong to hide from her friend. When Damian had left, it had been simple to suppress her true feelings, switching all her attention to Lily and her needs. When Lily died, Star's grief had doubled. If it hadn't been for Skylar, Star knew she would have collapsed, but the tiny baby her beautiful sister had left had needed her, and that was what had pulled her through.

But now Damian was back, and all those feelings she'd hidden from the world were now racing to the surface once again. It was suffocating. What was she going to do? Just the thought of Damian and their kiss had her body clenching with need. How was she going to face him and work alongside him day to day?

Laura squeezed her shoulder, before sitting down next to her.

"It will all sort itself out. Life has a funny way of doing that. Look at Toby and me," Laura said, just as a bundle of energy flew back into the kitchen.

∞∞∞

The next few days went by without incident. Star threw herself into the Morris project and kept out of Damian's way, while he seemed to have decided the same was in order. Star should have felt relieved, but instead she felt empty. She had to stop herself from looking for him. Every time she saw a dark head of hair, her heart would begin to race and she'd spend the next half an hour trying to calm herself down. It wasn't helping that her dreams were also peppered with the past. She was waking up every morning, her body trembling with longing. Damn Damian and that kiss; he'd awoken her body and now she was trapped.

By Friday, rumours had started to fly. The Board was unhappy; it had leaked that Lucas wasn't on vacation but had had a heart attack and was no longer in charge of the company. Stock prices had plummeted and rumours were flying around about hostile takeovers and clients leaving. Everyone knew they were exactly that – rumours – but Star knew the impact this would be having on Damian as he tried to keep the rumours from reaching his father. Lucas needed rest and a stress-free life after his operation. This was not going to help.

Star took Skylar's latest batch of cookies to Pam. Skylar had also drawn a picture for Damian and Star had awkwardly promised to give it to him, in addition to Skylar's handmade get well soon card for Lucas. Pam was on the phone when Star approached, but Pam waved at the seat in front of her, so Star sat down. It wasn't long before Pam put the phone down and grinned at Star.

"I thought you were avoiding me," Pam said mischievously.

"Not you," Star replied honestly, glancing at Damian's door and putting the cookies on the desk. "These are for both of you – Skylar was very clear about that," Star said, rolling her eyes.

"It seems he made quite an impression," Pam said, noticing the drawing that was clearly labelled "Damian".

"You could say that," Star said. "She hasn't stopped talking about him." Skylar was driving

Star mad with her constant chatter about Uncle Lucas's son. Skylar wanted to know all about Damian and how Star knew him. If Star didn't know better, she'd think Skylar had a crush on Damian Hunt. Not that she could blame her daughter – she had good taste.

"Well, I think the cookies will go down a storm. He's currently on with the Board," Pam said, pulling a face. "A few of them want to replace Lucas as CEO, and Damian is having none of it," Pam whispered. Damian and his father were majority shareholders, so Star knew this was something Damian could hold off, but that kind of pressure was never easy, especially as she'd heard Damian was also overseeing the New York office as well as the London one. He was stretching himself too thin.

Damian's door flew open, and the air around him seemed to crackle with the fury emanating from him. Star shrank into the chair, not wanting to be caught sitting and gossiping with Pam. Damian moved towards Pam's desk, his face like thunder and clearly unaware of her presence.

"Pam, I need Chris Hanson on the phone as soon as he gets into the New York office," he said.

"Is everything all right?" said Pam.

Damian's shoulders deflated at the sound of concern in his godmother's voice. "Just a few members of the Board needing a small reminder," he said, before noticing Star sat in the chair opposite Pam.

Star held up her hand. "Don't mind me," she said. "I'll be going, Pam."

"Star …" Damian started.

"Don't worry, I didn't hear anything," she said. Dark shadows circled his eyes. She clearly wasn't the only one not sleeping, although she their sleepless nights were for very different reasons.

"Thank you," Damian said, glancing down at the desk, the fight having left his body. He picked up Skylar's drawing and a small smile appeared at the corner of his mouth. "Thank Skylar for me," he said, surprising Star. "I'll make sure Dad gets his card."

"There are cookies there, too," Star said. "Make sure Pam shares."

With that, Star made a speedy exit. Every muscle in her body had begun to tingle at his arrival and she needed to get away to pull herself together. As she entered the lift, Damian was already grabbing the container of cookies from Pam, laughing at something she said. At least he looked calmer now. The draw to pull him into her arms and tell him everything was going to be okay had been a strong one, but that wasn't Star's place. Pam was there and she'd look after him. Star had given up that privilege years ago.

∞∞∞

After work, Star headed to the hospital. She'd been to the shops and picked up a fruit basket, knowing that Skylar's cookies were not what one should bring a man who'd just had open heart surgery. Star had been surprised when Mary had called her. She had stayed away, not wanting to rock the boat any further where Damian was concerned. He'd been hurt by her close relationship with his parents, and Star was loath to rub his face in it any further. Mary, however, had been insistent that she come and visit Lucas, especially after Damian had delivered Skylar's card. Mary said that Lucas wouldn't rest until Star had been in, and that Star should understand, as she knew how stubborn he was.

The private hospital was more like a five-star hotel with its plush seating area and wooden front desk. No NHS for Lucas Hunt – that's for sure. Star, following the instructions Mary had given her, made her way up to Lucas's ward.

"Star, so glad you could come."

Star was swept into a hug before she had time to react. Luckily, she had placed the basket down on the nurses' station so she could hug Mary back. Holding Star at arm's length, Mary gave her the once-over. "Beautiful as ever, although you look like you've lost some weight," Mary said and tutted. "I hope that boy of mine isn't working you too hard."

Star laughed. "I'm fine, Mary, I've just been busy with work and a six-year-old. Damian has been fine – he's definitely not breathing down my neck." A blush spread over her cheeks as Star realised how it sounded.

Mary's expression was contemplative, but she didn't say anything. Grabbing Star's hand, she led her down the corridor. "He's dying to see you. I've confiscated his phone to stop him working, but he is desperate to hear how everything went. The doctor has told me it would be better for his stress to let him work it out."

As Star entered Lucas's room, she was shocked at how frail he looked.

"Star! Thank goodness," Lucas said, straightening himself up in his bed. "Someone who will come and talk to me! They've banned all forms of communication – I'm a prisoner to the hospital."

Placing the basket on a side table, Star stepped up to the bed and grasped Lucas's outstretched hand. "It's good to see you, Lucas – you gave us quite a scare!"

"Hmph! It's all been blown out of proportion."

Star looked at Mary, who gently shook her head. Obviously not out of proportion at all, but simply frustrating for a man who, until a couple of weeks ago, had been the hands-on head of a multinational, billion-pound advertising company. Mary had pulled up a chair so Star could sit. Thanking her, Star turned back to her mentor and squeezed his hand.

"So how is it going?" he asked. Glancing at Mary, he added, "and don't leave anything out!"

"It's all good. Matthew Morris was incredibly happy with the presentation and the results of the focus group." Star gave him the rundown, leaving out all the negative press about Jackson. Damian had dealt with that; it was not something his father needed to be concerned about.

"Are you going to tell me what happened with Jackson Brown?" Damn, Damian had obviously filled his father in.

"It's nothing you need to worry about," Star said firmly. "He's gone and it's all been dealt with."

Lucas did not look pleased. "Damian said it had obviously been going on for a while. Why didn't you say anything to me? I'd have sorted out that upstart in a moment."

Star looked to Mary for support, but found none forthcoming. "There are certain battles I need to fight on my own. You can't fight all my wars for me, Lucas. If I want this promotion, then I need to earn it. Running to the boss isn't an option."

Mary looked pleased, while Lucas harrumphed again.

"Fine, fine. So how is that gorgeous little girl of yours?"

Star spent the next half an hour telling

them the story of the Tudor House, the grand burning, and Skylar's new best friend. Lucas chuckled and Mary cooed.

"So, Star, how are things going with Damian?" Lucas finally asked. Star froze as Lucas and Mary glanced at each other. "You two always did have enough chemistry to light up the room," Lucas said with a laugh and Star blushed.

"That was a long time ago ..." Star said.

"So he's not asked you out yet?" Lucas pushed.

The look of horror that passed over Star's face had Lucas sitting up straighter. "Damian will never ask me out again. I would be shocked if he did. We have a purely professional relationship now."

Lucas gave her a sceptical look. "But something's happened," he stated. Star felt the colour rise in her cheeks and Lucas clapped his hands. "I knew it! I told you, Mary!"

Mary came forwards and rested her hand on her husband's shoulder. "Enough! You're embarrassing Star, Lucas. Think about your blood pressure!"

"Well, he wouldn't tell me anything, but I knew something had happened. Now they're both acting suspicious."

Star shuddered to think of the third degree that Damian had obviously undergone at the hands of his father. Feeling the need to rescue him from future interrogation, she said, "Damian has been a great help. When Damian left for the US, you know I hurt him badly. There is no going back for us ... I'm sorry if that disappoints you."

"Listen to Star, Dad." Star froze at the sound of the new voice that had entered the room, colour flooding her cheeks at having been heard talking about him. "I'm surprised to see you here," Damian said, addressing Star this time.

"I invited her," Mary said, closing down any further argument.

Star stood awkwardly. She moved forwards and grasped Lucas's hand. "It's time I left and got back to Skylar anyway. You take care of yourself. We miss you. You need to listen to your doctors!" Leaning down, she kissed him on the cheek before collecting her bag.

"I'll walk you down," Mary said before Star could object.

"Good evening, Damian," Star said as she

left the room.

Damian refused to look at her, his eyes firmly on his father.

Mary stayed quiet until they entered the lift and descended down to the ground floor, "Have you got time for a coffee before you head off?" she asked.

Startled back into the present, Star said, "Of course, but don't you want to go back up to Lucas?"

Mary laughed. "Nope, they can bicker among themselves for a while. Damian won't take it too far with Lucas recovering, but they need to get a few things out of their system, and I could do with the break. They're two peas in a pod."

"I'd love a coffee, then," Star said. She'd left the office early, so still had time before she needed to collect Skylar.

∞∞∞

They decided on the hospital coffee shop, which, according to Mary, made a pretty amazing cup of coffee for the fact it was in a hospital. But then again, the price this hospital charged, it should be.

Once the Barista had brought their coffees, Star looked at Mary, waiting for the older woman to share her thoughts. Although her hair was now silver, Mary was still a beautiful woman. Her skin was soft and supple, with a natural glow, and the fine lines around her eyes were the only giveaway that showed she'd lived a full life.

"I want you to listen, take what I say on board, and not comment until I'm finished. Can you do that?"

Star nodded. It wasn't often that Mary wanted to be heard, so it must be important.

"Good. You are a beautiful, intelligent woman." She held up her hand before Star could open her mouth. "As such, you are always going to come across men like Jackson Brown. You need to be ahead of them. This is a dog-eat-dog world, and there are lots of useless people who want to ride on the coattails of others. What you did was brave and strong. Don't let anyone say anything different, and ignore Lucas when he said you should have gone to him – that's rubbish. That's just the alpha male in him wanting to be protective. His generation struggles to understand that we women are not damsels in distress! You were handling it and would have, if the weasel hadn't gone to Damian." Mary huffed. "It reminded me of the girl you once were, the one I was worried had disappeared. The years have been tough. You lost Lily, Damian, you took in Skylar, you got your Bachelor and Master's, all while working. You are not afraid of hard work. Lucas didn't just give you that promotion; he wouldn't. You earned it. You need to believe in yourself."

Star looked down at her coffee, unsure how to respond, a lump forming in her throat.

"Damian has told me how impressed he was with what he saw. What you had pulled together."

Star looked up and swallowed before Mary continued, "Don't get me wrong, he was very angry with his father and me for keeping our relationship with you a secret, but I told him it was none of his business whom we were friends with. With Lucas being ill, he's let it drop for now."

Star sucked in a loud breath, "No, you can't do that, Mary," Star said, horrified. "I hurt Damian, more than you can ever know. In order to get him to leave, I let him believe I didn't love him – that I never had."

"I know why Damian left, Star; I always have. I know you let him find you with Toby," Mary said gently. "It was smart and clever, and probably the only way you could have got my stubborn son to leave. It shows how well you knew Damian." Mary clasped Star's hand over the table. "Nothing short of you being unfaithful would have made him leave." Shaking her head, Mary continued, "I was so angry at Lucas for interfering, especially when I heard about Lily. Lucas was a different man then, too focused. All he could see was Damian needing to make a mark on his own, and he wanted nothing to stop him." A deep sadness tinged Mary's voice. Star was in shock; she had no idea Mary knew why she and Damian had split up.

Mary patted her hand. "I asked Damian a couple of years ago what had happened. It was then he told me. Lucas admitted to me he'd asked you to convince Damian to leave. I disagreed, but by then the damage had already been done."

"Oh, Mary, I don't know what to say."

"Do you still love him?" Mary asked.

"I don't know what I feel. My head tells me

I can't still love him, that he's a different man now. It's been so long, yet my heart re-breaks every time I look at him." Star stared at her hands. "So much time has passed and my life has turned upside down. I'm not the same person I was seven years ago. Damian has achieved so much, and I can only think of Skylar."

"That's where you are wrong!" Mary said, clasping Star's hand. "You have a child – that doesn't mean your life has to stop. You are young, beautiful, and intelligent. When Lily asked you to take care of Skylar, she didn't expect you to stop living, Star. Far from it. Your sister loved you, she loved Damian, and wanted the best for both you and her daughter. She knew you would be able to offer her daughter the unconditional love she was not going to be able to give her, but she would not have wanted you to give up on your own happiness. She fought so hard to stay on this earth with you both, but that wasn't God's plan for her. The last thing she'd want is for you to live a half-life."

Tears filled Star's eyes at the mention of Lily, and Mary patted her hand. Star knew Mary was right. Lily had fought to survive. She'd had such a thirst for life and adventure, something Star had always envied in her sister – that she'd always been the braver one. But Star wasn't sure how to do everything Mary was asking. At the moment, she couldn't allow for something to slip. Was Mary right? Had she put her life on hold? She had a plan, and once that was accomplished, then maybe she could start thinking about getting back into the dating scene. Until then, she had to get her job sorted and look after Skylar.

"Just think about what I've said. It's never too late. Open yourself up; don't lock yourself away."

Chapter Eight

Mary's talk continued to play on Star's mind over the weekend. Was she doing Skylar a disservice? Should she be looking for a father figure for her daughter? She knew better than to bring this up with Laura, as Laura and Toby had spent years trying to set her up with one friend after another, telling her constantly that she needed to get back out there. Star had pushed their matchmaking to the back of her mind, but maybe she needed to rethink. What harm could it do? She didn't have to introduce anyone to Skylar unless she was sure it was serious …

It wasn't until Star was collecting Skylar from after-school club that she finally bumped into Olivia and her dad. Skylar had run over and grabbed her hand. "Mummy, Mummy, Olivia's dad is here. Pleeeease can you arrange a play date." Star had been pulled across the hall and pushed in front of Olivia's father, who was surrounded by a couple of the other mothers. Andrew Dennison was in his mid-thirties, with short blond hair and brilliant blue eyes. He wasn't handsome in the traditional sense, but there was kindness to his face that instantly put Star at ease.

Greeting the other mothers who were congregating around him, Star stepped forwards and introduced herself, holding out her hand in greeting. She was more than a little embarrassed at her daughter's intrusion.

"Skylar's mum! Thank goodness," Andrew said with a smile, giving her his full attention. "I'm so glad to finally meet you. Olivia has been nonstop about having a playdate with Skylar, and I have to admit, I misplaced your number." The sheepish grin he shot Star was endearing and she found herself warming to him instantly.

"No problem, I know what it's like. All the bits of paper that come home from school!"

"May I take your number again?" he said, getting out his phone and unlocking it, before passing it to Star to enter her details. The other mothers slowly drifted away, leaving Star and Andrew alone. Even the girls had wandered off, content that their role in arranging a playdate was complete.

"So do you have a date?"

"Pardon?" Star said, startled at his question.

"For the playdate?" Andrew said, unaware of her awkwardness. Star felt the colour start to rise in her cheeks but stamped it down.

"I can either take Olivia home with us one evening for dinner, or she can come over one Saturday," Star said, mentally flicking through her diary.

"Well, I don't know about Skylar, but Olivia is dying to see the new Disney movie," he suggested.

"Is she ever," Star laughed.

"Well how about we take the girls to the cinema on Saturday, if you're free, that is?"

Knowing they had no plans this weekend, Star smiled and agreed. It would be nice to have some adult company for a change and it would solve two problems at once: Skylar would have the playdate she'd been on about for the past week, and Star could tick the movie off in one hit.

"Excellent, shall I pick you both up on Saturday? Save us both trying to find somewhere to park," Andrew said, before adding, "Maybe we can grab something to eat afterwards in one of the restaurants." The cinema was in a complex that catered to everything, from bowling and swimming, to a cinema and restaurants. It was a one-stop shop in entertainment.

"Sounds like a plan," Star said, scribbling down her address for Andrew. "I better get going. Skylar will be so happy we've finally managed to arrange something. See you Saturday."

Skylar chatted continuously about her playdate with Olivia all the way home, and accosted Laura and Toby with the tale as soon as they got in.

"So, you're going on a date with the new single dad?" Laura asked, when Skylar had left the room.

"What? No!" Star said, looking horrified. "We're simply taking our daughters to the cinema to see a film."

"And then dinner afterward?" Laura probed.

"You wouldn't be saying 'date' if it were

one of the other Mums," Star pointed out.

"True, but this is the 'hot' new dad, who is single," Laura pointed out, adding, "Don't get me wrong, I think it's great. You should go out on a date – it's about time."

"It is not a date! I don't do dates. This is two parents taking their girls, who happen to be friends, to the cinema and then for some food. No date! You can't have a date with two six-year-olds there!" Star said, suddenly concerned. She hadn't thought of it this way when Andrew had asked her. Surely he wasn't thinking about this as a date! This was a playdate, plain and simple. Just the cinema and then food. She was letting Laura, Toby, and even Damian get in her head! She'd show them – she could be friends with her daughter's new friend's single, good-looking dad.

"Okay, whatever you say," Laura said, sounding unconvinced.

"You'll see, he's picking us up on Saturday," Star said.

"Okay, so not a date!" Laura said with a smirk, before leaving the room.

∞ ∞ ∞

Friday came about really quickly. Star had relaxed a bit, as the team had all pulled together since Jackson had left, and she was able to trust that the tasks she delegated would get done. Life was looking up. After their impromptu meeting at the hospital, Star had managed to keep her distance from Damian, but was now being chased by Pam, who was complaining that she'd been abandoned. As it was Friday, Star had suggested they go for a catch-up lunch, which Pam jumped at, locking it into her calendar as an appointment.

They met in reception before heading to their favourite little Italian. The owner knew that lunch breaks were time restricted, so made sure the food came on time, which made it popular with the lunchtime crowd.

"So, what's new?" Pam said when they were seated at a table. "I know it's not me you're avoiding, so I can only assume it's Damian."

"I went to see Lucas in the hospital a few nights ago. Mary invited me, and then Damian showed up. Lucas was probing me about Damian and me. It was so embarrassing; I didn't know what to say. Then Mary took me for a coffee and told me I need to stop putting my life on hold."

"Well, Star, Mary has a point. When did you last go out on a date? When did you last truly let your hair down and enjoy yourself, and I'm not talking about the Christmas party or client drinks!"

Star was getting tired of everyone questioning her about her love life; it was her choice to be single. She was more than happy with just her and Skylar. "I don't need a man to fulfil my life."

"I'm not talking about fulfilling; I'm talking about enhancing. Having someone there to support and help you. Before you say it, I'm not talking about myself or Mary, or even Toby and Laura. I'm talking about someone for you, and someone who is above school age. I'm talking romance and orgasms!"

Star covered her face with her hands and laughed. It was beginning to feel like the world was ganging up on her. Before she had time to think it through, Star blurted out, "Well, as it happens, I'm going on a date tomorrow!"

"You are?" Pam's eyes lit up.

"Yes. Well, it's actually a date with Skylar and Olivia, her new best friend, and Andrew, Olivia's dad, who just so happens to be single.

He asked if we wanted to go to the cinema and he's picking us up. We are going to dinner afterwards."

Pam looked confused. "So you're going on a date with your two daughters?"

Star's shoulders sagged. "No, that's just what Laura said it was. I say it's simply a playdate for our daughters. If it were another Mum, no one would bat an eye lid, but because I'm a single mum and he's a single dad, everyone seems to be putting two and two together and coming up with five."

Pam laughed. "Don't worry," she said, patting Star's hand over the table as their food was delivered. "It may flourish into a romance, and if it doesn't, then it doesn't matter. However, if you don't go, you'll never know. Is he good looking?"

Star rolled her eyes and ignored Pam's question.

Before they knew it, it was time for them to get back to work.

Entering reception, there were plenty of people milling about, some coming and others going. Before they parted company, Pam shouted, "I hope your date goes well tomorrow!"

Star shot Pam a look of confusion, only to see Damian standing watching them both.

"Thank you, I'll let you know," Star said, unable to help herself.

Damian's eyes flashed, a look of annoyance crossing his face. For some reason, a sense of satisfaction enveloped Star. She was unsure what Pam was doing, but she felt the need to let Damian think she had a life, that she wasn't just some single mother left on the shelf. There was life after Damian Hunt, even if it was fabricated.

∞∞∞

The next day, Andrew arrived promptly at twelve-thirty. Laura rushed to the door to open it and let Andrew and Olivia in, offering them a warm welcome.

"Star's just coming," Laura said. "I'm her housemate and best friend, Laura. Pleased to meet you."

If Andrew was taken aback, he didn't show it. "You are also one of the teachers at the school?" Andrew asked, smiling at Laura.

"Guilty as charged. I teach Year 3," Laura

said. "Well remembered. Looking round a new school can be a little overwhelming. Come on in."

Star popped her head round the kitchen door, shooting her friend *the look*. "Don't mind Laura. We are having a bit of a shoe dilemma. Skylar has lost one of her favourite shoes and apparently no others will do."

Walking into the kitchen, Olivia immediately set about helping her friend try to find her shoe.

The shoe hunt had already been going on for half an hour, with Skylar refusing to wear any other pair. So when Andrew, Olivia, and Laura piled into the kitchen, it wasn't long before the shoe magically appeared behind the sofa in the conservatory with everyone hunting.

Olivia and Skylar were about to disappear upstairs when Star grabbed them both. "Ladies, we will be late for the movie if you don't get a move on."

Squeals of delight filled the air and both girls took off towards the door, only to be captured by Andrew. Star smiled at him appreciatively.

"Team work," he said, grinning.

Star couldn't help but smile back, finding

herself relaxing in his company. The joys of single parenthood, to have someone else around who understood and didn't need prompting. Star grabbed Skylar's booster seat and they headed for Andrew's car. Star took in a deep breath at the brand-new C-Class Cabriolet Mercedes, its top down. Skylar was jumping up and down in excitement, having never ridden in a car with its top off. Andrew smiled at her enthusiasm and showed her how the top went up and down using a button. Olivia was clearly also enjoying the show, happy her dad was able to impress her friend.

Once Andrew had taken the booster seat from Star and attached it, the two girls clambered into the back, and he strapped them in. Then he opened the door for Star. A real gentleman. It was something Damian had always made a point of doing, but, no, thoughts of Damian were not going to invade today.

Star climbed in, thanking Andrew, and allowing him to shut the door behind her. As the girls chatted nonstop, Andrew turned to Star, giving her a dazzling smile that left her breathless. This man could be dangerous, Star thought, as she returned his smile with one of her own. Looking over his shoulder at their two passengers, Andrew asked, "Are you ready to go, ladies?"

"Yes," both girls squealed, followed by another peal of giggles.

The cinema was packed. Andrew and Star sat either side of the girls, who sat happily in the middle with their large popcorn and drinks. The movie was not as bad as Star had feared. As with many of the new children's films, there was an underlying story, sarcasm, and innuendos that flew straight over the girls' heads but had both Andrew and Star laughing together.

The girls chose pizza for dinner. The restaurant itself was clearly set up for parents and their children, with a soft-play area for the children while they waited for their food to arrive. It didn't take long for the girls to make their choice before disappearing into the balls and tubes, leaving Andrew and Star alone.

"So, what do you do, Star? I take it you work, because Skylar is at after school-club every evening."

"I do. I work for an advertising agency in the City. How about you?" Star asked as the waitress delivered their drinks.

"I'm a cardiologist, heart surgeon," Andrew said. "We've just moved down from Yorkshire where I was based. I decided Olivia needed to be nearer my parents, and a position came up, so I took it."

"That makes sense. What about Olivia's mum?" Star said, and then immediately followed with, "Sorry, that's none of my business …"

"No, that's okay. Olivia's mum isn't in the picture. She never wanted children and found out too late that she was pregnant. She went ahead with the pregnancy, but when I told her I wanted to keep our child, she gave me an ultimatum. Her or Olivia. I told her it was Olivia, and that's the last I saw of her," Andrew said matter-of-factly. "How about you?"

"It's just me and Skylar," Star said, before adding, "and Toby and Laura, my housemates. My parents don't really help out, and Skylar's dad is out of the picture."

"I'm sorry, that's tough. But having met Laura, it looks like you have a great friend there."

"I do. It would have been much harder without them," Star admitted, surprised they were being so open with each other. "Skylar may tell Olivia, so I'll explain. I'm Skylar's mum, but

I'm also her aunt. My sister died not long after Skylar was born, so I adopted her."

Shock crossed Andrew's features. "Wow, that's some commitment. I don't mean to be rude, but you can't have been very old to take on that responsibility."

Star smiled. "I was twenty-one."

"You are raising a lovely little girl. Olivia adores her," Andrew said. "I get a run-down of everything they have done, every night."

"Glad it's not just me," Star said with a laugh. "Thank you. Olivia is sweet, too. Skylar has been so excited about today."

"It's good to be away from the hospital and doing something normal."

As they spoke, Star found herself relaxing and enjoying Andrew's company. It had been a long time since she'd been out with someone new, let alone talked so freely. Andrew was making that possible. He was easy to talk to and a great listener. It was only the arrival of the food that had the girls returning to the table, which caused a pause in their conversation.

Once the food was cleared away, the girls begged for more time, and with neither Star nor Andrew needing to rush home, they let the girls return to the soft-play area for another twenty minutes while they enjoyed a coffee.

"This has been really great, thank you for suggesting it," Star found herself saying.

"It has. It's nice to have someone else to share a day like this. If I'm honest, it's hard being a single dad. Olivia and I tend to be left on the side-lines, which is something I always feel guilty about."

"I agree, being 'the single parent' is hard, even as a woman." At Andrew's look of surprise, Star continued, "Skylar spends more time with Laura, Toby, and me than she does with any of the children from school. It's hard working full-time and trying to arrange playdates. I can't easily hold them during the week and at weekends, people want to spend their time as a family."

"Well, if I'm around, I'm happy for Skylar to come back to our house," Andrew said.

"The same goes for me," Star said, smiling in return. "I think we better round up these two munchkins before they get too tired."

"You are welcome, and I hope we can do it again sometime. We can form our own parents club. Single Parents United."

By the time Andrew drove them home, the two girls were fast asleep in the back of the car. "Thank you again for this afternoon. Our sleeping princesses have enjoyed themselves," Star said, looking over her shoulder at the two girls.

"Thank you – it's been fun," Andrew said as he climbed out. Opening the door, he scooped the sleeping Skylar into his arms and carried her to the front door. Star retrieved the car seat and followed. By the time she caught up, Andrew was handing an exhausted Skylar to Toby on the doorstep, who immediately turned and headed for the stairs.

Star and Andrew stood on the doorstep, staring at each other, neither one sure what to do, until in the end, Star broke the silence, "Catch you soon."

Touching her arm as a parting gesture, Andrew smiled before he turned and headed back to the car. "See you soon," he called, before getting back into the car and driving off.

"Well?"

Star jumped at Laura's appearance behind her.

"Well, what?"

"Don't play coy with me. How was it?" Laura said.

"We had a great time. The girls have had fun – they exhausted themselves," Star said, moving into the house.

"I'm talking about you and Andrew?" Laura said. "It looked like he was thinking about kissing you."

"No, he wasn't, and were you spying on us?" Star said.

"Guilty," Laura replied, unashamed.

Star shook her head. "We got on well. We talked a lot. He's easy to talk to, but before you get any ideas, that was it. We talked, end of. Please don't make any more of it than it is."

Laura raised her hands in surrender. One thing about Laura, she knew when to stop pushing.

"How was your day?" Star said, changing the subject.

"Good – we've ordered the crib and pushchair," Laura said, before going on to recount all the baby shopping they'd done over the day. Star tried to concentrate, but her mind kept wandering. It wasn't to Andrew her thoughts went to, though. She was thinking about Damian.

Chapter Nine

Star had received a number of messages from Andrew over the weekend. His messages had been fun and light-hearted, making her laugh. Laura had even commented about Star smiling more than usual, and Star had to admit when Monday morning came around that her time out with Andrew and the girls had lightened her mood.

Mary had also messaged an update on Lucas's recovery. Lucas was being kept in, as he'd developed a minor chest infection. His doctors were not too concerned, but his consultant wanted to keep him in for another couple of days, mainly to ensure he rested. Everyone at the hospital had learned Lucas Hunt was a force to be reckoned with, heart attack or not. He was not one to sit idly by and recuperate. If Star didn't know better, she would put money on Mary having got his heart specialist to keep him in to ensure he had to rest.

Star could hear the desperation in Mary's message, and promised to come and visit him later in the week.

Over the weekend, Star had had time to think. She'd decided it was best she stay as far away from Damian as she could, so refrained from visiting Pam when she got to work until she knew he'd left the building.

"About time you showed your face, young lady," Pam said, greeting her with a smile.

"I'm a busy woman, what more can I say," Star replied with sass, dropping herself into the chair opposite Pam.

"Come on, how did Saturday go?" Pam said sitting forwards, pushing her pile of work to one side.

"It was lovely, the girls had a great time," Star said.

"That is not what I'm asking. Did you have a *great* time?" Pam asked.

"It was fun. Andrew was good company, and we had a lovely afternoon with our daughters." Star decided not to embellish. Yes, he'd been in contact with her since. But she wasn't sure what that meant and didn't want to read anything more into it. Plus, she wasn't sure if she wanted anything more. Did she need the added complication? What would happen if she dated Andrew, and then it all went wrong – where would that leave Skylar and Olivia?

What was she thinking? Her friends had put ideas in her head; she needed to stop this right now.

"Changing the subject," Star said, "I'm heading over to visit Lucas one evening this week. Mary said Damian has a business meeting so I can visit without any awkwardness."

Pam pulled up Damian's diary, "Yes, he has a client dinner on Friday. You're good to go. You know, if you like this Andrew, then you should go for it. That's all I'm going to say on the matter."

Rolling her eyes, Star left Pam at her desk and headed back downstairs.

∞∞∞

Laura had volunteered to pick Skylar up after

school on Friday, and together they were going to bake some cakes for Laura's class bake sale. Star had promised to clear up when she got home as a thank you, which Laura and Skylar had jumped at. Star hated to think what kind of mess they'd make together.

Due to the rain, Star decided to take a taxi instead of the tube. When she arrived at the hospital, Star headed straight to Lucas's floor. His door was shut, so she knocked gently. Mary opened the door, looking much brighter than she had a week ago, but flustered. Lucas, although pale, looked more like Lucas on a day when things were not going his way.

"Maybe you can talk some sense into the stubborn old goat!" Mary said, stepping aside to let Star enter into the room.

"Don't you 'old goat' me, woman," Lucas huffed. "It's your fault I'm not at home right now, sitting in my own bed."

"Well, if I thought you'd stay in bed!"

Star stepped into the room, careful not to position herself between the waring couple.

"Okay, time out," Star said. "Mary, why don't you take a break and go and get yourself a coffee. I'm happy to sit with Lucas while you're downstairs."

A look of relief passed over Mary's face. "Don't put up with any of his nonsense!" she said, before grabbing her bag and heading for the door. "His specialist will be in soon and he needs to do as he's told. I'll be back later."

When Mary left, Star pulled up a chair next to Lucas's bed, and said, "You must be feeling better."

"Not really," Lucas muttered. "Everyone is treating me like I'm made of glass, that I'm broken."

Star had never before seen Lucas like this, his frustration and helplessness showing through. Since she'd first met him, Lucas had always been a dominant force, someone to be reckoned with. Now he appeared to be a shell of himself – pale and much thinner. The heart attack and surgery had definitely taken its toll.

"Well, it's for your own good," Star said. "Everyone loves you, Lucas, and you've given them a scare. They only want what's best for you." Leaning forwards, she rested her hand on his. He looked into her eyes and Star blinked, realising that Lucas Hunt, CEO of Hunt and Hunt Advertising, was frightened. His mortality was on show for everyone.

Lucas cleared his throat. Removing his hand, he patted Star's instead.

"How is that little munchkin of yours?" Lucas asked.

"She's good – she's sent you some cookies, but I'll be leaving those with Mary," Star said, knowing what a secret sweet tooth Lucas had.

"I hear Damian met her," the sly old goat dropped in, clearly fishing for more information.

Star raised her eyebrow, letting him know she wasn't fooled by his fishing. "He did. Skylar has a crush. She's been baking him cookies, too."

"Always did have a way with the ladies, my son." A twinkle appeared in Lucas's eye, but he didn't add anything else to the conversation. Before Star could reply, there was a knock on the door.

"Evening, Mr Hunt."

Star spun round at the familiar voice that had entered the room.

"Star? What are you doing here?" Andrew's eyes latched onto her, although he recovered quickly. "Well, obviously you're here to see Mr Hunt. How are you this evening, Mr Hunt?"

Lucas looked from one to the other, a

frown creasing his brow. "I'm fine, Mr Dennison. Just want to get out of this place. Tell me you're here to discharge me." Lucas's voice had once again taken on its commanding tone. The one Star was familiar with around the office. She was happy to hear he was still in there, even if his body was frail.

"We'll see," Andrew said, unfazed by Lucas. "I need to ask you some questions and run a few tests, but I think we should be seeing you going home very soon."

"I'll wait outside," Star said, glancing at Andrew, whose smile sent butterflies loose in her stomach. Feeling a blush rise into her cheeks, Star smiled back and made a quick exit, closing the door behind her. Leaning against the wall, she tried hard to get a grip on her raging libido. Star hadn't thought about Andrew as a surgeon. Until he'd walked into Lucas's room, she hadn't expected to see him in his scrubs at his place of work. Star leant against the wall and closed her eyes, taking a deep breath.

"What are you doing out here?" Star jumped at the sound of Damian's voice.

"Andrew is in with your father, so I'm giving them some space. I could ask you the same thing. I thought you had a client meeting?" Star stammered.

"It was cut short. And *Andrew*?" Damian raised an eyebrow. "You mean Mr Dennison, Dad's surgeon?"

"Yes, Mr Dennison." Star's cheeks were on fire and she once again found herself breathless. What was it about her traitorous body? For years, she'd had her feelings under control – now that seemed to be shot to hell. Two men had entered her life and she was acting like a teenager, all blushes and tongue-tied. "He's Skylar's best friend's dad," Star added, unsure why she felt the need to clarify to Damian her relationship with Andrew.

"Ah, the good-looking, single surgeon. I bet he sets a few tongues wagging in the playground," Damian said.

Star smarted at Damian's dig, surprised at how much he knew about Andrew. "I wouldn't know. I work and therefore don't listen to playground gossip."

They both stared at each other, neither backing down.

"Was he your date?"

"What?" Star felt the colour fly to her

cheeks once again.

"He was!" Damian said, as if he'd just uncovered something unpleasant.

"What business is it of yours whom I date," Star said before realising the trap she'd just walked into. Before either one of them could say anymore, the door opened and Andrew stepped into the corridor.

"All done," he said, smiling once more at Star, before realising Damian was standing next to her. "Good to see you again, Mr Hunt. Good news, your father is fit for discharge. I have given him strict instructions, which I've written down, but other than that, he'll be free for discharge in the morning."

"Thank you, Mr Dennison," Damian answered coldly, his usual warmth missing.

If Andrew noticed, he didn't let on, smiling once again before heading down the corridor. As Star was about to re-enter Lucas's room, Andrew turned and said, "Star, may I have a quick word?"

Damian glared at her, making her all the more adamant to speak to Andrew.

"Of course," she said, smiling at Andrew, before heading down the corridor.

"Sorry to pull you away," he said, not

looking in the slightest bit sorry, "but I'm off-duty in half an hour and was wondering if you wanted to grab something to eat? I have my car, so I can drive you home afterwards."

"That would be lovely." She'd enjoyed his company at the weekend, so why not. Laura was always telling her to get out. Star was sure her friend would be more than encouraging if she knew the reason for her babysitting extension. "Let me drop Laura a message and I'll see you when you're finished."

Andrew's face lit up with pleasure. "Fantastic, I'll pop back up when I'm done. Stay with Lucas as long as you want."

Star felt a smile take over her face. Maybe life was starting to look up.

∞∞∞

Before heading back into Lucas's room, Star fired off a message to Laura, who instantly replied telling Star to enjoy herself and all was good at home. Entering Lucas's room, Star was aware all eyes were on her. Mary had returned and was now sitting by Lucas's bed, while Damian was lounging against the wall.

"So you know my doctor?" Lucas said, leaving Star squirming under his gaze.

"I do. Skylar and his daughter Olivia are best friends," Star replied, although it wasn't really any of their business, but Lucas was a friend and she didn't want to offend him.

"They can't have been friends long – he's only just moved here," Mary said.

What was this, the third degree? Damian stood quietly, watching.

"No, he hasn't, but Skylar was Olivia's buddy when she joined the school and they hit it off. You know how children are – they make friends very quickly. Andrew and I took the girls to the cinema last weekend and that's how I know him ..." Star quickly changed the subject: "So, Lucas, when are you going to be discharged?"

Lucas looked a little disgruntled at the change of topic, while Mary simply stared at her. Surely they didn't begrudge her a male companion, especially one as nice as Andrew. She'd been on her own for the past seven years.

Lucas and Mary changed the subject as she requested, and they talked about what Lucas intended to do once he was free from the prison he was in, otherwise known as a first-class private hospital. Damian remained quiet, silently simmering in the corner. Star kept her gaze on Lucas but could feel Damian's eyes burning into her back.

Half an hour later there was a knock on the door and Andrew popped his head in, dressed casually now.

"Hi, are you ready to go?" he asked.

"Yes, of course," Star said, glancing around awkwardly for her bag. Damian picked it up and handed it to her. Their fingers touched, sending waves of desire spiralling through her body. Star diverted her gaze, not wanting to see the emotion written on his face – not when she was about to leave the room with another man.

Andrew smiled and waited, oblivious.

"We could have given you a lift home," Mary stated quickly.

"Thank you, Mary, that's very kind," Star said quickly, "but Andrew and I are going to grab something to eat before we head home. Laura has Skylar, so I get to play grown up for a couple of hours."

The temperature in the room dropped and Mary's eyes flashed to Damian. Star shot him a look, the tension in his jaw the only visible factor that he was unhappy with that answer. Deciding now was definitely the time to leave, she rose and dropped a kiss on Lucas's forehead. "Look after yourself and make sure you listen to everything Mary says. I want to be visiting you at home, not in here."

Lucas patted her hand, peering round her at Andrew, who was waiting patiently. "Have fun. But not too much," he said conspiratorially.

Star gave Mary a hug, "I'll see you soon."

"You too," Mary said, sounding off, but returning her hug.

"See you at the office," Star said to Damian as she passed him. Andrew held open the door for her, letting her pass. Star had never felt so visible in her life, as if the entire world were staring at her.

"Have a lovely evening," Andrew said as he left, shutting the door behind him. "Do you like Thai food? There's a great restaurant round the corner," he said, dropping his hand to her lower back as they walked down the corridor. Star jumped at his touch, but if Andrew felt her response, he chose to ignore it, guiding her towards the elevator.

"That would be great." Star replied, feeling awkward all of a sudden. What was she doing? She barely knew Andrew, yet she'd agreed to go to dinner with him.

∞∞∞

"So, how was your dinner with Dr Dishy?" Laura asked the next morning, when Star came down to the kitchen to make herself a cup of coffee. Laura swung her legs round, sitting up on the sofa where she'd been lying with her feet up.

"Not doctor, he's a Mister. Surgeons are Misters," Star replied.

"Doctor, Mister. Okay, how was your dinner with Mr Dishy Surgeon?" Laura waggled her eyebrows, making Star smirk.

"It was," Star paused, "nice."

"Nice! Nice is a biscuit! You can't go on a dinner date with a dishy surgeon and describe it as 'nice'!"

"Well, it was 'nice' – we ate, we talked, we laughed, and he drove me home. It was a 'nice' evening."

"Does that mean you're going to see him

again?"

"Of course I'll see him again – he's Olivia's dad, and she and Skylar are friends … Will I see him again, just him and me? No, I'm not ready for that kind of relationship. As I said, last night was nice, but it wasn't more than that."

"He isn't Damian," Laura said, not pulling her punches.

"No, he's not Damian," Star retorted, before sinking down into the chair opposite Laura with a sigh. "But that is also a good thing. Andrew and I discussed this last night – he picked up on the atmosphere between Damian and me when he saw us together and outright asked me what was going on. I gave him the short version, but he said our chemistry was off the charts and I shouldn't ignore it." Star looked up at Laura, who was watching her intently. "Andrew told me he likes me, but he thinks Damian and I have unfinished business, and he doesn't want himself or Olivia caught up in the middle, not that I blame him. I like Andrew, but found I couldn't say outright that Damian means nothing to me, or that Andrew's heart would be safe with me."

Laura got up and wrapped her arms

around Star. "Hey, don't worry about it. I'm just proud of you for getting yourself out there. Damian is here, and maybe he needs to be so you and he can finally put the past behind you and move on. Your relationship never really ended. It ended on a lie and that has never sat well with you." It was Laura's turn to sigh. "You've always put on a brave face – you did this for Damian, for Lily and Skylar, but in doing so, you broke your own heart." Laura's voice caught on the last word, her love for Star and her devastation at what her friend had given up evident. Composing herself, she continued, putting her finger to Star's lips, "I think you need to speak to Damian, tell him the truth, and move on with your life. For you, for Skylar, and for Damian."

Star's eyes burned with tears as she said, "I'm not sure I can."

"It won't be easy, but you owe it to yourself and to Damian. He loved you with every ounce of his being from the moment you met, and I know you felt the same."

Star swiped at the moisture that ran down her cheeks. "What am I supposed to say?" she whispered. "Sorry, Damian, you know you found me in bed with Toby – well that was all a set up to get you to leave and move to the US office. We still had our underwear on and weren't really having sex. I just wanted you to think we were. Your dad had asked for my help to get you to accept the job in the New York Office, but in the meantime my sister was diagnosed with cancer and I couldn't go with you so I tricked you into going by yourself and it worked." By the time Star had finished, her body was wracked with sobs. Laura held on tightly while her friend let out the pain of the past seven years. "He didn't even try to fight for me, Laura." The reality of the situation finally hitting home. For the first time, Star acknowledged that it wasn't what she'd done, so much as that Damian had given up on them at the first opportunity. The first sign of trouble and he'd left; he hadn't even wanted an explanation. He'd been on the next flight out and hadn't looked back.

Laura hugged her tighter, until a kick caused them both to fly apart. Laura giggled and Star stared in wonder at her friend's extended stomach. Placing her hand on Laura's bump, she was rewarded with another kick.

"Someone wanted to join in on the action," Laura said, laughing, easing the tension.

Star smiled, gently stroking the little bump knowing that her friend wouldn't mind. It was one of the reasons Star had never questioned her choice before. She'd been there when Skylar had started kicking Lily.

Star had found Lily crying late one night, so had climbed into bed and curled up next to her. Lily had taken Star's hand and placed it on her stomach, while Skylar had performed a merry dance inside her. Filled with wonder at the tiny miracle, they'd both given in and cried that night. Cried for the future they knew Lily couldn't escape, except by a miracle. They'd both loved the little bump that was growing, and it was at that point that Star had promised her sister that, whatever happened, she would always be there for them. She hadn't been able to save Lily, but she had been able to take her daughter and raise her, as she knew Lily would have wanted, surrounded by love.

Star wiped her face and smiled. "I remember Skylar kicking – she never gave Lily a moment's peace once she realised her mum would play with her."

"I remember too. Lily would be so proud of that little girl. What I should say, *is* so proud. You know I believe in guardian angels, and I know she's here with Skylar every day – and with you," Laura said softly.

"I like to think so. I hope she'd be happy with the way I'm raising her daughter. She gave her life to ensure Skylar made it into the world." Star looked up and smiled. "On a happier note, Skylar and I are heading into the office today. I have some appraisals I want to get finished and the office will be empty, so I thought I'd take her with me and she can use the desk to finish her project. She told me you'd helped her sort out all her baby pictures last night ready for her scrap book. I don't know how I'll ever thank you for all you do."

Laura smiled. "It was fun. We enjoyed looking at all the baby and toddler photos. I reprinted them all. Plus, we found some of you, me, and Lily when we were younger. I told her lots of stories about the mischief you and Lily used to get up to, and she lapped it up. Anyway, I'll be calling in favours once this little one arrives – you can count on it."

Chapter Ten

Skylar never complained when she had to go into the office. To her, it was an adventure. A trip on the tube and a walk to the office, often followed by a hot chocolate with all the trimmings and a muffin. What six-year-old was ever going to turn that down. Plus, she loved the staff, as they all spoiled her rotten. Today, however, was different, as it was Saturday. Star was not expecting anyone in today, which was why she was hoping she'd be able to get in, finish her tasks, and then she and Skylar would be able to grab something to eat and head home.

Skylar had brought her latest school project with her. They were creating a My Life book. Laura had helped Skylar collect photographs of family and friends, which she was sticking into a scrap book and labelling. They had bought a new glue stick and marker pens for her to use, so Skylar was super-excited to get on with it. Star knew it would offer her some time to complete her own work, which meant a win/win for everyone.

Star set up her laptop in the meeting room, and put newspaper down to protect the desk, before letting Skylar paste and stick to her heart's content.

Engrossed in her work, Star did not notice Damian's approach until Skylar squealed, "Damian!", snapping her out of her work trance.

"Hello, Skylar. Lovely to see you. What are you doing here today?" Damian had hunched down next to Skylar's chair and was looking at the photos she had spread out over the desk.

"I'm here 'cause Mummy had some work to finish, and I have a project to complete for school," Skylar told him.

"Ah, and what is your project?" Damian seemed genuinely interested.

"I'm creating a book about me," she said, flipping to the beginning of her scrap book, showing Damian all the pictures she had already stuck in. "This is me as a tiny, tiny baby. I was so small when I was born, I was in an incubator. I was only thirty weeks." Damian looked up and caught Star's gaze before returning his attention to Skylar. Flipping to the next page, she said, "This is Mummy Lily." Star froze. "Mummy Lily was very sick when I was born and she died. She's an angel now and it's why I live with Mummy."

Star watched as Damian swallowed hard, realisation crossing his features. "I knew your Mummy Lily," he said to Skylar.

"You did?"

Damian now had Skylar's full attention.

"I did. I knew both your mummies before you were born."

"Mummy Lily was an actress in the West End – did you know her then?"

"I did," Damian said, his eyes gleaming as he realised the joy he was giving the little girl who wanted to hear about her mummy. "I went with Mummy Star to watch her a lot – she was brilliant on the stage."

Damian had developed a close relationship with Lily, when it was obvious how serious he was about Star. Lily had been the protective older sister, giving him the third degree on his intentions for her sister, but he'd won her over within no time, and they'd all spent a lot of time together when Lily hadn't been on the stage performing.

Once Damian had exhausted his stories, Skylar went back to showing him more of her pictures. There were a number of pictures of Star, Lily, and Skylar together, although it was obvious how ill Lily was by this point. There were photos of a growing Skylar in her incubator, only Lily was no longer there. She'd died before Skylar had been released from hospital, so the photos switched to only Star and Skylar together. Damian didn't comment, but listened to the little girl telling her story. He kept his eyes averted from Star, for which she was grateful. Star knew the story; she'd lived it. But it still hurt to speak about Lily, and she wasn't ready to answer his questions – questions she knew he would have.

Skylar continued to talk and Damian continued to ask her questions. Star decided to shut them out and get on with her work. It wasn't until a little later she felt Skylar shake her arm.

"Mummy, can Damian come to dinner with us?" Star looked up, surprised to see Damian was still there. All the photographs had disappeared and Skylar's scrap book looked to be full. Glancing at the clock, another hour had gone by. Had Damian been here the whole time and helped Skylar?

"I'm sure Damian is busy, Skylar," she said, giving him an out should he wish to take it.

"Are you too busy?" Skylar asked Damian, a small wrinkle forming between her brows.

Damian smiled at her. "No, I would love to come to dinner with you. Where are you going?"

Star shot Damian a look. What was he doing? She'd just given him the perfect opportunity to get out of eating dinner with a six-year-old and he'd not taken it. "We were going to go to Mama's Pizza – it's my favourite," Skylar informed him.

It wasn't a fancy restaurant, not like the ones Damian obviously frequented.

"Mama's Pizza sounds perfect. I'll just pop up to my office and grab my things. Are you ready to go?" He directed this last part to Star.

"Yes, I'm all done. Thank you for helping Skylar with her project."

Damian smiled and rested his hand on Skylar's shoulder. "My pleasure. We had fun, didn't we, Skylar."

Skylar looked up in total adoration and Star's heart skipped a beat as she watched her daughter fall further under Damian's spell. He was winning her over. How would she cope when he went back to the US? How would either of them cope? She knew Damian was going to have questions for her. Thankfully he'd obviously left those for when Skylar wasn't present. Now they were having dinner together. So much for keeping Damian Hunt at arm's length. So much for telling Mary she couldn't love him … It was obvious she'd never stopped loving him, and now her daughter was falling for him, too. What was she going to do?

∞∞∞

They were immediately seated at one of the booth tables at Mama's Pizza. Skylar had held Damian's hand all the way from the office, which Damian seemed to take in his stride. For a man who had no children, Damian was very much a natural.

"Do you have any children?" Skylar asked Damian when he sat down next to her, as if she'd read Star's thoughts.

"No, I don't," Damian said. "But I have lots of friends with children."

"Ah, so that is how you knew how to do my scrap book," Skylar said before setting her attention to the colouring menu that the waitress had left for her.

Damian looked at Star for the first time since they'd left the office. "Not what I was expecting, and I'm sorry …" Damian said, clearly referring to Lily.

"It was a long time ago," Star said, swallowing past the lump that had formed in her throat.

"Did you get all your work finished?" Damian asked.

"I did, thank you. I didn't expect you to stay and complete Skylar's scrap book with her."

"It was my pleasure. It was lovely looking at the photos of her growing up. She really is a credit to you. Mum and Dad are obviously very taken with her, too."

"Your parents have been a tremendous support. I couldn't have done what I have without their continued support. Theirs, and Laura and Toby's."

Damian tensed again at Toby's name, but Star let it go. She needed to tell him the truth – Laura was right – but now with little ears around was not the time.

"How's your mum?" Damian asked.

Star rolled her eyes. Damian was well aware of the relationship she had with her mum. "Much the same, we don't see her often. Now Dad is on the scene permanently, she has her own life and has made that abundantly clear." Star struggled to keep the bitterness out of her voice.

Damian looked shocked. "Even after?"

"Even after," Star said, sending him a warning glance to shut this subject down. "I have a lot to tell you, but now is probably not the time."

Skylar looked up at Damian. "That means she doesn't want to talk about it in front of me," Skylar said, rolling her eyes, "She says the same thing to Aunty Laura, then stops talking until I leave."

"Well that told your mummy!" Damian said, his face softening as he grinned at Skylar, before raising his laughing eyes to Star.

Skylar grinned and looked at Star, "Please may I have the margarita pizza?"

It was Star's turn to roll her eyes, which made Damian laugh even harder. "Yes, you may."

After that, the three of them fell into an easy conversation. Damian asked Skylar about school, and she told him how she loved maths but hated reading. He questioned her about it, and by the end of the night, Skylar had decided reading was going to be her new favourite subject, mainly because Damian loved it and had promised to give her some of his favourite stories to read. After dinner, they made a trip to the local bookshop, and Damian had purchased a couple of books for Skylar which he thought she'd enjoy. Star had tried to step in, but he'd shut her down, telling her this was between Skylar and him. Skylar had clutched her bag of books all the way home.

Marcus was coming to pick Damian up, so he offered them both a lift home. Star was about to decline, but Skylar jumped at the suggestion, clinging to Damian, and one look at her daughter told Star she was exhausted and the ride was not going to hurt. It had been a hard day emotionally; it always was when Skylar brought Lily up to people who weren't aware of what had happened. Not that Damian was a stranger –

he'd known and loved her sister, but Star hadn't been able to tell him the whole story, and it was still sitting between them. Star surprised herself because she suddenly realised she wanted to tell him everything.

Skylar was excited to see Marcus when he collected them, but within five minutes was sound asleep, her head resting against Damian's arm. He shifted his arm around her to make her more comfortable.

"She's taken with you," Star said softly, knowing nothing would wake her daughter now she was asleep.

"She's a wonderful little girl and a credit to you." Damian looked down at the little girl asleep in his arms.

Silence stretched between them as they left the city and moved further out. Before long, Marcus was pulling into Star's driveway. The lights were all off, the house in darkness.

"Thank you, Marcus. Good night, Damian. I'll just open up and come back for her if that's okay." Star exited the car and headed to the front door. The security lights came on, making the journey easier. After opening the door, she turned back to collect Skylar, only to find Damian behind her, Skylar nestled in his arms, still sound asleep. He motioned for her to go inside when she tried to take Skylar from him, heading for the stairs.

Walking into the house, Damian followed. Star turned on the lights as they went. Laura and Toby were away for the bank holiday weekend, visiting her parents, so she and Skylar had the house to themselves. She motioned for Damian to follow her, and they ascended the stairs, heading to Skylar's bedroom. Pulling back the covers, Star motioned for Damian to lay her down on the bed. Slipping off Skylar's shoes, Star pulled the covers over her. Skyla's leggings and T-shirt could act as pyjamas for tonight. Star shut the door behind her and motioned for Damian to follow her back downstairs.

"Thank you again," Star said.

"No problem," Damian said. "I hope you don't mind – I sent Marcus away. Mum texted when we were in the car. She needs Marcus to collect something for Dad. He was finally discharged today, and is already driving mum up the wall. Marcus'll be back as soon as he's sorted it out."

"Oh, no problem," Star's heart skipped a

beat. She was alone with Damian for the first time in seven years. "Would you like a drink? I'm sure we have some wine, or tea, or coffee?"

"A tea would be lovely," Damian said, making his way through to the kitchen. "I can't believe you still live here," he said, almost to himself.

"Yes, Toby and Laura have been amazing. They've really helped with raising Skylar. I couldn't have done it without them."

"What about your mum?" Damian asked.

"Ha, what about her!"

"Well, Skylar is her grand-daughter. The daughter of the daughter she lost."

"Yes, and not her problem," Star said. Damian looked shocked and Star laughed. "You missed my father coming back into her life. His first wife died and Mum couldn't wait to step into her shoes."

It was Damian's turn to show understanding, "I'm sorry about Lily," he said.

"So am I," Star said, sighing, the pain still evident in her chest whenever she talked about her sister. "It was so quick in the end."

"Do you want to talk about it?" Damian was giving her the choice, and for the first time in what felt like forever, Star wanted to talk about Lily.

∞∞∞

Taking their tea into the sitting room, Star motioned for Damian to take a seat. Sitting next to him on the old sofa was like old times.

Damian sat back and waited.

"Lily didn't know she was pregnant at first. She had been feeling really tired, but had put it down to the number of shows she was performing, the late nights, and partying. She'd started getting bruises, but again had put it down to her clumsiness on set, multiple shows, and quick costume changes – it was part of the job. The theatre company was sending all its members for health checks, something to do with the insurance, and that is when the blood test came back to say she had non-Hodgkin lymphoma. She came straight home, and we went to see some specialists. They were really positive, telling her she was the perfect fit for a number of new trials. She was young, otherwise healthy – her prognosis was good." Star paused, taking a sip of her tea, the memories of that time flooding her mind.

"When was this?" Damian asked.

Star looked at Damian and sighed. "It was when you and your dad were in the US office for the month."

Damian took a deep breath, realisation hitting him. "You never said anything."

"I couldn't. I couldn't voice what was happening. If I didn't talk about it, it wasn't real. For weeks I was in denial." Star looked him in the eye. "By the time you came home, Lily had found out she was pregnant. They'd run some more blood tests, and her pregnancy had shown up. The doctor told her she would need to abort in order to have the treatment needed to save her life. She told them no way and walked out. I sat with the doctor while he explained the options to me. He wanted me to convince her, but I knew in my heart nothing would change her mind. It was that day I swore to stay by her side – that I'd support her decision and whatever else came from it."

"What about Skylar's father?"

"He wanted nothing to do with Lily once he heard she was pregnant. Or should I say, his family wanted him to have nothing to do with her or the baby. Two weeks after she found out she was pregnant, his engagement was spread all over a glossy magazine. His family had found the perfect match and that certainly wasn't an actress from a single-parent family. Lily was devastated. I think she knew she wasn't going to make it, and she was terrified about her baby's future." Damian pulled her into his chest as Star's voice caught. She took the strength he offered, resting her head against his heart.

"He didn't deserve either of them, whoever this man was," Damian murmured into her hair.

"No, he didn't. Lily was too good for him. I only met him a couple of times; she'd kept him a secret from us all the months they were together. He loved Lily – you could see that – but he was weak," Star said, admitting out loud what she'd never voiced before.

They sat in silence, Damian stroking her hair and Star letting herself fall into the comfort he offered.

Damian's hand paused, before he said softly, "Why did you sleep with Toby?"

"Damian," Star whispered, sitting up and holding his gaze, "I didn't. Lily needed me. You needed to go to the New York office. It is what we'd planned – it was your future and I couldn't ask you to put your life on hold for me, for my sister. Toby agreed to help me, although wasn't happy about it, and Laura to this day hasn't forgiven me ..."

"Did you not think I would have been there to support you, to support Lily? I wouldn't have gone. I could have gone at a later date." Damian sounded angry as the truth sank in.

"No, you needed to go," Star said calmly, placing a hand on his arm. She'd had seven years to come to terms with her decision not to hold him back and to let him go, however much it hurt her. "The Head of the New York office was looking to retire and you needed to be there. It was all we'd talked about for months. It was your future. I still had university to finish, but I knew I was needed here. I couldn't leave Lily, and then later, Skylar needed me."

"Don't you think I should have been given the choice? I loved you," Damian said, his frustration clear.

His use of the past tense struck a lance through Star's heart. "And it's because of that, that I had to do what I did. Our love would have died, resentment would have set in, and I couldn't have carried that. I looked after my sister throughout her illness. She gave birth as you saw at thirty weeks – it was touch and go whether Skylar was going to survive. Lily's cancer was everywhere by this point. Treatment was out of the question. Her pregnancy hormones had fed it, and she only lived for three weeks after Skylar was born. I was thrust into motherhood; I dropped out of college and spent all my time at the hospital. I prayed Lily hadn't given up her life for us then to lose Skylar, too. Skylar was a fighter and I brought her home from the hospital two days before my twenty-second birthday. I worked part-time and studied part-time as soon as Skylar was old enough. I wasn't going to drag you or anyone else into my chaos."

"You let Toby and Laura in," Damian said bitterly. Star watched as Damian looked around, taking in his surroundings. The decor was completely different to how it had been when they were students. There was no evidence that the house had been a party zone most weekends. Toby had invested in the property as soon as he knew Skylar would be joining them, getting the place renovated and child friendly.

"I did, but not by choice. Mum made it clear I wasn't moving back home with the baby. She wanted me to put Skylar up for adoption. Toby, Laura, and the rest of the housemates banded together. They wanted me to stay, so I agreed to cook and clean for them so Skylar and I had a roof over our heads. It was only supposed to be temporary – my father paid me an allowance which allowed me to pay my way, although he asked me never to tell my mother. But then I went back to uni part-time and your dad offered me a part-time role at the agency. The extra hands helped, and Toby and Laura became aunt and uncle to Skylar."

Star lay her hand against Damian's cheek, pulling his attention to her. "I'm sorry, Damian, I never wanted to hurt you. I loved you so much; I didn't want to drag you into my nightmare. You had so much to give the world. I wasn't going to hold you back. Look at you now – look how far you've come. I'm so proud of you and the way you've handled the Board."

"I would have been there for you, for both of you. We could have raised Skylar together," Damian said and Star's chest constricted.

Those were the words Star had dreamed

she would hear from Damian. She'd dreamed he'd hear the story and come back for them both, but Star knew in her heart that that would never be the case, as she had sworn everyone to secrecy. He was never to find out the truth.

"But you weren't. You left and you didn't look back. You believed what you saw, Damian, and so our relationship wasn't as strong as we thought. If you'd really loved me, you would have known that I could never have done that to you."

"That's not fair," Damian said. "You had been acting strange since I got back from the US. You'd been pushing me away. We hadn't been intimate for weeks. Seeing you with Toby made sense at the time ... I assumed you'd fallen in love while I was away. You and he were always so close." Damian ran a frustrated hand through his hair. "I did come back. Four months after I left, I came back and looked for you. I saw you with Toby outside the coffee shop. He was hugging you. You were obviously together, and so I made my decision to leave again and stay away. If you were happy, who was I to destroy that?"

A sob stuck in Star's throat. The "what might have beens" flashing through her head. Damian had come back; he'd wanted to fight for them.

Damian moved forwards, his thumb catching the lone tear that ran down her cheek. Star's breath hitched, her pain-filled eyes staring into his. Damian pulled her into his chest as the flood gates opened. Star wasn't sure how long she cried, but Damian stayed silent, stroking her hair and holding her close. Star pulled back and laid a hand over Damian's heart where her tears had soaked his shirt. He silently took her hand and raised it to his lips, his eyes never leaving hers. Turning it over, he kissed her palm before moving to her wrist, his eyes remaining locked on hers. His hands moved to cradle her head, his thumbs wiping away the remnants of the tears she'd shed. Moving forwards, he kissed her lips, causing Star to inhale.

Pulling back, he looked at her, the question clear in his eyes. Star licked her lips, which seemed to be all the signal Damian needed. His lips descended, possessive yet gentle in their caress. Star lost the ability to think as his lips claimed hers, his tongue seeking entrance. She allowed herself to open for him, demanding more, deepening the kiss. Her body and mind were in sync. She was finally home.

Chapter Eleven

Star linked her fingers with Damian's as she led him into her room before closing the door behind them.

Damian stepped forward, his arms wrapping themselves around her, pulling her body flush against his, the thick evidence of his arousal sending a burst of heat straight to her core.–Star's breath faltered, as she looked up, arrows of heat speared through her, at the raw hunger she saw in his eyes. "You are so beautiful," he whispered as his mouth descended on hers, his teeth scraping along her bottom lip, nipping, and teasing, asking for permission to enter.

Star's hands wound their way up Damian's body until she cupped the back of his head, her fingers sinking into his thick, dark hair, drawing him closer, deepening their kiss. Her head swam as his mouth devoured hers, their tongues and lips duelling and caressing.

Star shivered as Damian's mouth moved to her ear, nipping at her lobe, her body melting against his. Star could not suppress the moan that escaped her lips as Damian's hands gripped her hips pulling her closer, grinding her against him. Damian chuckled, trailing hot kisses down the side of her neck, "You always were so responsive," he said, his breath tickling her already over sensitised skin. Star's head dropped back; her swollen breasts pressed hard against his chest. She needed to feel him, she needed more.

The heat of Damian's hands seared through the material of her dress, making her squirm.

Damian raised his head, their eyes locking, desire pulsing between them. Star nipped at his jawline, causing Damian to groan. Closing his eyes, he recaptured her mouth with his, deepening the kiss as if the contact between them fuelled his own desperation. Star's weeks of erotic dreams were nothing compared to the real thing, and all he was doing was kissing her.

Star ran her hands over Damian's shirt, the material soft under her fingers compared to the solid muscles she could feel hidden beneath. Her fingers trailed down, pulling the material from his waist band, giving her access to the hard, bare skin beneath. Her confidence grew at Damian's sharp inhale of breath, as she drew her nails along his skin. Damian's hands moved to the front of her dress, his mouth never leaving hers as he made quick work of the buttons before pushing the material from her shoulders. Star's dress pooled around her ankles, Damian stepped back and a deep flush spread over her cheeks as she stood before his heated gaze.

Damian stared into Star's eyes. "Is this what you want?" he asked huskily, his eyes dark with passion.

"I more than want this, Damian. I need this; I need you," she whispered, a sense of power flooding her system as she watched his eyes darken. Unhooking her bra, Star exposed herself to his gaze before once again stepping forward.

Star squealed as Damian swept her into his arms and crossed the short distance to her bed. He placed her on the sheets, before kneeling next to her, his eyes never leaving her face.

"I never thought we'd have this chance again," Damian murmured, his voice choked with the same emotion coursing through Star. Star pulled at Damian's shirt, which he quickly removed and threw to one side, "Is that better?" he asked with a grin.

"Much," Star replied with a grin of her own.

Damian leant forward and gently ran his fingers over her stomach, Star's muscles contracted sharply at the sensation. She needed more, she needed all of him.

Star gripped Damian's shoulders as he bent down and fastened his mouth onto her aching nipple, Star groaned, pulling him closer. As if sensing her need, his fingers moved to her other breast, rolling, and pinching the hardened peak between his fingers, while his warm mouth continued to tease the other pebbled tip with gentle nips and sucks. He let out a low growl against her, the noise arousing her further leaving her body twisting and bucking below him. Star was not sure how much more she could stand. Her body needed him, all of him.

Damian moved his lips back to hers in another plundering kiss. Star sucked his tongue into her mouth, causing him to moan and grind his hips into her stomach, the rough denim of his jeans sent tendrils of pleasure over her skin.

Damian pulled back and Star felt the loss of his warmth immediately. What was this man doing to her? How had she ever let this go? Star watched as Damian made quick work of his jeans, ripping them from his body and throwing them to one side. Blood pounded through her veins as she took in the man before her. Damian re-joined her on the bed, stretching out next to her. Star's hips rose, clashing with Damian's, his arousal throbbing and pulsing between them.

Damian's lips found Star's again, only this time his hand slid down and across her stomach, soothing her skin, but lighting a fire in her belly. Heat coiled its way through her, her hips thrusting upwards in a long-forgotten pattern. Star moaned into Damian's mouth as his hand moved closer to her burning centre, teasing the edges of the small scrap of silk that covered her.

Damian's thigh moved between hers. "Is this what you need?" he asked, as his hand slid over the silk barrier, his mouth returning to hers. Star let out a whimper of desperation he teased her delicate and aching flesh through the material, while devouring her mouth.

Stars hips thrust upward, a groan of frustration piercing the air. Star's legs spread further apart, silently begging for more. Damian pulled the material to one side, exposing her moist heat, his fingers slowly sliding into her delicate softness. Star's eyes slammed shut at the sensations overriding her body, as Damian's skilful fingers demolished the last of her control. She could no longer think, only feel.

Clawing at his shoulders and back, tension built throughout her body, her legs shaking as her body readied itself for release. Star shattered and Damian absorbed her cry with his mouth, her body wracked with the mini detonations that flooded her system. Coming down, she opened her eyes, to find Damian staring down at her.

"I love watching you come apart in my arms," he said, dropping his mouth to hers. This kiss was gentle and slow. Star lowered her hand between them and ran a finger up Damian's rigid length. Damian grabbed her hand to stop her.

"I want to be inside you," he murmured, drawing her hand to his mouth and gently kissing her palm.

Star pulled back, shimming out of her panties, her eyes never leaving Damian's. Damian stood up, removing his own underwear before grabbing his wallet and pulling out a condom. Star took the gift from his hand and made quick work of disposing of the wrapping. This was the ritual they had always had. Leaning forward she dropped a kiss to the head of his swollen shaft before quickly sheathing him.

Damian moaned as he moved between Star's legs, rocking against her, the hard swell of his arousal leaving Star in no doubt of his desire for her. Damian looked into her eyes as he slowly pushed himself into her warmth, his eyes glazed with need. Star and Damian moaned in unison as their bodies finally came together. Star's eyes widened, her body stretching to accommodate him after so many years. She pushed up, needing, wanting more, as the tell-tale rise of tension began to build again at her core. Star wrapped her legs around Damian's waist, his arms encircled her, drawing her closer locking her in a ring of passion, as if he wanted to absorb her into himself. Damian's pace picked up, and he buried his head in her neck, gently nipping and sucking, as their bodies moved in unison. The sensation of him moving deep inside her after so long was enough to send Star spiralling over the edge once more. Damian's body froze and then shuddered, as he emptied himself deep within her core. Star held on tight kissing his neck and shoulders until his release stopped, and they were both left exhausted.

Damian pulled back and looked deep into Star's eyes. A single tear escaped, which he caught on his finger, a look of concern crossing his face.

"Are you okay? Did I hurt you?" Damian asked.

Star smiled and gently touched his face. "No, you didn't hurt me – that was a tear of passion. I don't think my body understands the pleasure it's just received."

Relief washed over his features and Damian leant forwards, kissing her nose before pulling out and disposing of the condom in her bathroom.

When Damian re-entered the room, Star was once again able to appreciate how truly beautiful he was. His body had filled out since they were last together. He grinned under her gaze before climbing onto the bed next to her, pulling the covers back over them both.

∞∞∞

Star stretched out, finding the space beside her cold and empty. Damian must have left at some point in the night, their lovemaking having exhausted her to the point that she hadn't even been aware of him leaving. Opening her eyes, she stared at the indent where his head had been, running her fingers gently over the pillow, and her heart quickened at the thought of what they'd done. Moving to get up and check on Skylar, Star was aware of her own body, a tenderness that reminded her how well loved she had been. Damian had never been a selfish lover, and their time apart had made him even less so. She didn't want to think about where that experience had come from, but she wasn't going to complain.

They'd talked well into the night, until sheer exhaustion had dragged her under. They'd talked about Lily and Skylar. Star had told him there had been no one else in her life since him, and he'd been shocked. When he'd started to speak, she'd placed a finger over his lips to silence him. She didn't need to hear about his past conquests; she'd read about them in Laura's magazines, even when Laura thought she'd hidden them from her. Damian was quite the sought-after bachelor in New York, with supermodels and actresses often accompanying him to red-carpet events. Star didn't need to feel any more insecure. She was a nobody in comparison to the string of beautiful women in his life. Last night had been her farewell to Damian, the way it always should have been. She didn't, *couldn't* expect any more from him; he wasn't hers and their lives were half a world away from each other. When his father was better, Damian would be returning to New York, and Star's life was here with Skylar. This had been their goodbye. Damian had protested, but Star wanted just one more night. She knew in her heart that she'd never find anyone else who made her feel like Damian Hunt did, but he wasn't hers. She'd made that choice many years ago when she'd let him go.

A noise in the hall indicated that Skylar was up and awake. Opening her bedroom door, Star was surprised to hear Skylar chatting in the kitchen. Laura and Toby weren't expected home until later, but Skylar was definitely talking to someone. As she drew closer, she realised the other voice was Damian's. When Star entered the kitchen, Damian was standing at the hob, making pancakes, while Skylar sat next to him still in yesterday's clothes. The shock must have been evident on her face, as Damian looked up and grinned.

"Mummy!" Skylar said, noticing Damian's attention had switched from her. "Damian came back. We were making you breakfast in bed!"

"Thank you," Star said, glancing shyly at Damian, her stomach jumping at the sight of him making pancakes with her daughter after last night.

"You look well rested," Damian said, flipping the latest pancake and adding it to the growing pile.

"I am, thank you. I slept remarkably well," Star said, heat flooding her cheeks.

Damian's eyes darkened in response. He knew how well she'd slept and why. The draw to kiss him was almost too great, but her gaze caught on her daughter, whose eyes were flipping back and forth between the two of them.

Star clapped her hands to deflect Skylar's attention. "Well, these look delicious," she said, grabbing a couple of plates from the cupboard and moving next to Damian. She leaned past him to snag a pancake. His hand brushed against her backside, sending a shot of desire straight to her core. Star swallowed a groan, closing her eyes briefly before pushing back into his hand. Skylar continued to talk excitedly the other side of Damian, unaware her mother had become a slave to this man. Star shot Damian a look. His touch was reigniting parts she thought would have been exhausted from last night, but her body clearly had other ideas. His gaze darkened as it dropped lower; her nipples had pebbled against her dressing gown. Star could feel the tension emanating from Damian's body. Maybe she wasn't the only one affected by last night. He was still here, standing in her kitchen, after all.

Skylar had decided the grown-ups were taking too long and now had her head stuck in the fridge looking for the lemon and maple syrup. While her back was turned, Star stood on her tiptoes, dropping a quick kiss on Damian's lips, "Good morning," she whispered. "I thought you'd gone?"

"No chance," he whispered back, stealing another quick peck before Skylar turned round. "I just assumed you wouldn't want Skylar finding me in your bed this morning."

Star looked ashamed. She hadn't even thought about that or the effect that might have had on Skylar had she found them together. It was not something that had ever happened in Skylar's life. Two minutes back in Damian's arms and she'd stopped thinking, only too happy to have him warming the bed next to her and reigniting her desire.

"Don't do that," Damian said, gently rubbing the creases she knew had formed between her brows. "No harm done. I saw to that."

Star nodded; he was right.

Skylar turned back from the fridge. "Mummy, we don't have any maple syrup."

"Yes, we do," Star said, happy for the distraction. "It's in the cupboard. We need a new one. Uncle Toby finished the last one."

Skylar grinned and turned to Damian. "Uncle Toby always finishes the maple syrup – it's his favourite."

For the first time, Damian didn't freeze at

Toby's name. Star relaxed. Damian had believed her when she said it had been for show. Toby was her friend and nothing more. Toby had been in love with Laura for as long as she could remember, their love having had its own ups and downs, and Star had made that clear to Damian last night.

The three of them sat around the kitchen table, with Skylar chatting as if this were a normal occurrence. Star couldn't believe the situation she was now in. How had they gone from enemies to lovers overnight?

The clattering of keys and the banging of the front door shattered the idyllic family picture. Star shot Damian an anxious look as Laura and Toby sauntered into the kitchen, drawing up short at the scene in front of them.

"Uncle Toby, Aunty Laura, we're having pancakes!" Skylar said, breaking the ice.

"Ooh, with maple syrup, my favourite," Toby said, sending Skylar into fits of giggles as she protected her pancake from Toby, who had started to stalk towards her. Toby grinned as he stood over Skylar, shooting a raised eyebrow look at Star. "This looks very cosy," he said, making a pointed effort of looking at his watch to show

how early it was for visitors.

"We weren't expecting you back until this evening," Star said.

"Obviously," Laura said, grinning. "Mum and Dad have developed a leak overnight and their kitchen is flooded. I wanted to stay and help, but Mum wouldn't hear of it. 'You're pregnant! You can't be crawling round on the floor or pulling out cupboards!'" Laura said mimicking her mum's voice almost perfectly, which made Skylar giggle even more. "As she was stressing over me and the baby and the leak, we decided to head home and get out of the way while they wait for the plumber."

"There are plenty for you, too," Skylar said, jumping up and pulling her aunt and uncle towards the table, no longer afraid Toby would steal her pancakes.

"That's okay, squidge," Toby said rustling her hair. "We've had our breakfast, but it's kind of you to offer."

Damian had remained silent, letting the scene unfold in front of him.

"Good to see you again, Damian." It was Laura's turn to break the ice.

"Morning Laura, Toby," Damian said.

"Sorry about the mess. We will be clearing up. Skylar has kept me well informed of the rules of the kitchen." Damian stood up and held his hand out to Toby. Toby looked surprised but accepted it as Damian added, "I'm sorry about the other day. No hard feelings."

"I take it a certain misunderstanding has been cleared up?" Toby said, directing his question at Star.

Star looked sheepish. "Yes."

"Good," he said, scooping Skylar up and heading for the door. "We have some presents for this little munchkin, from Laura's mum and dad," he said winking at Star as he removed a squealing Skylar from the kitchen before being quickly followed by Laura, who very obviously shut the door behind her.

Damian wasted no time in pulling her against him, her thin robe offering no protection against his hard body.

"Hum," he whispered, his lips against her neck, working their way towards the sensitive area under her ear. "Good morning."

Groaning at the sensations that were firing through her body, Star wrapped her hands around Damian's neck, pulling him closer. It didn't take long before their lips collided and his tongue dipped between her swollen lips. A knock on the kitchen door had them leaping apart. The door remained closed, although Toby's voice shouted through: "We're taking Skylar out to grab a milkshake."

Her colour high at the fact her friends knew exactly what she was up to, Star coughed, her voice sounding as dishevelled as she felt. "Great, thanks. Have fun."

"You, too. We'll be at least an hour!" came Toby's reply.

Damian pulled her back to him as the front door shut. "Toby is fast becoming my new favourite person," he said, grabbing her hand and pulling her towards the kitchen door and up the stairs.

Star went with him eagerly. She knew Toby, Laura, and Skylar would be gone at least an hour, if that's what Toby had said. Her best friends would keep her daughter entertained, so she could have some grown-up time.

"Mine too," Star replied, feeling free and content for the first time in a long time.

∞∞∞

Toby and Laura finally returned two hours later with a barbecue box from the local butcher, Skylar's favourite magazine, and a bag full of salad bits from the local greengrocer. He even whipped out a paddling pool for Skylar, shrugging when Star pulled a face at the amount of money they had obviously spent on her daughter.

"You spoil her!" Star moaned at Toby.

"Wasn't me this time," Toby said, pointing at his wife.

"Nope, it was all me." Laura winked. "Damian and Toby can spend some time setting it up while you and I prepare the salad and marinades," she said, linking her arm through Star's and dragging her towards the kitchen. "Plus, its glorious weather and this pregnant woman wants to dip her feet!"

"Sneaky!" Star said, laughing, as both the men were led outside by a very enthusiastic Skylar.

Star and Laura set to work in the kitchen,

listening to the men laughing and joking in the garden, while being directed by Skylar. It reminded her of their university days when Damian and Toby had been friends, often clowning around together.

"So? Spill!" Laura said as soon as she had Star alone.

"Your wish came true." Star sighed. "Damian came to the office and Skylar showed him her scrap book. The truth came out, or should I say Skylar told him the truth. He helped Skylar finish her scrap book while I finished my work, and we went for pizza, before Marcus drove us home."

"Melt my out of action ovaries," Laura said, fanning herself.

Star looked confused, until Laura huffed. "He helped Skylar with her scrap book. That, I would love to have seen."

Star shook her head at her friend. "That was all you got out of that statement."

"Well, it had to come out sooner or later. I'm glad it was sooner. Now down to the juicy gossip. How come Damian was sitting comfortably at our kitchen table at eight-thirty this morning?"

Star felt herself blush. "Skylar fell asleep in the car, so Damian carried her in and helped me put her to bed. Mary needed Marcus, so he left, and Damian and I started talking."

"Well, my friend, you looked thoroughly loved up this morning, so I'm taking a lot more than talking happened? Is your spell of celibacy officially at an end?"

Star felt her colour deepen further.

"Oh, lighten up, you look like a naughty teenager caught out by her parents. Toby and I are happy for you," Laura said, grinning. "So, what happens next?"

"I have no idea," Star said honestly. "When I woke up this morning, he wasn't next to me, so I assumed last night was closure sex. After this morning, I have no idea. I'm not sure what it can be, if I'm honest. Damian lives in the US. I live here. What future do we have?"

Laura looked at Star like she'd grown a second head. "Since when do you give up? If you and Damian are worth fighting for, then fight! You should never have split up in the first place, but I'm not going back over my thoughts on that. It looks like he's great with Skylar. She's already halfway in love with him. Open yourself up, Star.

Take a chance. There is only one chance in life. If nothing else, you should understand that – you had a front row seat!" Laura stopped, and Star knew her face showed the devastation she was feeling inside. "I'm sorry," Laura said, hugging her friend.

"No, you're right. But it's not just what I want. I have no idea what Damian wants," she said, looking out of the window as the two men and Skylar's laughter filtered through. "I don't even know if he's single, Laura. Last night happened. This morning happened. It was amazing, better than amazing, but I can't hold my hopes on it being something more." Star looked back at her friend, before adding, "I have Skylar to consider. It isn't just about what I want anymore." Taking a deep breath, Star said, "I'm just going to enjoy it while I can and protect my heart as much as possible. I never was strong enough to resist him." Her gaze flitted back to the window, and Damian looked up, as if sensing her. Damian shot her a smile that went straight to her heart. A frown appeared between his brow as if he could read the fear in her expression. Seeing his concern, she smiled and blew him a kiss, which he pretended to catch, his attention then drawn back to Skylar, who was asking another question.

For all her brave words, Star knew she was in trouble. Last night had made her realise, it wasn't Skylar who'd kept her single. It was Damian.

After their heart to heart in the kitchen, Laura backed off and everyone enjoyed the afternoon. Damian stayed late into the evening, catching up on the past seven years of gossip, and telling Toby about his life in New York. It was like old times, although this time Toby and Laura were married rather than simply her best friends. Somehow, Damian hadn't been surprised they'd finally got together. He'd seen their attraction years ago.

"You could have given me the heads up, mate!" Toby grumbled, pulling his wife in for a hug. "This one gave me the cold shoulder for years – she keeps telling me she was playing hard to get!"

When it was time, Damian helped get Skylar ready for bed, reading her one of the books they'd purchased the day before. To encourage Skylar to read with him, Damian promised he'd read three pages if she read one. She happily agreed until her eyes were rolling round her head. In a sleepy voice, she asked Damian if he'd be there for pancakes again in the morning. He'd told her he couldn't, as he needed to get home to see his father, but that he'd see her again soon. Star's heart melted as she watched him lean down and kiss her daughter's head before tucking her duvet round her. Backing out of the door, he closed it behind him before taking Star once again in his arms. They'd been restrained all day, trying not to be too tactile in front of Skylar. It had nearly killed Star to stay away from him. He was like a drug – one fix wasn't going to be nearly enough.

Star's hands wound their way round his neck and buried in his hair. "Do you have to rush off?" she asked, raising herself up and placing her lips against his. Damian deepened their kiss, until they were both breathless and panting. He didn't hold back or try to hide his desire, his mouth devouring hers, before making its way down her neck and into the sensitive hollow at the base of her neck.

"I can stay for a little while, but I should probably get back and ensure Mum hasn't buried Dad under the patio," Damian said, chuckling into her skin.

"Oh no!" Star said. "I'd completely forgotten your dad was back home."

"Good," Damian said with a grin, "it means I've distracted you." He pulled her body back to his, manoeuvring them both into her bedroom.

Heat flooded Star's body, her newly awakened libido showing no signs of letting up. Damian had reawakened a longing she thought had been extinguished. How wrong could she have been. He'd awakened a monster, one who had been asleep for far too long and needed feeding.

Chapter Twelve

Damian and Star lay encased in each other's arms, each unwilling to release the other. Damian finally raised his head, dropping a kiss on Star's nose, before gently pulling away and stepping into her en suite. Star lay staring at the ceiling, unable to fathom how this had happened and where they were headed. Before Star could think too deeply, Damian returned to the bed, pulling Star into his arms.

"I'm not staying, but I would like to just hold you for a while," Damian said against her hair.

A warmth spread through Star's chest. Maybe they did have a future. Maybe he wasn't as immune to her.

"I'd like that," Star whispered, settling back onto his chest, her hand resting above his heart, drawing lazy circles on his skin. Star found her eyes growing heavy, Damian's rhythmic heartbeat forcing her to relax. She swore she heard Damian tell her he had missed her, and life hadn't been the same without her. But she was too far gone to know whether that was her dream or reality, because when she woke a few hours later, the bed next to her was cold and empty. A note left on the pillow told her he would call her.

Star's heart sank. They'd been caught in a weekend dream, but reality was edging back in and fast. Lucas was home and on the mend; it wouldn't be long before Damian would be heading back across the water. Where would that leave her and Skylar? Within twenty-four hours, Skylar had already become attached to Damian, reading with him, asking him to help her rather than asking Star, Toby, or Laura. What would happen when he left? Her six-year-old would be left with a gaping hole in her life and she'd be left to pick up the pieces.

A painful realisation dawned on her as Star stared at the empty place beside her. How was she going to be able to help Skylar when her own life would be hollow without him in it? To the world, Damian was an eligible bachelor, gracing magazines in the US and sometimes the UK, attending red-carpet events and rubbing shoulders with the rich and famous. Star, on the other hand, was a single mum from a dysfunctional family, still living in her best friends' house. Damian had always been from a rich family, an enigma who'd bucked the trend and had her falling head-first in love with him. Damian had never worn his family wealth on his sleeve; he'd always been grounded, preferring the local curry house to dining at The Ivy.

They'd met during Star's Freshers Week. The university had set up a meet and greet where the freshers could talk to students in their final year. Star had been set to miss it, not really interested in listening to others' opinions. She was there because she wanted to be; she'd researched all the courses and this was the best. In her mind, that was all she needed to know at the time. Her new friends and course mates had other ideas, though. It was Freshers Week – a time to spread your wings, drink far too much, and get laid. Star had no intention of doing any of those things, but Lily convinced her she needed to put herself out there and make new friends. No one at university knew her family history and she could finally move past the snickering and gossip they'd both been plagued with since childhood. University was going to be lonely if she made no friends, so after some convincing, she went along with the crowd.

The hall had been packed, tables and students everywhere. It hadn't taken her long to find the Marketing Course table. She would never forget the first time she laid eyes on Damian. He'd stood at the back, looking as bored and disenchanted with the whole thing as she was. She'd been about to make her escape when she'd heard her name shouted across the room. Laura had come barrelling towards her, drawing everyone's attention to them both, before throwing her arms around Star in greeting. Star remembered the warmth that had spread through her body at seeing her childhood best friend again and it must have showed on her face. Her gaze had caught Damian's, his interest riveted on her. Their eyes had locked over Laura's shoulder and every cell in her body had sparked under the scrutiny of his gaze, leaving her breathless and slightly confused. She'd dated before, but no one had left her aching with the need to get closer to them, with a longing to make a physical connection.

But Laura had drawn her attention away from Damian, sweeping Star out of the hall and into the Student Union bar before she'd been able to give Damian a second thought. They'd spent hours catching up and re-establishing their friendship, and by the end of the evening, university life had taken a new turn. No longer were the next four years looking to be all studying, but instead exciting and full of fun. It hadn't been until later that evening Star had returned her thoughts to the young man with the piercing eyes. She had doubted she'd see him again, but how wrong she had been.

It had been weeks before Damian had reappeared in her life. Mr Forboys, her Visual Thinking lecturer, had convinced Damian and some of his peers to assist in his lecture. Damian had swept into the room and Star had found herself breathless, her heart pounding, colour riding high in her cheeks. He'd captured her eye and smiled, and if she hadn't been sitting, she would have melted in a pool at his feet. They hadn't spoken until after the lecture, although the majority of the girls had been tittering about how he was Damian Hunt of Hunt and Hunt Advertising. Star, of course, knew who Hunt and Hunt were. They were an international advertising firm – it was every students dream to get an internship with the company. She supposed Damian's pathway was already mapped out. He'd be walking into a high-paid job in the family firm.

Star had been lost in her own world after the lecture and hadn't seen him approach. She'd finally dragged her eyes away from his and kept them focused on her lap in order to pay attention to the lecture. She'd answered questions, but had averted her eyes, so as not to appear like a lovesick puppy, unlike some of the others around her.

"Hi, I wondered if I'd see you again." Star had jumped at his voice, dropping her pen, leaving her scrambling to find it. Damian had picked it up and passed it back to her calmly. Colour had flooded Star's cheeks.

"Er, thanks," she'd said, nearly dropping the pencil again as he returned it to her.

"You never made it to the stand for a chat

about what life is like over the next four years. Do you have any questions?"

"No," was all Star could say, embarrassment flooding her system. How unprofessional – she hadn't taken the time to find out about the class and it had been noted. Just great! And now, she'd found out that he was the son of one of the marketing company greats!

Damian must have seen the look of despair on her face, because he leant in, whispering "Can I let you into a secret? I didn't attend during my first year either, and it hasn't done me any harm. If you know what you want to do, then why do you need someone else telling you it's the right choice for you. From what I saw today, you seem to know what you're about."

"It is, I do …" Star stammered, before finding herself relaxing in his presence. There was something about him, not just his good looks and charm, but it felt like he got her.

They talked for a little while, and the theatre had emptied out, a few of the girls shooting her envied looks as they left. Unsure why Damian had singled her out, she simply sat and watched as their conversation meandered away from advertising to more general topics.

They continued talking until the lecture hall began to fill up again with new students. Star glanced at her watch, her eyes widening. "Damn, I have a lecture about to start across campus. Sorry, I've got to go."

She'd grabbed her bag and headed for the door when Damian touched her arm and said, "May I see you again?"

Star had looked at him with a frown, before asking, "Why?"

"Honestly. You're refreshing and I've enjoyed talking to you," he'd said, his cheeks colouring with embarrassment.

"Okay, I've enjoyed talking to you too." She'd grabbed his arm and used her rescued pen to write her phone number on his hand. "Message me." With that, she'd turned and run, her heart pounding. She'd just given her number to a virtual stranger, a gorgeous virtual stranger. Her insides warmed at the thought, an unfamiliar pull forming low in her belly.

She'd only just made her lecture, getting a short look from her lecturer as she burst through the door. It wasn't aided when her phone pinged loudly in the middle of his monologue. Hiding her phone under her textbook, she opened the message.

Damian: *Can I take you to dinner tonight?*

Closing her phone, Star had placed it back in her pocket. Did she want to go to dinner with Damian Hunt? Should she go to dinner with him? She didn't really know him. She'd waited until after class before sending Laura a message.

It had taken Laura all of ten minutes to call her back and demand to know what was happening. She'd told Star she categorically had to go to dinner with Damian. She had of course Googled him and told Star he was gorgeous and she'd be an idiot not to. Uncomfortable with the whole scenario, Star had agreed and messaged Damian back.

Star: *Okay, what time?*

Her phone had buzzed instantly.

Damian: *Be ready by 7. I'll pick you up.*

After lectures, Laura had torn Star's wardrobe apart, trying to find the perfect outfit. Her friend's enthusiasm did little to remove the sick feeling Star had been experiencing all day since agreeing to this mad date. By the time Damian arrived, Star's nerves were on edge. It hadn't been her imagination; his presence definitely caused her stomach to contract. A warmth she'd never felt before had enveloped her whole body. When he captured her hand in his, her response had been electric; she wasn't the only one to feel it – of that she was sure. Damian had gazed down at their joined hands before his eyes had returned to hers, a small smile playing around his lips. They'd left then, Damian never relinquishing her hand. He'd touched her whenever he could and she'd relished in his attention, glowing with the need to be close to him. That evening had been the start, and their relationship had only gone from strength to strength. They had been inseparable. She'd met his family, who she'd found to be remarkably normal and welcoming. She'd even introduced him to her sister and mother. Her mother had actually been welcoming for once in her life, lavishing Damian with the Daphne Roberts first-class treatment.

Star had never questioned if falling in love was easy. With Damian, it had been inevitable, natural. For nearly three years, they'd been together, surviving Damian graduating and starting work, and supporting each other's dreams. Star would never have foreseen what was to come.

∞∞∞

When Star woke up the following morning, the pillow still held an indent where Damian's head had been, but the bed itself was cold. Running her hand over chilled space, a deep ache spread through her chest. What was she doing? They'd gone from mortal enemies two nights ago to insatiable lovers, it would seem. Flopping onto her back, Star covered her eyes with her arm. Had she lost her mind? It had taken her years to recover from Damian's departure the first time, if she ever had, and that was with all the distractions at the time. Now she'd opened herself up to all the hurt and heartache again, but she couldn't resist him or stay away; he was the air she breathed. The only difference this time was she'd invited Skylar along for the ride, so it wasn't only her heart on the line now.

Star heard Laura and Toby's bedroom door open and close before someone headed downstairs. She needed to speak to another grown-up before her mind drove her insane. Grabbing her dressing gown, Star headed out, catching Laura entering the kitchen.

"Good night?" Laura asked with a grin on her face. "I haven't seen you look as relaxed as you did yesterday in a long time."

Star collapsed into one of the kitchen chairs, burying her head in her hands with a groan. "What am I doing?"

"Hey," Laura said, the amusement in her voice disappearing, as she moved closer, placing a hand on Star's shoulder. "What's going on? You seemed so happy yesterday. Did you and Damian have a row last night?"

Star shook her head as she sat up and stared at her friend. "No, everything was great," Star said, searching for the right words to explain her turmoil.

"Then I'm at a loss. Was the sex no good?" Laura asked.

"What? No!" Star replied, colour flooding her cheeks. "I mean ... it was amazing, mind-blowing."

"Great," Laura said, laughing. "So, what's the problem? You haven't had a row, sex is 'mind-blowing', and you seemed comfortable in each other's company. Even Skylar is a Damian fan."

"There lies the problem. Skylar is already

falling under his spell. What happens when he ups and leaves to go back to the US? How do I explain to a six-year-old that he has to go?"

A knowing look crossed Laura's face. "Oh, hon, you're thinking too much. No one can predict the future. Damian may decide he's not going to go back to the New York office. Have you asked him?"

"He will. His life is there. His clients are there. It's not like he just works there, Laura. He runs the New York office.

"Well, you could always go with him," Laura said.

Star shot her a look.

"Friday, he hated me; today, who knows. I've let him back in my heart, Laura, and I don't know how to protect myself, or Skylar. I have to accept this is a temporary thing and build some barriers. I know I can't stay away from him; I'd be lying if I said I could, but I can protect Skylar from any more hurt."

Laura nodded. "Life itself is only temporary. Sometimes we need to take a chance. Please don't close yourself off. As your friend, watching you yesterday, you were more alive than I have seen you in years. That is not something you should hide from Skylar. Showing her life is more than just hard work, that relationships make people happy and content – that is a lesson she needs to see whatever the outcome. Worry about the future when the time comes. Live for each day – that is what Lily would have told you to do."

"That's low, and she sees you and Toby 'happy and content'."

"Yes, but she wants that for you, too. Do you know why she was taken with Andrew and why she likes Damian? It's because they make you smile and laugh."

"She said that?" Stars eyes filled with tears.

"She mentioned it when we were getting her photos together. She wants you to be happy. I'm not telling you this to make you cry," Laura said, her own tears escaping as she looked at her friend. "We all want the best for you. Don't put roadblocks in the way. Enjoy Damian's company; let it go where it needs to. If I didn't think he reciprocated your feelings, I'd be telling you to run, but one look at that man and he's invested. He always was."

Star hugged Laura around the waist, letting her head rest on her friend's growing bump, "What would I do without you?"

"Well," Laura said, suddenly laughing as a foot or tiny hand pushed hard against Star's cheek.

Star removed her head, rubbing where the little bump had appeared.

"You're one lucky little bump. You have an amazing Mummy and Daddy," she whispered, another kick letting her know she'd been heard.

Laura moved to the kettle and switched it on before turning back to Star. "Love, Star. It's what you were designed to do. Watching you hold yourself back has been painful. Damian is your soulmate. Life got in the way. If you've got a second chance, then go for it. Don't let fear stop you."

Star had expected to be berated when she came down this morning. She'd been set to hear what a bad idea she and Damian were. How could she involve Skylar so soon … Instead, she'd been told to "go for it", throw caution to the wind, and follow her heart. She'd done that years ago and her heart had been broken, albeit by her own hand. Now she had a second chance. Even if their relationship was not destined to be, maybe she would find some closure if he did leave this time, and finally be able to move on with her life. Maybe this was fate's way of resetting her life.

∞∞∞

Damian sent messages throughout the day. Skylar asked if he was coming around again, that they'd had fun, and she wanted to read some more with him. Star struggled to believe how well Skylar had adapted to Damian's appearance; she knew it was early days and their future was uncertain, but perhaps Laura was right – she should simply embrace the here and now and let fate run its course.

Damian didn't come round, but he had a Facetime reading session with Skylar instead. Star set up her tablet and sat with Skylar and their book while Damian sat on the other end of the connection with his old copy of the book, which Skylar thought was amazing. They took turns reading, and even Star was roped in. Everyone had to read a page until Skylar's eyes began to droop and Star called it a night tucking her in. Star made her way back to her room with the iPad, settling herself on the bed.

"Thank you," she said, smiling at Damian.

"Don't thank me. She's a great kid, and if it helps her, I'm happy. Mum talks about Skylar like she's her granddaughter."

"Your parents have been amazing throughout it all."

Damian's face hardened, leaving Star with a hollow feeling churning in her stomach. "What is it? Why that look?" she asked tentatively.

"It's nothing …"

"It's not nothing, Damian. I thought we'd decided to be honest with each other."

Damian laughed, but the sound was hollow. "Honest. That's the problem. No one was honest with me. I'm beginning to realise I was excluded from the biggest secret. A secret that impacted me. Everyone I cared about made a decision, not allowing me to make up my own mind about what was best for me."

A heaviness weighed on Star's chest. She knew he was right. If the boot were on the other foot, she'd have been annoyed. Control was something she'd always valued and her lack of it had made it difficult to think or see straight after Lily's diagnosis. But nothing she could say now would make it any different. "I can only say

I'm sorry. I'm hoping one day I can make it up to you."

The screen rocked as Damian rubbed a hand over his face. "I've just got things to work through. What I thought was true isn't, and I've got to get my head back in the game. But, Star, I want us to try. We can work through this. But we need to build trust again. It's not just with you; it's also with my parents."

"No, Damian, don't blame your parents—"

"Don't cover for him, Star. He admitted to me the part he played, and it was underhand. He coerced us both, and if he weren't so ill, I'd be giving him a piece of my mind. He played me, for his own gratification, and he used you to facilitate it all."

"Please don't be cross with him, Damian. He wanted the best for you. We both did."

"No, Star, what my father omitted to tell you was that I'd already told him I didn't want to go to the US office, and that I intended to work my way up here. He manipulated you into manipulating me. Tell me you would have sent me away if my father hadn't suggested it."

Star wiped her cheek, surprised at the dampness that was there. She couldn't lie to

Damian anymore. The lies and games were over. "No, I wouldn't have sent you away." Tears were now streaming down her face, and Damian reached his hand towards the screen, as if wanting to reach through and remove Star's pain. "I was desperate for you to be there with me. All I ever wanted was your arms around me, telling me everything was going to be all right."

They sat in silence for several minutes as Star's words sank in. It was the first time she'd admitted this to herself, let alone said it out loud. She knew she was throwing Lucas under the bus, but their relationship would survive. Lucas had been the instigator. He'd told Star that Damian had been enthusiastic about his move to America. That this would hamper his development, that she'd hold him back. She'd been in such shock that she'd gone along with it. Especially when Lucas had arranged for Lily to see some of the top cancer specialists in London. How could she have denied him his – and what she thought was Damian's – wish. Now she could see more clearly. She didn't hate Lucas; she couldn't. She knew how ruthless he was in business – why wouldn't he be even more so where his family was concerned. Lucas had been protecting Damian, like he had protected her later when she had been left with a new born. He'd helped and shielded her, enabled her to finish her degree, had given her a job, had even paid for childcare. She was beginning to wonder if it had been done to assuage his own guilt.

"Don't be too hard on him," Star said, finally. "He did what he thought was for the best. Nothing can change the past. I would love for us to simply move forwards."

"Me too. I wish I were there with you now," Damian said.

"I do, too. This weekend has been amazing," Star said smiling.

They talked about everything and nothing for the next hour, sharing insights into the life they had shut each other out of. Star ribbed Damian about his magazine covers and being deemed one of the most "eligible bachelors" in New York, although deep down the thought made her wonder what he was doing talking to her when there was a stream of models and actresses waiting to be seen on his arm. Damian had laughed, telling her it was something the magazines over there loved to do with the young, single, wealthy men. It meant very little. Star couldn't help with the feeling of unease. This was too good to be true.

All her deepest wants and dreams had come true this weekend, but she couldn't shake the sense of foreboding that sat heavily on her chest. After they finally said goodnight, Star lay on her bed, staring at the ceiling, wondering how long her fairy tale was going to last.

Chapter Thirteen

Tuesday morning came about in a flash. Skylar had been enthusiastic about going to school, asking if she could take her new book to show her teacher.

Star had made it into the office before the rest of the team, giving herself time to plan out her day and the coming week. The project was on schedule; the client was happy. It was just the loose ends that needed tying up. With her current team, she had no fears – they were all invested and hard-working, which meant she could ease off the pedal just a little bit and start reviewing some of the new business that was coming into the firm. She'd already discussed with Damian that they would keep their distance in the office. She'd had one bad experience with Jackson, which fortunately Damian had witnessed, and she didn't want anyone else questioning her professionalism or whether Jackson's gossip had teeth. As it stood, she was keeping her private life just that – off limits to the office gossips.

When Damian returned to the US office, Star didn't want any kick back of any kind. She already knew it would be hard enough to say goodbye.

It was mid-morning when Pam rang down.

"Greeting stranger," she said. "I've pinged you a meeting request but you haven't picked it up. Damian is chasing."

"Hi Pam, I've been working away from my desk. Let me take a look," Star said, butterflies raging through her stomach. "Yes, that's fine. I've accepted."

"Excellent, I'll let him know," Pam said ending the call.

Star looked around, hoping that none of the team noticed the flush that had erupted all over her body. So much for staying away from each other. She seriously needed to get a grip of herself if they were going to have a relationship and work together. She couldn't be swooning like someone out of a romance novel. What did Damian want? He hadn't mentioned a meeting last night. What was going on?

Star made her way to Damian's office, stopping at Pam's desk.

Pam looked up, giving Star a quizzical look. "Are you okay? You look a little flushed. You're not coming down with anything, are you?"

Star felt her colour rise further. Her palms were sweating, her panties damp at the mere thought of seeing Damian face to face after the weekend. "I'm fine," she coughed, then tried to divert the conversation onto safer ground. "Do you know what this meeting is about?"

"New client, I think," Pam said. "Are you sure you're not getting sick?"

Just then, Damian's door opened. Star didn't dare look at him as he ushered her into the room, sure that Pam would see the sparks flying should their eyes meet. Damian closed the door firmly behind her before pulling her towards him. Star melted into his body, his mouth descending on hers with a passion that took her breath away. When they finally broke apart, they were breathless, their bodies still touching.

"Sorry," Damian said with a cheeky grin. "That wasn't why I asked you to come up."

"No apology necessary," Star said, pulling back and smoothing her skirt, her self-doubt washed away in the tide of Damian's passion.

Damian ushered her towards the chair placed in front of his desk. He reluctantly headed to his side of the desk, but not before dropping another kiss on her lips. Working together and keeping their distance was going to take a lot of willpower.

"I have a new client," Damian started, changing the subject and pushing a folder across his desk.

Star picked it up, her eyes clashing with his as she saw who the new client was.

"Wow! Felt Beverages, the drinks company! Impressive!" Star said, unable to keep the surprise and awe out of her voice. This would be a massive account for the firm if they could capture their business.

"I was in talks with them in the US before I came over," Damian explained. "They want to start the ball rolling, so they're flying over. They want us to meet with them to discuss some of the finer details."

"Us?" Star jolted, her heartrate picking up at the thought.

"Yes, us. They want to include the UK office. This is to become a joint project, and I'd like you to work on it with me."

"I'm not sure what to say," Star said, her brain and heart racing at the prospect. This was a career-changing client. "Why me? There are many more members of staff who have more experience than me."

"That may be so, and before you say anything, this has nothing to do with us. They've seen your work and they're impressed. They've asked to meet with you."

"I'm flattered, but I'm still working my way up ... I'm still learning."

"My father is on board with this, and believe me, he wouldn't be if he didn't think you were up to the task. This client's business is huge, he's not going to risk losing them on a whim. He has every faith in you, as do I."

Excitement at the prospect of being part of this flooded Star's body. Lily was obviously looking down on her and Skylar.

"Okay, I'm in," Star said with a grin.

"Excellent," Damian said, getting up and

stalking towards her, pulling her out of the chair and against his hard body. "Now, I don't want you to leave here like you've been thoroughly kissed, as I know we need to keep this on the down-low. However, you are going to let me drop you off at home this evening. No more getting the train. I want to spend as much time as I can with you."

Star stared up into his eyes, passion and determination staring back at her. How was this happening? All her dreams were coming true.

Without waiting for her answer, Damian dropped a kiss to her ear, whispering, "Marcus will be in the underground car park at five fifteen. We'll wait for you and grab some takeaway on the way home. Skylar can then read to me before I leave."

Star nodded her agreement. Damian's thoughtfulness towards Skylar was stealing her breath. How was she going to be able to resist this man? The answer was, she wasn't. It was time to stop being a control freak and let life take its own path.

"No takeaway," Star said. "I'll cook."

∞ ∞ ∞

Dinner had turned into a family affair. Skylar had been so excited when they arrived at school to collect her that she hadn't stopped talking the whole way home. She told Damian all about her book and the conversation she'd had with her teacher that morning about the story. She wanted to read to Damian in the car, but Star had drawn a line, telling her that they needed to pick up some ingredients and that she could read to Damian while she prepared dinner for them all.

Star grabbed the ingredients from the local supermarket, while Damian purchased some wine, even though it was a "school night", as Skylar pointed out. When they got home, Star lay out the ingredients on the kitchen counter and began chopping while Skylar got changed out of her uniform. Damian slid his arms around her waist and nuzzled her neck, sending tingles rocketing throughout her body.

"I've wanted to do that all day," Damian whispered against her neck, sending shivers down her spine, before sliding his hands up and capturing her beaded nipples between his fingers. Star's eyes closed and she let out a groan, her head dropping back on his shoulder, giving him greater access to her neck, pushing her breasts into his hands. Lowering the knife, she turned in his arms, sliding her hands over his shoulders and into the soft hair at the nape of his neck. Nibbling his chin, she made her way to his mouth where she demanded entry, letting Damian know he wasn't alone in his desire.

The sound of pounding footsteps broke them apart as Skylar ran back into the kitchen. Coming up short, her gaze flitted between Damian and Star, a sly smile playing across her face. "Were you kissing? Mummy, you look like Aunty Laura when Uncle Toby has kissed her."

Star felt her face darken in embarrassment. Out of the mouths of babes …

"Yes, I was kissing your mummy," Damian said. "Do you mind?"

"Do you like her a lot?" Skylar asked.

"I do," Damian replied.

"Nope, I don't mind. You make her smile," she said before moving to the cupboard to grab a glass, the conversation clearly over.

Damian grinned down at Star, who was both embarrassed and shocked at having been caught out by her daughter. Damian dropped a kiss on her nose before moving to help Skylar with her drink. "Do you have any homework?" Damian asked Skylar, remembering her conversation in the car.

Skylar pulled a face.

"Skylar Roberts," Star said in her sternest voice.

"Okay, okay, I have some maths and history, but they're not due in until next week," Skylar moaned.

Crouching down to her level, Damian said, "Well, how about you and I attack the maths and history while Mummy makes dinner. I was hoping we'd be able to go out together this week, and if you haven't done your homework then we may have to postpone."

Skylar didn't need any further encouragement, shooting out of the door to grab her school bag, dragging it back into the kitchen.

When Toby and Laura got home, homework was complete and the table laid, and everyone sat down to dinner, discussing their day. Skylar's excitement at Damian collecting her from school had both Laura and Toby raising their eyebrows at Star. Someone was clearly smitten with Damian, although, after today, Star's fear of their future was less pronounced. Nothing was going to be able to keep her away from Damian; she'd tried that and failed.

Before Damian left that evening, he promised to pick her up in the morning, although Star had told him she was quite capable of getting the Tube into the office.

"If you get the Tube, then I don't get to see you. I appreciate you want to keep our private life out of the office, but with the hours we work, we don't get any time to talk. Plus, we can discuss the new client brief."

Star found it very hard to argue with Damian, as she too wanted to spend as much time as she could with him. To be honest, Skylar did take up all her time outside the office, which left little time for socialising.

"Okay, and I'll speak to Laura and Toby about looking after Skylar when we have the business dinner."

"About that," said Damian, "I spoke to Mum and Dad about that. They'd love to have Skylar that night. Rosy has just had puppies, and Mum thought Skylar might like to come and play with them."

Rosy was Lucas and Mary's German Shepherd. She was a guard dog, but also as soft as a brush when it came to family. Skylar had been part of her life since she'd been a pup and they'd grown up together.

"Oh, she'll love that. The only problem is, she'll want to bring one home," Star said.

"Don't worry, Mum and Dad are going to keep one of the pups. Maybe Skylar can help them choose which one. That way she can come to the house and help them with the puppy training." Her body tingled as Damian dropped a kiss at the base of her neck. "And while she's playing with the puppy with Mum, maybe you and I can find something else to occupy our time …" Star moaned her response, and Damian chuckled, before spinning her round and deepening their kiss. "I really need to go," he said sounding pained at the thought.

"I know," Star said, and pulled herself away. "I'll see you in the morning."

Damian adjusted himself, his arousal obvious. He grinned. "I can't seem to resist you."

Star let her hand slide over the aching bulge, unable to stop herself. Her mind filled with wonder over the effect she seemed to have on this man. Damian let out a low growl as his eyes closed. Star pulled him into a nearby room, before pushing him against the now-closed door.

She unzipped his trousers, and pushed them down his hips, while massaging his burning flesh. Damian's fingers tangled in her hair as Star dropped to her knees, using her mouth to tease him, and his head fell back against the door, swallowing a moan. Star's thighs clenched at his response as his hands pulling her closer. It wasn't long before she felt him harden further and attempt to pull her away.

"I want to be inside you," Damian whispered, his eyes clouded with passion.

Damian pulled Star to her feet, dragging her against him, his mouth claiming hers. Liquid heat pooled at her centre, leaving her quivering with awareness. Damian's hand glided over her thigh and under her skirt, shooting pleasure through her nerve endings. Star's skirt bunched around her waist as Damian teased her swollen nub with his finger. Star gasped, shifting her hips towards him, silently begging him for more. Star felt Damian's smile against her lips as he moved a finger to her opening, circling and teasing before finally giving her what she craved the most. Damian's moan matched Star's at the warm, wet heat awaiting him. Moving them both towards the sofa, Damian spun Star away from him, holding her back to his chest, before running tender kisses down the slender column of her neck. Star shivered at the dual sensations flooding her body. This man could drive her body insane with just the slightest touch.

"Damian..." she whispered, aware Toby and Laura were only metres away in the other room.

Damian seemed to understand her unspoken plea, bending her forwards over the sofa before slipping between her folds, coating himself in her need. Star gasped, biting down on her hand as Damian slid home, leaving them both breathless. Damian froze, allowing her time to adjust to his presence. Needing more, Star moaned and pushed back, letting Damian know she was more than ready. Damian didn't need any further encouragement, pulling out before pushing back in a desperate rhythm. Star followed his lead, feeling the pressure building low in her body, the sensation of what he was doing to her overriding her ability to think. Her orgasm clenched him tight, causing his own release to explode out.

Damian rested his body on top of hers, his arms encircling her waist, pulling her into the warmth and shelter of his body. Neither one of them seemed capable of moving, both trying to get their ragged breathing under control. Damian finally pulled away, grabbing a nearby tissue box, tenderly cleaning Star. Star stood up and readjusted her clothing, a shy smile playing over her lips, her eyes hooded as she stared at the man in front of her. Rising up on her toes, she placed a gentle kiss on his lips, before pulling away.

"We didn't use any protection," Damian said.

"It's fine, I'm on the pill ..." Star watched as a look of disappointment crossed Damian's features before it was replaced by a smile.

Damian pulled her into his arms and kissed her once more. "I don't want to leave, but I really need to be going. Marcus is outside," he said, clearly in no hurry to leave, despite his words.

Star laughed and pushed him off. "Go - I'll see you in the morning."

Damian looked like he wanted to say more, but instead backed out of the room.

"I'll see you and Skylar in the morning. We can drop her off together."

With that he turned and left, leaving Star standing in a post-coital bliss, loving this man more than ever before. She really was in trouble.

Chapter Fourteen

The rest of the week saw Star and Damian fall into a routine. Damian would pick Star and Skylar up every morning before dropping Skylar at Breakfast Club, and then in the evenings he would drive her home and they would spend the evening together, either at Star's house, or they'd travel further out and stay at his parents' estate.

On the Friday, Star and Damian were preparing for their business dinner. They'd collected Skylar early and headed to his parents in order to get changed and settle Skylar in for the evening. Lucas was recovering fast, and Star could tell he was dying to get back into the throes of the business. Andrew Dennison, however, had other ideas and had demanded his hard work not be in vain, telling Lucas he needed more rest and time off, and that going back to the office too early could set Lucas back and have him retiring permanently. Star had silently celebrated. The longer Lucas remained off, the more time she would have with Damian.

Mary had taken the threat seriously, even if Lucas hadn't, and she'd coerced him into resting. Damian had agreed to spend longer in the UK office while his father recuperated.

Marcus drove them back into the City, ready for their meeting. This was a more informal meeting, the American Office and the UK office coming together to discuss their high-level plans and desires for the campaign. Damian and Star discussed their strategy in the car, their personal relationship pushed to one side for the evening. Tonight they were professionals, neither one wanting to let this opportunity slip by.

Arriving at the hotel, they were escorted to their seats. Star's palms were clammy and she had a strong desire to wipe them down the side of her dress to dry them. Instead, she made her excuses and headed to the ladies room in order to freshen up and calm herself before the meeting.

She still wasn't convinced that this client really did want her to be on the team.

Star took a deep breath and composed herself in the mirror. Her cheeks looked flushed and butterflies jumped nervously around in her stomach. She reapplied her powder and stepped towards the door. Opening it, she was surprised to see Damian waiting for her.

"Ready?" he asked, as if knowing why she had needed to escape. "You've got this."

"Tell that to the monkeys having a party in my stomach," Star replied with a tight smile.

Placing his hand in the small of her back, Damian directed Star into the dining room, the maître d' leading them to their table. Two men and a woman were already sitting at the table, and they rose to their feet as Damian and Star approached.

Damian stopped next to the tallest of the men, smiling brightly and holding out his hand. "Henri, great to see you," he said, before moving to shake hands with the woman who Star quickly realised was Henri's wife, Patrice, and the second man, whose presence froze Star's blood. Damian was now introducing her, but Star's gaze was fixed on the third guest, Christian

Dupree. It had been nearly seven years since Star had last seen Christian and their meeting in a solicitor's office had been short and abrupt, as he'd signed his daughter's adoption papers, handing all responsibility for his new-born child to her. Damian touched her arm, capturing her attention, concern visible on his face.

Star shook her head. "Sorry," she said, snapping herself back into the present, forcing a smile onto her face before shaking everyone's hand. Christian didn't look shocked at her presence but refrained from saying anything to let the others know they knew each other, for which she was grateful.

The rest of the meal went well. The discussions were open and honest. Henri mentioned his close friendship with Matthew Morris, who had clearly sung Star's praises. Together, they pitched their ideas and thoughts on the new marketing campaign, listening to Henri and Christian's take on the trans-Atlantic campaign.

Towards the end of the meal, Star again made her excuses and escaped to the ladies room. Her emotions were frazzled. Keeping up appearances while facing her daughter's father was not easy, especially when their previous meetings had been hostile. Now she was expected to sit there and make polite conversation with him. Pulling herself together, she exited the ladies, to find Christian waiting outside the door.

"Can we talk?" he asked, pushing himself away from the wall.

"I'm not sure what you want to talk about," Star said, moving to step past him.

"How is Skylar?" Christian said, his voice catching at the end of the sentence, which had Star spinning towards him in surprise.

"She's well," she said, unsure what he wanted. "I really should be getting back." Star moved towards the restaurant.

"I'm sorry, I know tonight hasn't been easy for you," Christian said. "When I realised who was going to be at the meeting, I couldn't believe it. I've wanted to reach out for so long."

A hollow feeling settled in Star's stomach. What was happening? This man had signed away all rights to his daughter like she was nothing but an inconvenience to be swept under the carpet, and had had nothing to do with her for the past six years, but was here now talking about reaching out.

"Well, it's been over six years, Christian, and there were nine months before that – plenty of time for you to find out about your daughter. Instead, you got married and turned your back on Lily," Star said, her voice hitching in her throat. "Now I really need to get back, otherwise Damian will wonder where I've got to."

Star turned and walked away, leaving Christian in the hallway, her stomach doing somersaults and threatening to evict the gourmet food she'd just eaten.

Damian looked up, a frown marring his face. Star shook her head quickly and smiled, before retaking her seat and striking up conversation with Patrice. Christian took a while to come back, although he too looked pale and was much more withdrawn when he sat down.

It wasn't long before the evening was over, and they were heading to the front of the hotel where Marcus was waiting.

∞∞∞

Once inside the car, Damian turned to Star,

his eyebrows pulled together. "Want to tell me what's going on?" he asked,

"Nothing," Star told him, wanting to time to think and sort this out in her head. She needed to speak to Toby urgently.

"Don't give me that, Star! You looked like you'd seen a ghost when we walked in and were shaking when you returned to the table after you visited the ladies room. Not to mention that when Christian came back from the men's room, he looked like he was going to be sick. I know you – something happened!"

"No," Star said. "You *knew* me. Seven years is a long time, Damian. People change."

"No, you haven't. You are still the same person. Putting everyone else first." He sighed, before saying, "It's one of the main reasons I fell in love with you all those years ago. What did Christian say to you? And don't say nothing, because I don't believe you. Did he make a pass at you?"

"No, he didn't make a pass; it would be better if that was all it was," Star said, looking out of the window and wrapping her arms around her stomach.

"Then what? Something spooked you,"

Damian said resting his hand on her arm, his thumb rubbing small light circles.

Turning back to look at Damian, Star captured his hand in hers and brought it to her lips. "Christian Dupree is Skylar's biological father."

It was Damian's turn to look shell-shocked. His mouth opened as if he were about to say something before closing it again. "I think you'd better explain," he finally said.

"It's not a pretty story," Star took a deep breath. "When Lily moved to London, she starred in that small play. We went to see her in it a couple of times. It wasn't one of the main West End shows, but she had a reasonable part and the show was getting some good reviews. Christian went to see the show with his friends and took a shine to my sister. He started sending her flowers and invited her out to dinner. Lily became a challenge when she didn't fall straight into bed with him. She said he was relentless in the ways he was trying to win her over, and found herself laughing and falling for him. He was charming." Damian huffed before sending Star a look of apology. "After about two months, she agreed to go on a date with him. He worked in

London, was attentive and loving … He'd phone her every night after her show and showered her with presents. Not expensive, but thoughtful presents. He won her heart."

"Go on," Damian said.

"About six months in, Lily started to feel really tired, all the time. She was losing weight. Initially, she thought it was the theatre hours she was keeping and the partying with Christian. The rest you know. She no longer had the strength required for six shows a week, and so she left the production and came home. The producer was great, offering her a leave of absence. He thought she was an amazing actress."

Damian's hand clasped Star's, the warmth of it radiating up her arm, offering her his strength.

"What happened with Christian?" he asked.

"When she initially spoke to him, she didn't know she was pregnant. She only found out as her treatment was about to start."

"But Christian knows about Skylar?" Damian asked.

"When Lily found out she was pregnant,

she went to see him at his family home. She felt he had the right to know that they'd created another human being together. She was so in love with him. Christian's father slammed the door in her face and called her a lying, filthy whore. Christian simply stood there. She was devastated." A growl emanated from Damian, but he let Star continue. "She had hoped he would at least care for his child should she not survive ... Instead, something broke inside her. It was then that I promised her I would love and care for her daughter should anything ever happen to her. Lily's body gave up towards the end and they had to bring Skylar into the world earlier than expected. Lily got to see her daughter but the cancer had progressed so far, that it was simply a matter of days, not weeks. We had already arranged guardianship – Toby's dad helped. The paperwork was signed. Christian came to the office, signed the papers, and left, and that was the last time I saw him. Lily passed later that day. I think once she knew Skylar was safe, she let herself rest. She'd fought so hard, Damian, at the end it was a relief to see her pain-free."

Damian pulled Star into his arms,

cocooning her against his chest, his warmth soothing the pain engulfing her. Star could hear the rumble through Damian's chest as he offered soothing words of comfort. Eventually, Star pulled herself away, wiping her face with her hands and giving an apologetic smile. Damian shook his head.

"So what did Christian say tonight?" he asked.

"He simply asked after her. It made me feel uneasy. Why after all this time when he has shown no interest in his daughter would he suddenly want to know how she is? He even said he's been thinking of getting in contact for a while. What if he wants to take her away from me?"

"No one is going to take Skylar away from you. You've adopted her. She is your flesh and blood, too."

"But his family have so much money, they may decide he can give her a better life than I ever could. Look at me, Damian. I live in the same house I lived in when I was at university, a house that I share with my best friends." Star's heart beat faster, panic overtaking rational thought. "I can't lose her, Damian."

"He signed his rights away, from what you've said. Skylar is your daughter."

In Star's anxiety, she wondered if Damian was regretting getting involved with her again and being embroiled in all this drama. She pulled away from him, moving towards the door of the car.

Damian turned to Star, taking her face in both his hands. "Don't," he said, "don't begin to doubt us. I'm here now and I appreciate you being honest with me. Don't let Christian Dupree cause you to doubt yourself or your ability as a mum. You are amazing, Star, and Skylar is lucky to have you. Thank you for trusting me. Most people would not have done what you've done. Let me help you – you are not alone. Should Christian get in touch, I want you to let me know."

Star nodded, feeling exhausted. Damian interlocked their fingers, dragging their hands to his lips before resting them in his lap. This was not how she'd expected this evening to go. Potentially, she would now be working with Christian Dupree. She wasn't sure Damian had realised that. Was she strong enough to fight the Dupree family alone?

∞ ∞ ∞

Arriving back at Damian's parents' house, Star left Damian to check on Skylar while Damian went to update his father on the meeting. Skylar was sound asleep, curled up in a four-poster bed, in a room larger than both of their bedrooms put together. She looked so peaceful, totally unaware of the chaos that had erupted this evening. A sense of pain sat heavily on Star's chest. Christian had asked after Skylar. He'd seemed genuine. Yes, it was six years too late, but surely late was better than never. Maybe she should have given him more time to talk, to find out what he wanted.

The door opened behind her, chasing her thoughts away as Damian came into the room, wrapping his arms around her from behind and dropping a kiss on her neck. "She looks peaceful," he whispered.

Star smiled, resting her head back against his shoulder. "Skylar has always slept well. Her head hits the pillow and she'll remain there for the next twelve hours."

Bending down, Star kissed Skylar's head. It was then she noticed her daughter cuddling a stuffed German Shepherd teddy.

"Ah, Mum must have given it to her," Damian whispered. "I saw it in one of the shops. She may not be able to take one of the real puppies home, but she can have a stuffed version."

Star's heart clenched at his thoughtfulness. What were they going to do when he returned to the New York office …

∞∞∞

Star awoke early, aware she didn't want her daughter to find her sleeping in Damian's bed. They'd made love before talking late into the evening. Falling asleep in Damian's arms felt comforting, like coming home after a long period away, and her body knew it was where she was supposed to be, as she'd slept better than she had in years.

Star got showered and dressed, before walking into her daughter's room, only to find her bed empty. Panic flooded her body as she wondered if Skylar had gone looking for her and couldn't find her. Where would she be? Perhaps downstairs playing with the puppies? At the bottom of the sweeping staircase, Star stopped. She could hear faint laughter coming from the kitchen. Walking down the wood-lined corridor, Star headed in the direction of the noise, her daughter's giggles becoming louder the closer she got. Star paused outside the heavy door. She could hear Lucas and Skylar chatting in the kitchen. Mary was trying to be stern with Lucas, which seemed to be sending Skylar into even greater fits of giggles. A smile blossomed on her face as she pushed open the door and entered.

"Everyone seems in bright spirits this morning," she said as a greeting.

Skylar jumped down from the marble-covered island and flew towards Star. "Mummy!" she yelled, throwing her arms around Star. "Aunty Mary is making me pancakes, but she'd told Uncle Lucas he's not allowed any, as he's on a strict diet." Then, conspiratorially, she whispered loudly, "But he says he's going to share mine."

Mary rolled her eyes and Lucas burst out laughing again before huffing, "I'm being ganged up on!"

Star sat next to her daughter, noticing she was not in her pyjamas but already dressed for the day. "Wow, you are up and dressed early this morning," Star said.

"Yes, Aunty Mary helped me," Skylar said between mouthfuls. "She said I could play with the puppies again, but only if I got washed and dressed. She didn't want me putting dog fur in my bed tonight," Skylar giggled.

Star was shocked. She'd expected they'd be heading home today. Just then, Damian came into the kitchen, sliding his hand around her waist from behind and kissing her ear. Star jumped at his open show of affection in front of his mum and dad. Skylar grinned at him and Lucas looked smug. Mary winked and led Skylar towards the boot-room, where the puppies were currently residing in a pen with Rosy.

"Mum's spoiling us this morning," Damian said, snagging a pancake from the pile Skylar had left. Turning to face him, Star was shocked when he then dropped a kiss on her lips.

Lucas coughed. "Glad to see you two have made up ..."

Star felt herself blush. What was Damian

playing at? Was he declaring them an item? She had spent the night in Damian's room. His parents had actually given her a room next to Skylar's, but Damian had threatened to abduct her if she hadn't gone with him willingly. Star had intended on heading back to her own room later, but had fallen asleep and hadn't woken until her alarm had gone off.

"When you two love birds are ready, we can discuss last night in my office," Lucas said, winking at them both, just as Mary returned to the room.

"No," Mary said firmly.

"What do you mean, No?" Lucas looked at his wife in surprise.

"What I said, No! There will be no meeting today, or tomorrow. It is the weekend, and we are having family time," she said, hands on her hips.

Star sat back awkwardly; she'd never heard Mary contradict Lucas before.

"Don't be silly – it's only talking," Lucas said, frowning.

"No, it's not just talking. It's work. You've just had a heart attack and major surgery. Nothing was said last night that cannot wait until Monday morning when the office opens."

"You are being silly Mary," Lucas said, his tone taking on a firmness that Star had often heard him use in the office.

"No, Lucas, I am not being silly. You nearly died because work has been all you care about," Mary said, her voice cracking.

Star watched as Lucas got down from his stool and approached Mary.

Mary held up her hand as if to stop him, but Lucas ignored her and pulled her into his arms.

"I'm not prepared to lose you because you are a stubborn old goat!" Mary mumbled into his chest.

Damian looked shocked, as if it were the first time he had seen his mum openly emotional about Lucas's heart attack. Star gripped his hand and squeezed.

Mary pulled back and looked up at her husband, a new firmness in her voice. "I don't want these two young people to take a leaf out of your book. It's their weekend. They need to be able to enjoy themselves, not be talking to you about work! There will be plenty of time for that on Monday. They should be taking Skylar out, having fun. You may not care if you kill yourself, but there are other people who do!"

Star looked at Damian awkwardly. His mum had just suggested he spend the whole weekend with her and Skylar. They had not even talked about what they were doing. Star didn't want Damian to feel obliged to spend his free time with her and her daughter.

As if sensing her unease, Damian wrapped his arm round her waist again and whispered in her ear, "I can almost hear your brain whirling. I want nothing more than to spend the weekend with you both. I was going to suggest it after breakfast – Mum just beat me to it."

Star spun around in Damian's arms to face him. "You don't have to," she said. "I'd understand if you have something else planned."

"Do you?" Damian asked.

"Do I what?" Star said confused.

"Have other plans?"

"Of course not, I was going to take Skylar bike riding in the park, that's all."

"Excellent. Mum and Dad bought a bike for Skylar last week, and what better place for her to cycle than our grounds. We can go for a run and Skylar can ride with us. I also thought we could clean out my old treehouse together. I'm sure

Skylar would love that."

"We'd love to spend time with you," Star said, a little breathlessly, before remembering Mary and Lucas were standing watching them. Star turned to them, embarrassment flooding her face. "That is if it's okay with you?" she directed at them.

"I wouldn't have made the offer if it weren't," Mary said, smiling at them both, her cheek still resting on Lucas's chest.

"Well, it looks like we'll be having that meeting on Monday morning, if that's okay with you, Star, Damian?" Lucas said, smiling down at his wife, love radiating from his eyes.

It was at that point Skylar came running back into the room.

"Mummy, can we stay?" she said, obviously having heard some of the conversation.

"If you want to," Star replied. This wasn't just about her, after all.

"Yes," Skylar said, before throwing her arms around Damian, who let go of Star and scooped her up into his arms.

Chapter Fifteen

Monday morning came around far too fast. They had spent hours cleaning the treehouse and running round the grounds, with Skylar cycling next to them. Star loved that Damian still enjoyed running; it was something they'd spent many weekends doing when they had been students. Lucas and Mary's seventy acres surrounding the manor house was perfect for running.

When Star came down for breakfast, she saw that Skylar was already dressed and ready for school. They'd popped home, and grabbed a change of clothes and Skylar's uniform the day before.

"Mummy, Marcus is going to drop me at school and so I don't need to go to Breakfast

Club," Skylar said. "I can go just in time for school to start. It's even better 'cause now you're up, we can have breakfast together before I go. Uncle Lucas wants to have a meeting with you here." She looked up and added in a loud whisper, "He's not allowed in the office, so he needs to speak to you in the house."

Star looked at Mary over the top of her daughter's head. "Mary, are you okay with this?"

"As if I can stop the old goat. I'm never going to hear the end of it. If you're happy for me to take Skylar to school with Marcus, then maybe you and Damian can stop this man's pacing and he will calm down. I got my way over the weekend, but it's now Monday and life has to get back to normal." Mary rolled her eyes, shooting her husband a glance.

"Yay," Skylar squealed. "Aunty Mary, can we see the puppies now. Please!"

Star was about to protest, but Mary held up her hand to stop her. "Let me enjoy this time with my favourite little girl," Mary said, coming round with a facecloth to wipe Skylar's face and hands. It was such a grandmotherly thing to do. They took such great care of her. Star knew they would be doting grandparents when Damian gave them children. The thought sent a hollow feeling flooding through Star's body. The idea of another woman getting large with Damian's child made her sick to the stomach. They'd always talked about children before she'd ruined their chances.

Damian came into the kitchen, his hair still damp from the shower. Dropping a kiss on her lips, he helped himself to a large bowl of cereal and sat down next to her.

"I sent an email to the team, letting them know I would be having a face-to-face meeting with Lucas, so no one is expecting me in this morning," Star said. "Friday night's client meeting wasn't a secret, so there should be no repercussions or gossip. If anyone asks, you dropped me home Friday night and then I drove out here this morning."

A strange look crossed Damian's face. "That's very thoughtful of you," he said before going back to eating his breakfast.

Damian's response left Star feeling uncomfortable. She nibbled at her toast before getting up and washing her plate in the sink. Damian had made her no promises, and with Lucas starting to get involved in projects,

Damian would no longer need to stay. The speed with which their relationship had restarted meant they hadn't discussed any long-term plans. The past weekend had shown her what she had lost. She wasn't sure how she was going to cope when he was gone.

Trying to hide her discomfort, Star plastered a smile on her face. "Skylar is really excited about your mum taking her to school," she said, before turning to Lucas and adding, "Give me a moment. I'll just finish getting ready and then we can begin. Are we meeting in your office?"

Both Lucas and Damian nodded, although Damian's face held a quizzical look. He'd obviously picked up on her discomfort; she couldn't hide anything from him.

"I won't be a moment," she said before making a quick exit.

Once outside the door, Star sagged against the wall, a sickening grief filling her chest. Rubbing the pain that had taken hold around her heart, Star pushed away from the wall and headed back towards the sweeping staircase that led to the upstairs.

She remembered the first time Damian

had brought her here. The house looked like something out of *Downton Abbey*. It was a real country manor with oak panelling, a west and east wing, and acres of land. But the Hunts, unlike her own mother, lacked the snobbery of their station; they'd always been warm and welcoming. Damian had never flashed his family's wealth. If anything, he'd kept it hidden, and Lucas had made him work for what he had. When Star had arrived, she'd been the first girl Damian had brought home to meet them, or that was how Mary had described her, and she'd been welcomed with open arms. Star had joined them on holidays, at parties, and no one had ever made her feel less. She'd felt loved.

Making her way back to Damian's room, Star sat down on the bed, and rubbed her chest to ease the tension. When Lucas returned, Damian would leave. She had no right to feel sad; they'd made no promises to each other. But the hollow feeling burrowing its way through Star left her in no doubt she was not going to walk away unscathed. She had fallen in love with Damian all over again – if she'd ever fallen out of love with him in the first place. Swiping at the single tear that had escaped, Star jumped at the gentle knock.

"It's Mary, dear. I just wanted to let you know Skylar and I are about to leave."

Star took a deep breath and headed to the door. Mary took one look at Star, and patted her arm. Star bent down and hugged Skylar goodbye.

"Be a good girl, munchkin, and I'll see you after school," Star said, giving her an extra squeeze.

"Are we coming back here?" Skylar asked excitedly.

"Not tonight, we need to go home." Star watched as Skylar's face fell.

But Mary jumped in: "You can come back with Mummy and Damian at the weekend. I know Rosy and the puppies are going to miss you."

Skylar beamed at Mary, her excitement clear. "Can we, Mummy?"

Star shot Mary a look, which Mary returned with an unapologetic glance.

"I'll discuss it with Aunty Mary before we leave, but I'm sure that will be all right."

Skylar skipped off back towards the stairs and Mary turned as if to go, before swinging back round, and saying, "Don't despair yet …"

Star smiled, but her heart wasn't in it. It was time to pull on her big girl pants and get to work. She had Skylar and her future to think about. Damian had become a distraction. It was time she refocused and thought about what was best for them. She'd proven herself more than capable with the Morris project, and her promotion was now guaranteed. To land Felts Beverages as a client would be a game changer, affirming her rightful place as a top executive at the firm. All her dreams were finally coming true. She no longer needed to rely on Toby and Laura's generosity, and for the first time since Skylar had arrived she was going to be independent. Why then, did she feel so empty inside?

Damian and his father were talking at Lucas's desk when Star returned. Both men stood as she entered, and Damian directed her to the seat next to him after giving her a kiss on her cheek. Her heart fluttered at his open sign of affection; he certainly wasn't hiding their relationship from his father anymore. Lucas was beaming from the other side of his desk, which took Star by surprise, leaving her feeling as if she'd missed some major announcement.

"So, Damian has informed me Friday night went well," Lucas said, looking at Star. "I'm also aware that Christian Dupree is Skylar's father. Is that going to be an issue, Star?"

"No," Star replied, holding his gaze. "Damian and I checked with Toby – the adoption is watertight. As far as the law is concerned, Christian signed away his rights to Skylar the day he signed the papers." Star's voice sounded convincing even to herself, but her insides churned uncontrollably. The "what if"s were still flying round her head, feeding the little devil sitting on her shoulder. Despite what Toby had said, Star was still petrified.

"Good. You know you have our full support should there be any backlash," Lucas added with a nod.

Star was a little taken aback. She could not and would not let this undermine the company's chances of winning this business. She couldn't do that to Lucas, Damian, or her colleagues. This opportunity was huge. If the time came and there was an issue with Christian, she had already decided she would resign. She just hoped it wasn't going to come to that.

They talked about the meeting for the next

hour and a half before agreeing it was time to pull together a team and bring the clients into the office. Star was surprised when Damian and Lucas asked her opinion; she had been sure Damian had only invited her to bring them closer, but instead they both made her feel like a valued member of the team.

∞∞∞

"Don't look so shocked," Damian said when they finally returned to his room to grab their things before heading to the office.

Star spun round, her wash bag in her hands. Damian grasped her hands, pulling her towards him. "You spent that entire meeting looking shell shocked that we'd included you. You seem to have a very warped idea of your worth. You are where you deserve to be, Star. Not because you are in my bed, but because you're good at what you do. More than good. Dad recognises that. He wants you on the team. You wouldn't be here if he didn't have total confidence in your ability."

Star looked up into Damian's face for any

sign he was playing her. There was nothing but honesty. "It's just hard to take in. I'm one of the newer members of staff. There are many more who have years more experience than me," she said, looking down.

Damian grasped her chin, forcing her to look at him again. "Experience isn't everything. You should know that by now. It is a gut instinct; it's about understanding the client's wants and needs. You have that in bucket loads. Plus, you are so creative! You proved that on Friday night. I've already had Henri on the phone singing your praises this morning and telling me how he wants you on the team. You made that impression, not me. You need to start believing in yourself. What happened to the girl I met – the one who wanted to take on the world and believed she could? You still can, Star. You have the talent to do it."

Star stepped back, a warmth spreading through her chest at Damian's praise. But she wasn't the same girl he had known seven years ago. She was a shadow of that person, although she was fighting hard to get her back. The fact he'd noticed worried her. Maybe she wasn't what he wanted anymore; maybe the old version was the one he loved and he was now realising that version no longer existed.

"Stop it," Damian said pulling her close again. "I can see where your mind is going. You are not less than you were, Star, you just need your confidence back. I get it! You ended up as a single mum at twenty-one, not through any fault of your own, and you've done an amazing job. You need to start seeing what everyone else can see." Damian kissed her forehead before continuing, "Jackson was jealous – that is why he spread the rumours he did. He knew he'd never shine as bright as you. Your understanding of the job and clients was superior to his, so he tried sabotage instead. You are going to be up against it. Some people are not going to like you being in charge on this project – they are going to sling mud, but it doesn't have to stick. Rise above it, and do the job you know you can do."

"You sound like you know what I'm about to go through," Star said, looking closely at Damian.

He grinned in reply. "Boss's son, remember. It's one of the reasons Dad wanted me to work away, so I could prove myself. I know about the conversation he had with you seven years ago, Star, and I'm pissed. I can't change it, though, so there is no point looking back. I want us to look forward." With that Damian dropped his head, his lips capturing hers in a kiss that left them both breathless.

Stepping back, Damian ran his fingers through his hair and said, "We really need to get ready for work otherwise, we'll end up back in that bed and won't make it in at all."

Both their eyes flitted to the bed.

"Dammit," Damian said, pulling her to him. "Who said we aren't still in a meeting."

Chapter Sixteen

Star and Damian made it into the office a couple of hours later. Star's team were hard at work, although excited to see her when she arrived. After fielding questions about Friday night's meeting and questions regarding Lucas's health, she finally sat down at her desk and saw she had a missed call on her mobile.

When she accessed the voicemail, her heart stopped.

"Star, it's Christian Dupree. I'm sorry to bother you at work, but I didn't know how else to get hold of you … Look, I'm sorry about Friday night. I didn't mean to ambush you. I spent a lot of the weekend thinking how my appearance must have seemed." Star held her breath at his pause. "I really want to talk. I was wondering if you'd be willing to meet me? I know it's a lot to ask, but if you can bring yourself to speak to me, you can contact me on this number. I really hope I hear from you."

Star listened to the voicemail several times, before staring blindly at his number on her mobile. She didn't want to meet with Christian Dupree or have anything to do with him. But if the company won the contract, she knew that was going to be impossible – they would be working together.

Star opened her emails and tried hard to put his call out of her mind. After half an hour, she gave up. Picking up her mobile, she motioned to her team that she would be in one of the meeting rooms. For the conversation she was about to have, she needed privacy.

"Toby, it's Star,"

"Hey, how was your weekend with Damian?" he asked slyly.

"We had a great weekend, thank you," Star said, but she knew her voice held more weight than she hoped to convey.

"What can I do for you Star? You never ring me at work."

"Christian left a voice message on my

phone this morning," Star said flatly.

"Are you OK?" Toby's voice softened.

"Not really, I have had horrible thoughts rushing round my head all night and now—"

"Take a deep breath. Before you panic, as I explained yesterday, your adoption of Skylar was all legal and above board. He signed away any rights to her years ago. The law doesn't allow for him to change his mind and come back for her. If he wants a daughter, then he'll have to have one with his wife." Toby practically spat the last words out. After the way the Dupree family had treated Lily and Skylar, Star knew he had no time for them.

"But they're so wealthy. He is the UK CEO of the biggest drinks company in the world. What can I offer that he can't automatically give her?"

"Stop right now. No one is going to take Skylar from you. What exactly did he say? I can get a restraining order placed on him if you want?"

"Oh gosh, no!" Star said in a panic. "Hunt and Hunt are trying to win their business. I don't know what I want, but I just needed to be able to talk to someone, especially after his message."

"I'm listening. What did he say to you, Star?"

"He simply asked me to call him. What do I do, Toby? I don't want to jeopardise the contract with the company, but I can't risk Skylar."

"Have you spoken to Damian?"

"No, I haven't told him about this morning's call. I tried to do some work, but I just couldn't concentrate. I think I needed to hear you say that the adoption was okay, that he can't just decide he wants her back." Star tried to take a deep breath.

"Are you going to talk to Damian?" Toby asked.

"I honestly don't know. I need to think about it. I don't even know what he wants …" Star gave a hollow laugh. "Why does life have to get so complicated just as I thought it was coming together."

"Don't rush into calling Christian back. You hold all the cards here, Star. Talk to Damian."

"I can't! If I speak to him, he's likely to call Christian and ask him what his game is. This is huge business, Toby. You saw how horrified Damian was over the whole thing. I can't involve him."

"Okay, okay, but remember, Laura and I are always here for you and Skylar – you know that. I think you should let Damian be, too, but it's not my call. You shut him out once before and you've been unhappy ever since. But, Star, I'm glad you called me."

Star sighed, feeling better now she'd managed to get someone else's perspective.

But she didn't feel right pulling Damian into her family dramas. He'd only just come back into her life, and she did not want to burden him with her problems or split his loyalties. She wanted their relationship to be perfect, at least for the time they had left together. He had enough issues with helping get his dad back on his feet, landing this client, and keeping the Board happy. He didn't need to jeopardise anything for her; she wouldn't let him.

∞∞∞

Star got through the rest of the day in a daze. Damian questioned her in the car on the way home, but she simply told him she was tired. He had smiled knowingly and accepted her excuse.

When he dropped her off at home, he promised to pick her up in the morning, telling her tomorrow he'd be driving himself as his mum and dad needed Marcus for check-ups.

Still on a high from Damian's kiss, Star stumbled inside the house.

"So, did you tell him about Christian?" Star spun on her friend, before shushing Laura and looking around for Skylar. "Don't fret, she's upstairs doing her homework."

"I see Toby updated you! No, I didn't tell him. I don't even know what Christian wants. I'm not risking the company and a huge deal for my private life. Where would that leave us?"

Laura shook her head. "If Damian is your partner, then it's called sharing your problems. It's not burdening him. Damian is not stupid – he's not going to do anything that will jeopardise the company. He will, however, be able to support you through this."

"I don't want his advice – this is my decision," Star snapped.

"Fine," Laura said quietly, "but remember I watched you implode a perfect relationship before. I don't want to watch it happen again because you won't let someone in."

With that, Laura returned to chopping vegetables for dinner.

"I'm sorry," Star said, walking up behind her friend and resting her head on her shoulder. "I need to decide what to do, and I'm scared."

"I know you are," Laura said, resting her head against Star's. "Why don't you ring Christian? Find out what he wants. Not knowing is always far worse."

"I'll wait until tonight when Skylar is in bed and find out what he wants." Star stepped back, moving to stir the onions browning on the stove.

The decision to call Christian made Star feel lighter. She needed to know what she was up against. Maybe he only wanted a photograph. Whatever it was, Star owed it to Skylar to find out. He was Skylar's biological father and Lily had loved him. Staring upwards, Star sent up a message to Lily asking what she should do? As always, silence prevailed. Lily had always said she trusted Star to raise Skylar to be the best person she could be. She just hoped her faith in Star was warranted.

∞∞∞

Later that evening Star sat on her bed, staring at Christian's number. Taking a deep breath, she opened her screen and dialled before she had a chance to rethink.

"Christian Dupree," the voice answered almost immediately. Shocked at hearing his voice, Star was suddenly unable to find her own. "Hello?" Christian's voice came across quieter, almost as if he realised it was Star.

Star cleared her throat. "Christian, it's Star Roberts,"

"Star, thank you for calling. I wasn't sure you would." Christian's voice was soft, as if he was scared she would spook and disappear.

"I wasn't sure I was going to either," Star replied honestly, her heart pounding wildly. "Why did you call, Christian?"

There was another silence at the end of the phone. "I thought this was going to be easier than it is," Christian said with a self-deprecating laugh. Star could almost hear him shaking himself on the other end of the line, as if to clear his head and get his thoughts together. "I wanted to know about Skylar, find out how she is," he said, the words coming out so fast Star barely caught them.

"I don't mean to be rude, Christian, but why now? Skylar is six. You didn't want anything to do with her before. What's changed?"

"I know, and I'll have to live with that forever."

Star held her breath, readying herself to jump in.

But before she could Christian continued, "Star, I know I gave up my rights to Skylar. She is your daughter, and for that I am eternally grateful. I know you have sacrificed a lot to raise her."

Star didn't know what to say; she didn't want his pity, so she remained silent and let Christian speak.

"This is so difficult ..." He sounded dejected.

"Just say what you need to say, Christian." Star sounded tired even to herself.

After a minute, Christian coughed, as if trying to clear his throat and get the words out. "I know I have no right, but I'd like to know about

Skylar."

Star's heart sank. This is what she'd always feared, that at some point Christian would want his daughter.

"Why now?" she managed to spit out, failing to keep the hostility from her voice.

"I'm not asking to meet her," Christian said with a sigh. "I just want to know about her. Can you and I meet? I have a lot to explain, and I would rather do that face-to-face. Please, Star, I understand I'm asking a lot."

Lily's heartbroken face, her weak body … Skylar's tiny body helpless in the incubator, her first steps, her first words … all these images flashed in front of Star's eyes. The one that stuck the most was her sister crying on her shoulder, the devastation Christian had caused, but throughout it all Lily had still loved him.

"Okay, I'll meet you, but only because Lily would have wanted me to. But, Christian, I'm trusting you."

"Thank you, Star," Christian whispered.

"Don't thank me. I've agreed to meet, nothing more," Star said abruptly, not wanting him to get the wrong idea.

"Thank you anyway."

After they'd arranged to meet at a hotel close to Hunt and Hunt, Star ended the call and sat back on the bed, looking at the phone. An internal battle waged within her, a deep sense of foreboding weighing on her chest. She knew she should call Damian and let him know what was happening, but the part of her that had been independent for so long told her that Damian didn't need her problems and that she was better off keeping him out of this. As she had told Laura, she wasn't willing to jeopardise the biggest deal the company had ever seen for personal reasons. She would resign before she let that happen.

∞∞∞

Damian picked up Star and Skylar as usual in the morning. This had become a beloved part of their daily routine. She loved the time they spent together, talking about everything and nothing on the way into work. The past couple of days, they'd been discussing ideas for the pitch to their new client. Star never saw Damian as animated as when he was deep in the throes of discussing and spinning ideas. She used his excitement as a distraction this morning to ensure that Damian didn't pick up on her low mood. Although she had slept, she'd spent a lot of the night tossing and turning, mulling over what she was going to say to Christian this afternoon, and what his true motives were after all this time.

"So, do you want to meet in my office for lunch today?" Damian asked as they pulled into the underground car park.

"I can't," Star stammered, trying hard to think of an excuse.

"Oh, okay. No problem. I just wondered if you wanted to continue this discussion, plus I have something else I wanted to discuss with you," Damian said, before adding with a laugh, "Don't look so worried, it's not an issue."

"I'm sorry," Star said quietly. "I've made plans with the girls to meet and do lunch today." She and Damian were on different floors so he'd never notice when she slipped out alone.

Star stepped out of the car feeling flushed and flustered. Why had she lied? She should have just told Damian the truth.

"Damian," she said, calling after him and making him turn.

"Yes?" he said smiling back at her, making

her heart sink even further.

"It's nothing," she said. "Have a lovely day and I'll see you this evening."

They went their separate ways, still careful to keep their private life private and away from the rest of the office.

When lunchtime finally came, Star grabbed her bag and left the office, wanting to get clear of the building as fast as she could. Her stomach threatened to bring up that morning's breakfast the closer she got to her destination.

When she entered the hotel lobby, she saw that Christian was already waiting in the far corner of the lounge. He stood up as soon as he saw her approach, motioning to a chair near him. Star tried to walk with an air of confidence that she didn't, couldn't feel. It was only when she looked at Christian that she realised he wasn't faring much better than she was. There were dark circles under his eyes and his skin was much paler than the last time she had seen him, even though that had only been a couple of days ago. His blond hair was ruffled, as if he'd spent the morning running his hands through it. He looked broken, not the powerful CEO she knew him to be. Christian's obvious discomfort helped

Star to relax. Maybe this was no easier for him than it was for her.

"Thank you for coming, Star," he said. "I honestly wasn't sure whether you would stand me up – and if you had, I wouldn't have blamed you."

"I wouldn't have done that, Christian, it isn't my style." Star clasped her hands in front of her, "So I'm here. What do you want to know?"

"Do you have any photos of Skylar?"

His question took Star by surprise. She'd been expecting demands, intimidation. Instead, he sat there quietly asking for a photo.

Star grabbed her phone and opened her photo app, showing him the latest picture of Skylar playing with the puppies. She handed her phone to Christian and was shocked when his eyes filled with tears. He swiped a stray one away with the back of his hand.

"If you swipe forwards, there's a video of her playing with the puppies," Star surprised herself by saying.

A heart melting, watery smile appeared on his face as he tried and failed to get his emotions under control. Star knew what he was seeing as Skylar's excited voice came across the speaker and she giggled. Star had captured the moment Skylar had been attacked by all the puppies and had been giggling as they nipped at and licked her as she went to feed them. Skylar's laugh was one of Star's favourite things.

"She looks so happy," Christian said, his voice clogged with emotion. He handed Star back her phone. "Thank you for sharing that."

"Why, Christian? Why now?" Star was confused by the man who sat in front of her. A man who had turned his back on her sister and child, a man who now sat with damp cheeks, looking lost and alone.

Christian looked up and captured Star's gaze. "I suppose you could say I've grown a backbone." He laughed harshly before continuing, "I finally stood up for myself. I've divorced my wife, although let's just say that it was by mutual agreement, and I've taken over my father's portion of the company and have crawled out from under his shadow."

Star's heart sank, she had a horrible feeling she knew where this was going. Christian must have seen something in her face because he held up his hand. "Please, Star, don't look like that. I don't want anything from you or Skylar. I just wanted to see her with my own eyes. I let others dictate my future – take it away from me and I will have to live with that for the rest of my life." He gave Star a half smile. "But Skylar looks happy, and for that I can only say thank you. I've been a terrible human being, but I want to make it right. I want to help you, if you'll let me."

Leaning forwards, Christian grasped Star's hand in his. "I know it can't have been easy for you, taking on your sister and my child when you were a student, but you did without hesitation." He paused, looking up at the ceiling, "I want to help you, help Skylar. Let me pay you maintenance – I have more than enough money, too much. Before you stop me, Skylar is my heir and what is mine will be hers one day, that is one thing I will make sure of."

"What?" Star said shocked. How dare he after seven years come back, cry over a photo, and then offer to throw money at the situation. Star started to stand, but Christian held onto her hand.

"Please, Star. I'm sorry, that came out wrong. I just want to help my daughter and you. I can't take back what has happened, and I can't change the past, but I hope I can change the future and try to make amends."

"You broke my sister's heart, why should I trust you or want anything from you? You stood by and let your father insult my sister and throw her out. We don't need your help, Christian. Skylar and I are fine!"

Christian had the decency to look ashamed. "I will have to live with that for the rest of my life. What I did to Lily." Christian's face fell as he struggled to hold his emotions in check. "I loved your sister with all my heart, and what I did can't be excused. The only thing I'll say is I made a lot of wrong decisions and I want to try and make up for it now. If you'll let me." The last part almost came out like a plea.

Star looked at the broken man in front of her. She didn't know what to think. For years, she had seen him as the villain, but he couldn't be all bad, could he? Her sister had loved him, had died still loving him. They had produced a beautiful child with a pure heart.

"What do you really want, Christian?"

"Honestly Star, I'm not asking anything of you. Maybe the odd photo so I can see how she is. I'm happy to keep my distance but help support her. I want to be able to help give her all the things I should have been giving her all these years."

"Is that really going to be enough?" Star asked, suddenly feeling like the villain in this picture. What was she going to say when Skylar asked about her father? Hers was far from a standard adoption. When Skylar had asked, Star had told her that her mummy and daddy had split up before Lily had known she was pregnant and her father hadn't known about her. Skylar had accepted that. But what was Star going to do now? Clearly Christian wanted to be part of his daughter's life. Could she really keep her away from him? Was that in Skylar's best interest? Lily had hoped until her last breath that Christian would come round and want their daughter. Now it appeared he did.

"Why now again?" she asked.

"It might sound cliched, but I've done a lot of soul searching and found out a lot of things about myself I wish I hadn't. I've spent a lot of time in counselling and there are things I can't go into, but …" Christian paused again. "I have spent too much time being manipulated and I've taken back control. I know my past is not your fault, and it certainly wasn't Lily's or Skylar's, but

I truly want to make amends."

Star wasn't sure whether she was being a sucker, or if Christian was genuine. Her heart was telling her this man meant everything he said. Star sent a prayer up to Lily hoping what she was about to do was the right decision. Toby, Laura, and Damian would not understand, but she had to do what was best for Skylar.

"I need to think on this. If, and I mean it's a big if, would you want to get to know Skylar? Do you want to be part of her life?"

Star was shocked as the grown man in front of her crumbled. Tears slid down his face as he grasped her hand tightly, before pulling her into a hug.

He eventually let her go, and said, "I would do everything and anything in my power to make that happen. But I understand it is not what I want; it is what is best for Skylar. I don't know what she knows about me, if she'd even want to speak to me after what I did."

Star wiped a tear from her own cheek, holding up her hand. "She thinks you don't know about her. I decided early on it was better that she thought you were unaware of her existence than that you had rejected her." Christian's face was a picture of gratitude, although a guilty sadness swept over his features. "If you want to do this, Christian, this is for life. You cannot choose to come back into her life and then leave again." Christian started to speak, but Star held up her hand. "I want you to go away and think about it. If you can truly commit, then I will arrange for you to meet Skylar."

Star stood up. Her lunchtime was over, and she had just made an enormous decision that was going to affect both herself and her daughter for the rest of their lives. She hadn't consulted Toby, and she knew he was going to be furious, but somewhere in her heart, she knew this was the right thing for Skylar. Her father wanted to know her; it was only right she gave him the chance.

Christian stood, pulling Star into a hug. "Thank you."

"Don't thank me yet. Think on it, Christian," Star said, pulling away from him. "I'm doing this for Skylar, not you."

As Star turned towards the lobby, Star spotted Damian standing by one of the pillars, his face a mask of fury. Star took a step towards him, but he turned abruptly and left.

"It's okay, I'll tell him it was a personal meeting," Christian said, clearly thinking Damian was angry because he thought she was visiting with a client behind his back.

Star spun back to him. "He knows it will have been personal," Star said. "He knows about Skylar. I just didn't mention to him that I was seeing you."

Christian's face gained a look of understanding, although he refrained from making further comment.

"Well, if you need me, you know how to contact me," he said.

"Thank you," Star said, before turning and leaving. It was time to face the music once again and hope Damian would listen.

Chapter Seventeen

Damian was nowhere in sight when Star exited the hotel. What had she been thinking? First, she'd lied when she blew him off for lunch. Now he'd found her with the one man who was not only a potential client but also her daughter's biological father. To top it all off, she'd just offered that person access to her and her daughter's life.

Before heading to the office, Star walked into the park to sit on her usual bench. She needed to get her head straight. What was she going to say? How was she going to explain this almighty mess to the man who meant the most to her?

After taking several deep breaths, Star asked Lily for her support before returning to the office. She felt like she was on a death march as she walked towards Damian's office. The door was firmly closed, creating an even deeper sense of foreboding. Walking up to Pam's desk, she waited until Pam finished her call.

"Is he in?" Star asked, tilting her head towards Damian's door.

"He is, but he's just come back from lunch in a foul mood. You may want to hide downstairs for a bit," Pam said quietly.

Star nodded, but knew she needed to see him. "That may be the case, but I really need to see him," she said, again glancing towards the door as if willing the man himself to appear so she could set the record straight.

"Be it on your head. Let me call through," Pam said picking up her phone.

"I asked not to be disturbed," Damian barked.

"I know, Damian, but Star is here asking to speak to you."

A silent pause followed.

"Send her in," he said.

Pam looked up and made a sweeping gesture towards the door. Star grimaced, pausing a moment outside the door before she bit the bullet and entered.

"What do you want, Star?" Damian sounded exhausted.

"I wanted to explain," she said quietly.

"I think what I saw was quite evident," Damian replied.

"Really?" Star said, a small amount of sarcasm entering her tone.

"Tell me you weren't meeting with Christian to discuss Skylar; tell me you haven't agreed to let him meet her?" Damian said, his eyes never leaving Star's face.

"Well..."

"When, Star? When did Christian contact you? It was obviously before this morning, as you were having lunch with the girls!" Star didn't like the tone in Damian's voice, but she understood his growing anger.

"Yesterday," she said, breaking his gaze and looking at the floor. She felt like a naughty schoolgirl, who had been caught cheating in a test.

Damian shook his head. "Were you ever going to tell me?"

Star stayed silent; she didn't want to lie. She would have told him this evening, but she wasn't sure that was what he wanted to hear.

"I thought we were past this," Damian said sadly. "Did you not trust me enough – is that it?"

"It's not that," Star said quickly.

"What is it then? I don't understand." Damian paused, before running his hand through his hair and saying, "I can't do this right now, Star. I need you to go."

"Please, Damian, we need to talk about this." Star sounded desperate, even to herself.

"No, Star, we don't. You've made your decision. I hoped I meant enough to you for you to include me in your choices going forward, but I was wrong. *Fool me once, shame on you. Fool me twice, shame on me*. You made a decision for us seven years ago that changed both our lives. You have done the same today. You don't trust me, Star, and without trust we have no future."

"Damian, please, this is about Skylar."

"No, Star, this is about you." Damian got up from his desk and walked towards her. Taking her face in his hands, he dropped a chaste kiss on her lips. "I'm sorry, but I can't do this anymore."

A sob caught in Star's throat and she raised her hand to his cheek. "I'm sorry, Damian," she whispered.

"I know you are," he said flatly, before taking her hand and walking her to the door. "Goodbye, Star."

∞∞∞

Star stumbled out of Damian's office in a daze. Her mind was racing, unable to keep up with what had just happened. Damian had broken up with her.

Pam got up and came round her desk, taking her arm and leading her away from prying eyes.

"Want to explain what's going on?" Pam asked.

"Not really, but I've messed up and I need to find a way to fix it," Star said, her voice cracking.

"I'm not blind, beautiful girl. I know when two people are in love, however much you've tried to hide it." Star stared at Pam in shock, but she just smiled in return. "Don't worry, I don't think your secret is out with anyone else. But whatever the issue is, I'm sure Damian will come round."

Star shook her head sadly. "I don't think it's going to be that easy. I've really screwed up this time, Pam."

Maybe this was for the best. Damian was going to head back to the US soon; their time together had always had an expiration date. Maybe this was the easiest way for them to part. Her heart, however, had other ideas. The pain was suffocating. Star knew it would be a long time before her heart recovered from Damian Hunt and she had no one but herself to blame.

∞∞∞

At the end of the day, Star decided to go up to Damian's office and try one last time to apologise to him. Pam wasn't at her desk when Star approached, but her screen was on, a flight manifesto clear before her eyes. Looking up, Star noticed Damian's door was open. His desk sat straight ahead, immaculate. The office was empty. Too empty.

∞∞∞

When Star got home, the joyful sound of Skylar's greeting helped lift her, and she opened her arms for the incoming hug.

"Careful mummy, you're squashing me," Skylar laughed, wriggling from her grasp. "Uncle Damian came to see me on his way home. He told me he had to leave the office. He said he has to go back to America, so he won't be able to see me for a little while, but he made me promise to keep reading and he looks forward to hearing me read when he gets back." Skylar looked at her mum, her eyes wide. "I'm going to miss him."

Stars throat closed over, and she swallowed hard around the lump that had formed. Damian was a good man. Whatever had happened between them, he had tried not to hurt Skylar with his departure. Star deserved his disdain. What had she been thinking?

Coughing to clear her throat, she said, "We will both miss him ... Why don't you go and get your book and maybe we can read together for a bit?"

Skylar trotted off up the stairs.

"Want to talk about it?" Laura asked, appearing in the doorway.

"Not right now," Star said. "I screwed up

and now he's gone. You can say 'I told you so,' if you like."

"He'll come round," Laura said, resting her hand on Star's shoulder.

"I'm not sure he will. I lied to him this morning and then he caught me in that lie. The worst part was, I was with Christian," Star admitted. Not even Laura had been privy to their meeting.

"You were with Christian? As in Dupree Christian?"

"Yes ... I arranged to meet him over lunch, he wanted to ask about Skylar. Damian asked me to lunch, but I told him I was going out with the girls. Somehow he came across us in the hotel lobby. I don't know whether he followed me, or if it was by chance. Anyway, he left and when I spoke to him ... he told me he couldn't do this anymore. Pam booked him flights back to the States. He's gone, Laura."

Laura pulled Star in for a hug, her ever-growing bump making it more awkward than usual.

"I can't believe he has just upped and left," Laura said, sounding confused. "He knows the danger of misunderstandings."

"It wasn't a misunderstanding, Laura. He guessed what was going on. I hurt him. Maybe this is for the best – now he can walk away. Close this chapter in his life for good and move forward."

"I don't believe that for one minute. I've seen the way that man is around you, the way he looks at you like he wants to devour you. There is no way he would just walk away. He loves you, the same way you love him."

Star wasn't sure her friend was right.

"I'm sure he'll be back. What I want to know is what did the sperm donor want after all the trouble he's caused?" Laura's face turned hard.

Star shot a look behind her to make sure Skylar wasn't within earshot. "This wasn't Christian's fault; this was all down to me. I'll talk to you later," she said, just as Skylar came rushing into the room with her book.

∞ ∞ ∞

Reading, dinner, bath, and then bed. Damian still hadn't called, and Star began to think he never would. It really was over. Tucking Skylar into bed, Star's heartstrings pulled as Skylar added Damian to her goodnight list. He had made such an impression; hopefully time would help ease the pain when he didn't come back. She hoped the same for herself, although she wasn't so sure this time that she'd be able to put him behind her and simply move on. She'd forced him out of her life for so long, but letting him back in had opened wounds long closed and scars never healed as well the second time.

Star headed downstairs to find Laura and Toby waiting for her. She grabbed a chair at the kitchen table and the glass of wine they had poured.

"I went to see Christian at lunchtime today," she said, waiting to see their expressions.

"We know that much," Laura said, encouraging her to continue.

"As you know, Damian saw us together and left. When I spoke to him after, he broke up with me," she said, pausing and taking a large swallow of wine, "and has returned to the States."

"Let me park the Damian situation until later. What did Christian want, Star?"

"He offered to pay me money to help raise

her. In return, he asked for updates on her progress and photos." Eyebrows shot up across the table, and Star intervened before Laura could say anything: "I've agreed to let him meet her – that is, if he decides he wants to be part of her life."

Star let them shout their arguments quietly at her. Neither wanted to wake Skylar after her mother had made this monumental mistake in their eyes. Star waited until both Laura and Tobias had calmed down before she continued.

"We had a long chat. I saw a different side to Christian, the side my sister loved. He wants to support Skylar – how can I keep him away from her if he wants to be part of her life? That is not what Lily would have wanted."

Laura opened her mouth and then closed it again, rethinking her comment.

"The decision is yours at the end of the day Star," Toby said, grabbing her hand. "We weren't there. I trust your judgment and I know you'd never do anything to hurt Skylar. We both know that," he said, looking at Laura pointedly. "If this is what you think is best for her, then we will support you, but we want you to be cautious."

"Thank you. It's not going to be easy. I've never had to share Skylar before, but I know in my heart this is what Lily dreamed of." She looked to Laura for understanding, adding, "How do I explain to Skylar in the future if she goes in search of him that I had kept him from her for all these years? I can't look her in the face and lie to her about her father not knowing about her if he wants to be part of her life."

Tears rolled down Laura's face, which she swiped at madly. "These pregnancy hormones! Lily would be so proud of you," Laura said, grabbing Star's other hand. "I'm sorry I questioned you. I get it, and I know Skylar will be made up when she finds out he knows about her and wants to be part of her life. You have raised a very special little girl – she deserves the best."

They sat discussing the logistics and Toby asked Star to give him some time to check out any legal implications there might be. The adoption was watertight, but he wanted to ensure that if Christian Dupree came back into Skylar's life with anything other than pure intentions, he would be in for a nasty shock. Star agreed, thanking both her friends for their unwavering support, before making her excuses and heading to bed.

Damian would probably be in the air now, flying away from her. She placed her phone on the nightstand as the first tears fell. She should have trusted him, but she hadn't.

∞∞∞

The next week at the office crawled by. Damian had returned to the States, much to everyone's surprise. There had been no explanation: simply one day he was there, and the next he was gone. Lucas had reclaimed the reins of the London office, although he was still working part-time hours and from home, where Mary could keep an eye on him.

Lucas and Mary stayed silent about Damian's disappearance, neither saying a word to Star. Star decided they probably wanted to stay out of it. As promised, Mary invited Skylar over to play with the puppies, who were growing at a rate that Star couldn't believe.

"Careful, Mummy," Skylar warned as one of the more boisterous puppies came bounding up to her. "They have razor-sharp teeth; you don't want to get cut."

Star smiled at the seriousness in her daughter's voice. It was easy to forget she was only six.

"Thank you for the warning," Star said as one of the puppies sank his teeth playfully into her hand. Mary laughed, handing her one of the toys so she could exchange flesh for plastic. They stayed several hours, although the house felt empty without Damian in it. It felt like the heart had been removed, or maybe that was her heart.

But she'd already cried too many tears into her pillow this week. So instead, with Mary watching Skylar, Lucas and Star discussed the new business opportunity which was beginning to look more and more like it was going to happen. The Creative Service team's preliminary mock-ups had gone down well both with the US and the London offices. They were now waiting for the Account Services Team to do their bit.

"It's all going well," Lucas said, looking up from the latest update.

"It is, everyone seems very happy," Star replied.

"Excellent," Lucas said before adding, "I take it there are no issues with Christian

Dupree?"

Lucas's phone rang, cutting Star off before she could reply.

"Lucas speaking," he answered, putting the phone on speaker, as he always did.

"Hi, Dad."

Star's heart stopped in her chest, the sound of his voice making her stomach contract and heat flood her body and face.

Lucas looked up awkwardly at Star. "Damian, I'm in a meeting. Can I call you later?"

A husky female voice came over the phone, and Damian muffled his reply before saying, "No problem, Dad, I'm at the apartment. Call me when you get a minute."

Lucas cut off the call, before turning back to Star. "Where were we?" he continued, as if nothing had happened.

Star's brain was in free fall. Damian was in his apartment in New York with another woman. What an idiot she was! She'd never asked him if he was involved with anyone. She'd assumed he was single, simply welcoming him back into her arms and bed. She felt sick to her stomach at the thought. There had been a couple of times they hadn't used protection, although she was sure Damian would be clean, but it was not a risk she was willing to take. She would need to get herself tested. It was only then that she realised Lucas was talking to her. "Star, is everything all right with Christian? Are you okay?"

"No, yes, I mean I'm fine, I just remembered I have to get something for Skylar on the way home. No, there are no issues. We've spoken multiple times and there are no problems," Star said, repeating herself, but not wanting to go into any further details. She needed to get out of here and regroup.

When Star walked out of the office, she took a deep breath and looked at her mobile. Christian had messaged while she'd been in the meeting.

Star had been speaking to Christian throughout the week and he was more than happy to keep their personal and private lives separate. She had begun to enjoy their daily chats – discussing Skylar and what she had done that day, as well as reminiscing about Lily and the past, which was both painful and uplifting. It was also helping to keep her mind off Damian.

Star hadn't realised how much she'd

missed talking about Lily. It was not just the passing mention of her name – that was something that happened a lot; it was the in-depth memories, talking about her fun-loving side, her amazing talent as an actress, her love for animals and how she'd stop and rescue anything she found in need. Christian had clearly loved her sister. She could tell that from the way he spoke about her, how his voice caught when the loss got too much.

Star kept Lily's memory alive for Skylar; she needed her to know she had been wanted and loved. With Christian in her life, Skylar would have someone else who could share their memories of her mother.

Star had kept her plans quiet from Laura and Toby, as she was not sure of their response, but she had arranged for him to visit the house to meet Skylar. She had yet to tell her six-year-old the plan as she needed her to sleep, and she knew that once she opened this door, it would be impossible to get the horse back into the stable.

Chapter Eighteen

Friday night came about all too quickly. It had now been a week and a half since Damian's departure and still no word from him. Star went into professional mode when working with Lucas, and so Damian never came up unless they were discussing the client, and then, it was if they were simply talking about another employee. Star found it odd but decided it must be Lucas's way of trying to return their relationship back to pre-Damian levels.

Today, however, she needed to put Damian out of her mind, although she wished he was there to offer her comfort and let her know she was doing the right thing. Laura and Toby were both on hand to deal with any questions and to hopefully share in Skylar's excitement.

"Skylar, I have a surprise for you tomorrow," Star said to her daughter over the dinner table.

Skylar looked at her, her eyes wide in anticipation. "What surprise Mummy? Is Damian coming back?"

Star faltered, her chest suddenly tight. Skylar had been asking after Damian all week and she was running out of excuses.

"No honey," she said, "Damian is still very busy in America." She hated lying. "I think you'll like this surprise even better than Damian coming back."

Skylar tilted her head in an expression that reminded Star so much of Lily, it made her jaw ache. "What surprise?"

"Well, your daddy wants to come and meet you."

"My daddy?" Skylar stared at Star open mouthed.

"Yes, your daddy," Star replied, smiling

"You found him? He knows about me?" she asked.

"Yes, munchkin, and he really wants to meet you."

Skylar's eyes suddenly filled with tears.

"He wants to meet me?" she repeated, making Stars own eyes fill up.

"Yes, angel, he wants to come and see you tomorrow."

Skylar burst into tears. Star panicked, looking at both Laura and Toby for support. For the first time since Skylar was born, Star didn't know what to do.

"Hey, squidge, why are you crying?" Toby said as he squatted down next to Skylar.

"I prayed asking for a daddy. I thought God might make Damian my daddy, but instead he brought my real daddy home." Star caught the sob before it escaped, her chest burning under the pressure. Laura had moved round the table to grab her in a hug, her own face wet with tears.

"Well, your real daddy wants to meet you," Toby said, taking charge of the conversation, realising Star and Laura needed a moment to pull themselves together.

Skylar wiped her face on her sleeve and beamed up at Toby. "Uncle Toby, my daddy really wants to meet me? When is he coming?"

Star marvelled at her daughter's ability to recover and flip her emotions from one to the other.

"He does, squidge, and he's coming tomorrow morning." Toby said, pulling the little girl into his arms.

Skylar's eyes flew to Star. "What's wrong, Mummy?" Skylar said, concern covering her little face.

"Nothing's wrong, angel," Star said, smiling through her own tears. "I'm just happy that you're happy." Pulling Skylar in for a big hug, she kissed the top of her head, breathing in her clean, child scent.

"Can I show him my room and my toys?" Skylar's eyes flitted from one adult to the next, her growing excitement contagious.

"Yes, but you may want to tidy your room up a bit," Star said, knowing her dolls were strewn across the carpet.

Skylar jumped up and raced for the door. "I'll do that now."

"Don't you want to have your pudding first?" Laura asked.

Skylar stopped and tilted her head again, as if weighing up the options. "Yes," she said, "Tidying can wait as I have until tomorrow morning."

∞ ∞ ∞

The next morning when Star awoke, she was surprised that Skylar wasn't already up and about. Having tossed and turned for a large portion of the night, she felt far from refreshed, but knew that her daughter's excitement would help get her through today.

Star crept into Skylar's room, expecting her daughter to be asleep, only to find her sat at her desk surrounded by paper and glue.

"Good morning, munchkin," she said.

"Good morning, Mummy," Skylar said, not looking up, her tongue poking out from between her lips as she manoeuvred tissue paper on the cardboard in front of her.

"What are you doing?" Star squatted down next to her daughter, holding the card in place as it lifted off the desk, stuck to Skylar's finger.

"I'm making a card," she said, holding up a 3D card that popped out as she opened and closed it. "Mrs Robinson showed me how to make this at after-school club. I thought it would be nice to give Daddy a card."

"That's such a lovely idea, I'm sure your daddy will love it." Star dropped a kiss on top of her head and headed to the door. "Pancakes will be ready in ten minutes."

Star just hoped Christian would appreciate what a gem he was letting into his life.

Pancakes and tidy up took longer than expected. Laura and Toby had joined them, everyone feeding off Skylar's energy.

Star breathed a sigh of relief when at nine fifty-five the doorbell rang. She didn't know how many more times she could respond to Skylar's "How much longer?" questions.

Skylar ran to the door but froze before she opened it. She waited for Star to join her, shooting her looks of panic. Star took her hand in hers and gave it a gentle squeeze before opening the door.

Christian stood in the doorway with an armload of presents. Skylar had moved to stand behind her, peeping round Star's side, but staying silent. Christian smiled at her, causing her to grip Star's hand even tighter. Stepping back and trying not to squash Skylar, Star welcomed him into the house. "Come on in, Christian."

"Thank you," he said, stepping through the door, allowing Star to close it behind him. "Hi, you must be Skylar, I'm Christian," he said, kneeling down in front of Star and looking at his daughter.

Star could see the raw emotion crossing his face as he stared at his daughter for the first time.

Skylar looked at Star, confused. "I thought you said this was my daddy?"

"He is," Star said with a frown.

"Then why did he call himself Christian?" she said in a loud stage whisper.

Star and Christian laughed. "Shall I start again," Christian said. "Hi Skylar, I'm your daddy and I'm so happy to finally meet you."

A grin spread across Skylar's face and she rushed forwards, throwing her arms around his neck, sending presents flying as he caught her. Christian hugged his daughter close, tears welling up in his eyes as he held on to this miracle.

Looking up at her father's face, Skylar wiped away the tear that had escaped. "Don't cry, Daddy. You've found me now," she said, taking his hand and leading him further into the house, the presents he had bought forgotten on the floor. He looked at Star in panic, and she smiled and ushered him forward, bending down to collect the presents and the flowers that had been abandoned.

Laura and Toby were sitting at the island in the kitchen when Christian entered. "Uncle Toby, Aunty Laura, look – my daddy is here."

Laura and Toby stood and shook hands with Christian. Toby had already spoken to Christian a number of times on the telephone, reiterating that Star was Skylar's parent, and whatever his plans, they had to fit in first and foremost with her. Christian had been incredibly receptive, thanking Toby for caring, and ensuring him that his intentions were good and that he simply wanted the chance to get to know his daughter.

After everyone had made small talk, Toby and Laura made their move. "Be good, squidge," he said, ruffling her hair.

"Always, Uncle Toby," she replied giving him a leg hug.

Star had told Toby and Laura they didn't need to leave, that this was their home, but both had been adamant that they needed to buy baby furniture for the nursery.

Skylar showed Christian all her things and gave him the card she had made for him that morning. It was still sticky, but he didn't complain, his face taut as he tried to hold back the emotion he was feeling.

"I bought you some gifts," he said. "I'm not sure what you like, but—"

"It's not my birthday," Skylar said, her attention now on the wrapped presents in front of her,

"No, but I have missed quite a few birthdays, so I thought you could have these now," Christian said. "I won't miss any more." He shot a look at Star.

Star simply smiled in reply. Her daughter was happy, Christian seemed happy. She was sure Lily was there, happy that Christian had finally come round and was wanting to take an active part in their daughter's life. She had been created in love and had so much love to give. There was more than enough for Star to share.

Skylar opened her presents while Star put the kettle on. Skylar was squealing at the American Girl doll and accessories that Christian had bought her.

"Mummy, look what Daddy has bought me! He has bought me the 'Doll of the Year' and all the bits that go with her," Skylar said, hugging Christian before rushing to share her bounty with Star.

A warm sense of relief spread through her as Skylar came to share her joy. She had to remember she would always be her mummy and nothing could take that position away from her.

Skylar ran off to get her other favourite doll, leaving Christian and Star alone together in the living room.

"I wasn't sure what to get her," he said, staring wide-eyed after his daughter. "She is so beautiful ... She looks so like Lily," his voice caught.

Star laughed. "I think you're safe, that was a complete hit," she said, resting a hand on his shoulder as she handed him his coffee.

"You've done an amazing job in raising her; I'm sorry I've not been around."

Star's eyes shot to the door. "No more talk of that – it's ancient history. I'm only interested in what happens going forward."

"I am, too. I want to be part of her life if you will let me?" Christian asked.

"I think Skylar has the final say, but the way she has been today, I think she will want you in her life."

"I hope so," Christian said as Skylar came flying back into the room with her favourite doll. She also carried her scrapbook.

"Daddy, would you like to see my scrapbook," Skylar said jumping onto the sofa next to him and snuggling into his side. Christian wrapped his arm around her shoulder as she placed the book on his knee and her doll by her side.

"So, what's in your scrapbook?" Christian asked, his attention once again focused on Skylar.

"This is my scrapbook," she told him. "I had to make it for school. It's lots of pictures of me from birth until now."

Christian's eyes flashed to Star, who watched him swallow. "I'd love to see your scrapbook."

Star watched as he fought his emotions at the pictures of Lily holding Skylar, and the ones of her next to the incubator, her illness and fragility clear for everyone to see. It was in those moments Star came to realise that everything

Christian had explained was true. He hadn't chosen to leave Lily; He had clearly loved her; he just hadn't been strong enough. Star hurt for the pair of them. Love was so easily shattered.

Christian stayed for most of the day, and they took Skylar to the park and out for a Chinese, where Christian taught her how to use chopsticks. Skylar wanted to show her daddy everything she could. When the time came for him to leave, Skylar cried, but Christian promised he would be back and that he would always be a part of her life now he had found her.

Christian pulled Star into a hug before he left, "Thank you," he whispered into her ear, the emotion he was feeling clear in his voice.

Star felt her own voice catch as she hugged him tighter. "You're welcome. She's a special little girl and she deserves all the love she can get."

∞∞∞

Laura and Toby had returned halfway through the afternoon, the car loaded with equipment and baby items. Skylar had shown Laura her new doll and accessories, promising she would share it with the baby when it arrived, as long as the baby was careful with it. Skylar had fallen asleep on the sofa, having exhausted herself talking. Star had carried her to bed, easing her out of her best dress and slipping on her nightgown. She was so tired; she had barely stirred.

Laura and Toby waited for Star in the living room. "That seemed to go well," Laura said.

"It did – they hit it off almost straight away," Star replied.

"But?" Laura questioned.

"No buts … I think he's genuine and I think he will now be a part of her life. Blood is thicker than water. They share so many mannerisms – it was interesting to watch them together. I see so much of Lily in her, but I could also see Christian today," Star said with a sigh.

"You aren't going to lose her, Star, she loves you. You are her mummy. No one can take that away from you and I don't get the impression that's what Christian wants."

"No, I agree with you, but it's going to be hard to share her with someone else," Star said honestly. "But I know it's what Lily would have wanted."

"Hold on a minute – this isn't about what Lily would or wouldn't want, Star. You are her mummy and you have been for the past six years. It has to be what you want too," Laura said, looking at her friend.

"No, what I want, is what is best for Skylar. Her daddy being in her life is always going to be the best thing for her. I need to let it go. I'm just an emotional wreck at the moment," Star said as tears started to track their way down her cheeks. The more she swept them away, the faster they fell. Laura moved closer, pulling her friend into her arms.

"Still no news from Damian?" she asked.

"No, nothing." Star sniffed. "He's gone. It's time for me to get back on with my life."

Star cried on her friend's shoulder, deciding this was the last time she was going to shed a tear for Damian Hunt. She loved him, she always would, but it was time she put him in the past and moved on with her life. With the new project, she knew she would finally have enough money available for her and Skylar to find their own place nearby. Tobias and Laura wouldn't like it, but she needed to do this for herself. She needed to go back to her original plan.

∞∞∞

Over the next three weeks, Star threw herself back into work and motherhood, pushing Damian from her mind. Christian had become a constant fixture at weekends, but proved himself to be a hands-on dad, helping with homework, reading, and even Skylar's latest project. He even proved himself a dab hand in the kitchen, cooking a meal for everyone with Skylar's help, as well as adhering to the household rules that everything had its place, and the kitchen must be kept tidy.

Lucas and Mary invited Skylar and Star round to see the puppies, who would soon be heading to their new homes. Skylar talked nonstop about Christian and there were several glances between Mary and Lucas that set Star's nerves on edge.

"Are you sure Christian is above board?" Mary asked when she got Star alone, making Star's skin prickle.

"He appears to be," Star said vaguely, not

wanting to discuss Christian with Mary or Lucas.

"You haven't done this just for the firm, have you," Lucas said coming into the room.

"No! I've done this for Skylar," Star said, feeling her stomach and chest start to bubble at their questioning.

"I wanted to check, because you didn't need to."

"Lucas, this has nothing to do with the firm and everything to do with my daughter's father. I am a grown woman and can make decisions for myself. Please accept that."

"We're sorry, dear," Mary said. "We are just worried about you."

"Well, you don't need to be. Skylar and I are fine."

Mary rubbed her arm, the pair dropping the subject, and moving on to the puppies and the new homes they were heading to.

Star headed home later that afternoon. She had things to do before Christian arrived. He had asked if he could take them out to dinner. Star had declined for herself, but felt it was time that Christian had some time alone with his daughter. If this was going to work, she knew she needed to start to let go.

Star jumped as the doorbell rang. Christian was early, although that was not unusual. "Don't worry, Mummy, I'll get it," Skylar shouted as she thundered down the hallway.

Star stepped out of the kitchen into the hall. She didn't allow Skylar to open the door unless they knew who it was, and as they weren't expecting anyone and the mailman had already delivered, Star was pretty certain it was Christian.

"Damian!" came the excited scream from the doorway. Skylar launched herself into his arms. "I've missed you," she said.

"I've missed you, too," Damian said, bending down and scooping her into his arms. Star's body froze at the sound of his voice.

"Mummy! It's Damian – he's back," Skylar yelled, not realising Star was behind her.

Star's eyes locked with Damian's, a traitorous warmth spreading through her body pooling at her core. Would she ever get over this man?

"I can see that, sweetheart," Star said, her eyes never leaving Damian's. "Why don't you go and get ready – Daddy will be here in a moment."

Skylar hugged Damian before saying, "My

daddy found me, Damian. He's going to take me to the park," she whispered, her voice unable to hide the excitement she was feeling, before wriggling out of his grasp. Damian let her go and watched as she ran off up the stairs.

"Why are you here, Damian?" Star said as she struggled to keep the pain out of her voice.

Damian's eyes returned to hers. "I wanted to see you."

"Well, you've seen me," Star said.

"Don't be like that," Damian said, touching her arm.

Star shrugged him off. "Like what, Damian? Dismissive? Short? Rude? How would you like me to be, Damian? You've ignored me for the past four weeks and you just waltz up to my front door and expect me to welcome you back into my life as if nothing has happened. You turned me out of your office and left the country without a backward glance. Sorry to disappoint, but that's not how this works."

"I just want to talk, I've done a lot of thinking," Damian said.

"Talk. I tried to talk to you four weeks ago and you shut me out. If you've been thinking, I'm pleased for you. I've done some thinking of my own and I'd like for you to leave. Christian will be here in a minute to collect Skylar and I have things to get ready." Star moved to shut the door, but Damian blocked it with his foot.

"Please, Star. I was angry, hurt. I know I was wrong to walk away. Give me a chance to explain."

"I don't want to hear it, Damian. You hurt me. I've hurt you. Let's just call it quits and leave it at that. I can't do this anymore. I have Skylar to think about."

"I can see that – and Christian, it seems," Damian muttered.

"And what's that supposed to mean?" Star asked incredulously.

"It means you've let him into your and Skylar's life without a pause." Damian said hotly.

"He's Skylar's father! I'm doing what I feel is best for my daughter, not that it's any of your business!"

"Really, that's not how it's felt for the last two months when we were doing things together as a family. When you were sleeping in my bed. Or has Christian taken that position, too?"

Star's hand struck out before she could

stop herself, the crack of her hand hitting Damian's cheek resounding off the walls. A look of shock crossed Star's face.

Damian looked at her, his expression hard, his cheek reddening before her eyes.

"Sorry," she whispered, but Damian turned and walked away, passing Christian on the driveway. Christian went to greet him but stopped at the look Damian shot his way.

Heading to the doorway, Christian took one look at Star and realised something was wrong. "Are you okay?"

Star brushed away the traitorous tear that had escaped. "I'm fine. Skylar, Daddy's here," she shouted up the stairs.

Christian put a hand on her arm and pulled her round to face him, "You don't look fine."

"Maybe not," she said giving him a watery smile, "But I will be."

Skylar came flying down the stairs and threw herself at her father, who scooped her up into his arms. "Are you all ready?" he said, shielding Star while she wiped her face.

"Yes, Daddy. Can you push me on the swings? I want to see how high I can go."

"Of course. Say goodbye to Mummy and we'll see her later."

Star gave Skylar a big hug, reminding her to be good and stay with Christian. Shutting the door behind them, Star sank to the ground, an animalistic howl escaping her lips before she could stop it.

Arms encircled her, lifting her from the ground. She knew it had to be Toby. A few moments later, she felt softness beneath her, but she curled herself into a tight ball.

She had done the right thing sending Damian away. Who did he think he was? He had no rights. They didn't need him in their lives. But if that was the case, why did it hurt so much, and why did she feel like she'd lost Lily all over again.

∞∞∞

Christian returned Skylar several hours later. Star had managed to pull herself together, Laura and Toby giving her the space she needed. The hollow feeling she had inside had not left her; she knew she was grieving but she also knew that, like before, she would recover and come out stronger.

Christian had come in to speak with Toby. He clearly knew something was amiss, but had not pried, for which Star was grateful.

A half an hour later, Christian and Toby emerged from Toby's office. Christian gave Skylar a hug goodbye and pulled Star in for a brotherly hug, "If you need anything, let me know," he whispered in her ear before letting her go.

They'd begun to develop a strong relationship over the past few weeks, one that a brother and sister shared. Christian had been Lily's love, and Star could understand why. He was charming and friendly with a kind and generous streak. She now understood the power his father had over him and how he had extracted himself over the years.

Star knew the power her own mother wielded and how years of being undermined had left its mark on her soul and confidence. It was only after the birth of Skylar and her need to protect an innocent child that she had broken away, but the previous years had still affected her.

It was evening before Toby pulled Star to one side. She'd just put Skylar to bed and was about to retire herself. She didn't fancy discussing her earlier breakdown; she wanted to hide in her room and lick her wounds. Toby, however, was having none of it.

"Star, can I have a word?" Toby called as she headed towards the stairs, her peppermint tea in hand.

"Sure," Star replied, heading in the direction Toby had just gone. She entered his office to find him by his desk, a document in his hand. "What can I do for you?"

"It's not for me," Toby said, handing her the document he had in his hand. "Christian had me draw up this document. He wanted to make this legal."

Star took the document from him, her heart racing. What did Christian want to make legal? She thought everything had been verbally agreed. Was he going to back out of their current arrangement and go after custody of Skylar? He could certainly offer her more than she could.

"Stop your brain working!" Toby said. "Do you think I'd have drawn up anything to hurt you or Skylar?" Star took a deep breath, realising Toby was right. She'd have had the heads-up from Toby long ago if that were Christian's plan.

"Read it."

Star dropped herself down into one of the chairs in the office. She realised the document she was holding was a financial agreement on Christian's part to help raise Skylar, by offering Star monthly payments. Star also saw he had clearly included that it was without strings attached. He wasn't asking for anything in return, only to help assist in easing the financial burden of raising a child alone. Not that Star had ever looked at Skylar as a burden. It was then Star saw the amount he was offering per month and her mouth fell open, her eyes flying to Toby's.

"This is ridiculous," Star spluttered. "He can't mean to pay me this – this is outrageous."

"I said the same," Toby said with a laugh. "But he was determined that he wanted to do right by you and Skylar. He said you have managed brilliantly for the past six years, but he understands that it can't have been easy, with studying, childcare, working part-time. He has the money, and he wants to ensure that his daughter and the woman who is raising her have the best they can have. He wants to make amends – he can't change the past, but he can improve the future. He knows you want to move out and buy a place for the two of you – he wants to make that easier. I had my doubts about him in the beginning, but he seems like a genuinely nice guy."

Star was speechless. Toby was no one's fool. Christian had already signed the documents. Christian meant every word he had said to her over the past couple of weeks.

"I need to speak to him," Star said. She wasn't comfortable taking money from someone, whether it was Skylar's dad or not.

"I told him you'd want to. Remember, he is Skylar's dad – he's not some stranger offering you money. He was the love of Lily's life. Because you agreed to raise your sister's daughter, he now has access to Skylar. If you'd given her up for adoption, she would have been lost to him forever. You've opened your home to him and let him in. Doing that is going to disrupt your life; sharing her is not always going to be easy. You love with all your heart, Star, and you give with such generosity, even to your own detriment. You didn't blink when Lily asked you to adopt Skylar and raise her as your own, irrespective of what that meant for your own life and what you were sacrificing. Take this as karma if you will –

one good turn deserves another."

Star knew she could never have followed a different path; this was her destiny. Had probably always been her destiny. She'd speak to Christian and think on his more-than-generous offer. She could put the money aside for Skylar, set her up a college fund, something she wanted to do but didn't have enough money currently to put to one side, not if she was to finally get them a place of their own to live. Christian's financial assistance would move the timeline up; she might even be able to look at the house that had come up around the corner, which would mean Skylar's routine would not be compromised. It was a fixer-upper, but she and Skylar would have some fun choosing colours for the walls and a new kitchen. It would be their home.

"Okay, but I still want to talk to him," Star conceded.

"Good and, Star, you need to talk to Damian, too."

The elephant that had sat in the house all day had finally entered the room.

"No," Star said getting up and heading to the door.

"I think your breakdown earlier tells me

something different," Toby said, following her.

"Stay out of it, Toby," Star said. "I can't play games with him anymore. I can't deal with the emotional swings."

"I'm not asking you to. I'm asking you to talk to him. I mean, really talk to him. Don't throw away what you have, not for a second time without knowing for definite that you are making the right decision. I love you, Star, but you've made some poor choices where Damian is concerned. That man has strong feelings for you, but you keep pushing him away. You have surrounded yourself with so many barriers. Maybe you need to drop the drawbridge and talk to each other. Find out what you both want and if you can make it work."

"It can't work." Star sighed. "He is in the States and I'm here. Now Christian is in Skylar's life, I can't move her across the world – that wouldn't be fair to anyone. So there is no point in extending the hurt."

Toby ran his fingers through his hair letting out an exasperated sigh, but remained silent.

Chapter Nineteen

Star came downstairs to the sound of raised voices.

"No, I'm not going to stay out of it, she's my best friend and she's sabotaging her own happiness," Laura was standing, arms folded, facing her husband, as Star entered the kitchen, her back resting against the sideboard, her now very visible bump jutting out in front of her.

"Say what you want to say," Star said, looking her friend directly in the eye.

Laura huffed. "Do I actually need to? Damian came here yesterday to talk, and you threw him out. For seven years, you've pined for that man, lived half a life. The past few months, you've come alive, blossomed back into the person you were before. You love him, but why are you so afraid to let him love you back?"

"Have you forgotten that he's the one who left?" Star said calmly.

"No, but he came back! Star, you are far from innocent in all this. He's only ever asked you to be honest with him and you keep hiding yourself from him. Please talk to him," Laura said.

"Okay, I'll talk to him," Star said. "But I'm not promising anything, but I'll try and see if he'll speak to me."

Laura threw her arms around her best friend and pulled her in tight, so much so a gentle nudge was felt between them. Junior had decided tight hugs were cramping their style. Both laughed as Star placed her hand on her friend's stomach, soothing the little foot that was now playing football against her skin. "Okay, little one, I'll speak to Damian."

Toby and Laura grinned at each other.

Star laughed at her friends; they had everything all planned out. She didn't want to burst their bubble – she'd let them think they'd won the battle. Not that she'd spent a large part of the night tossing and turning. She knew she had overreacted at his sudden reappearance. She had to make things right, whatever that meant.

A quick message to Mary had let her know Damian was at the Manor and not in London. Mary had called her, and invited them both over for a late breakfast. Skylar was already dressed, excited to be seeing Damian, and hoping to get one last play with the puppies before they left for their new homes.

As Star grabbed her keys from the sideboard, it was Laura and Toby's turn to look shocked.

"No time like the present," Star said with a wink, both realising they'd been duped. "Skylar, we need to go," Star called up the stairs.

Skylar came trundling down the stairs, the teddy Damian had bought her in one hand and her backpack in the other.

"What's in your bag?" Star asked.

Skylar rolled her eyes. "It's all the books I've read while Damian has been away, I need to show him."

Star's eyes glistened at her daughter's words, "I'm sure he'd love to see what you've been reading," she said, hoping he wouldn't reject her daughter's affection even if she herself had blown any chances with him.

∞ ∞ ∞

Pulling up outside Kingston House, Star switched off the engine. She took a deep breath before turning to Skylar. "Can you stay with Aunty Mary and Uncle Lucas while I go and find Damian?"

"Of course, Mummy," Skylar said, her eyes shining in excitement. Silly question when there were puppies involved.

Mary met Star at the front step, ushering Skylar into the house, who took off immediately as if she owned the place.

"He's on his usual running path," Mary said. "I haven't told him you were coming. You two need to talk."

"We do," Star said, pulling on her trainers and removing her jumper dress. Underneath, she had her running gear on. She'd known, or at least suspected, Damian would be running – it was something they'd done every Sunday morning. The greenery was good for the soul and helped calm the mind. She knew the grounds almost as well as he did; she'd made him explore them with her whenever they got the chance. Star knew this would be the best place for them to meet.

Mary took in her dress and shoes, nodding her approval as Star set off in the opposite direction. She knew she'd never catch him, but if she could meet him halfway round, then she hoped they could talk.

Twenty minutes into her run, Star began to worry that Damian had changed his route or that Mary had got it wrong. It wasn't until she saw him as a speck ahead that she was able to relax, picking up her pace. She was hot and sweaty by this point, but it wasn't glamour she wanted to sell to Damian; he had that in America, surrounded by actresses and models. She wanted to sell him the warts and all. If what they had was real, then he needed to see the sweat, blood, and tears that were her life. She needed him to see the real Star Roberts.

Damian's pace didn't ease up, even when Star was sure he had seen her. They met halfway, both pulling up, dragging in air. Star leant forwards, resting her hands on her knees, her heart fluttering as Damian smoothed away a piece of hair that had stuck to her cheek as if it were the most natural thing in the world for him to do. Reaching up, her hand snaked behind his head as she pulled his lips to hers. The salty taste of his workout and hers was like nectar to a honeybee as their lips collided, and Damian didn't wait for a further invitation, pulling her body flush against his own. One hand nestled in her hair, the other sliding over her bottom and down her thigh, hitching her leg around his waist. Star jumped, her legs wrapping themselves tight around Damian's waist, the evidence of his pleasure at seeing her nestled close to where she ached the most. Star moaned deep into his mouth as their tongues battled for supremacy, their hands frantic as they sought out flesh.

Damian manoeuvred them into the Dell at the side of the path. Away from prying eyes, they made short work of each other's clothes before Damian dropped to his knees, his mouth latching on to the moist folds between her legs. Star's head swam with the sensation, her knees buckling, her breath coming out in pants. This was not what she had expected when she'd come in search of him; she knew she needed to speak to him, but their desire for each other was overwhelming. Damian lowered her to the ground, his body moving back up hers, locking his mouth to hers, allowing her to taste herself on his lips. Spreading her legs Star locked her ankles behind his back, angling herself up to draw him in. Neither of them had the power or will to wait. Damian did not hesitate, thrusting himself deep, leaving them both breathless and moaning as the sensation of coming together overwhelmed them. Star rolled Damian onto his back, sitting herself astride him, taking charge as she teased his head with her opening before sliding up and down his hard length. Damian's eyes remained locked on hers, his raw desire plain to see.

Tension coiled in Star's belly as Damian's hands reached for her breasts, his thumbs stroking her tender nipples, warming them against the coolness of the morning breeze. Star continued to move up and down in a rhythm only their bodies knew. A moan escaped her lips as she rested her hands on his shoulders, digging into the solid muscles she found there. Damian reached up, taking a puckered nipple in his mouth. Star's muscles began to tighten around Damian, her body shattering as her orgasm hit her. Damian's own followed quickly behind. Star dropped her forehead to Damian's as she waited for his shudders to stop. Her own muscles were still fluttering inside with the intensity of what they had just shared.

Star rolled off and lay panting on the grass next to Damian.

"That was not what I expected when I left the house for a run this morning," Damian said, rolling onto his side. Taking her hand, he interlocked their fingers before bringing it to his mouth.

"I take it you don't usually ravish ladies while you're on your morning run then?" Star said cheekily.

"Only woodland sprites," Damian said, bending down and reclaiming her lips.

Placing her hand on Damian's naked chest, she eased herself away, "We need to talk."

Damian flopped back onto his back and stared at the blue sky above, the sunlight flickering through the leaves above them.

It was Star's turn to move. Sitting up, she hugged her knees to her chest, offering herself some coverage against Damian's heated gaze. "I want to apologise. I flew off the handle yesterday when I should have listened."

"You did," he said, taking her hand again as she tried to withdraw, "but I deserved it. I'm sorry I didn't stay around to listen."

"We need to work on our communication," Star said, drawing his hand to her mouth and placing a kiss on his palm.

"We do. Probably with clothes on," Damian said, grinning as he hauled himself to his feet, pulling Star up alongside him. Cradling her face in his hand, he stared deeply into her eyes. "I love you, Star. I want us to work, whatever it takes. I don't think I can cope with losing you again."

Stars eyes prickled and her breath caught. A warmth spread through her chest, defrosting the ice that had been present since his departure. Star moved into Damian's arms, encircling his waist and resting her head against his bare chest. His heartbeat was erratic as hers.

"I love you, too. I never thought I'd get to say that to you again." They stood locked in each other's arms until a cool breeze whipped through the trees, causing goose bumps to rise on their skin, making them laugh .

"We better get back," Star said, "Your mum is going to think we've killed each other. But,

Damian, we still need to talk."

Damian smiled down at her. "We will, but let's get back. I have a surprise for Skylar."

"You spoil her," Star said, frowning. "Oh, and she wants to show you all the books she's read since you left. She brought them with her in her backpack."

"I want to spoil her. I love her mummy. She's part of you, and she holds a special place in my heart."

Gathering up their clothes, they redressed in silence.

"Race you back," Star said not waiting for Damian to finish putting on his trainers, before she took off down the trail. Damian called after her but Star ignored him. It wasn't long before his larger stride had closed the distance and they made their way back to the manor together, where Mary was waiting.

"Get washed up, breakfast will be ready in fifteen minutes," she said, smiling, happy her intervention had so clearly worked.

Damian grabbed Star's hand and pulled her up the stairs, heading for his room where they decided it would be much more time effective to share the shower. Or maybe not!

∞ ∞ ∞

Breakfast went off as though none of the past few weeks had occurred. Skylar was incredibly vocal, talking continually about all the books she had been reading. Damian in his usual manner remained focused and encouraging in ways Star couldn't believe. This was a man with no siblings and no children of his own – as far as she was aware. Her body tensed as she remembered the woman's voice from the phone call. What if Damian had another life? What if he was in a long-term relationship? What if she had inadvertently become the "other woman"?

Star's brain went into overload, her breathing increasing.

"Are you okay?" It was Mary whose voice broke through the haze.

Star looked up, and her eyes must have flashed the panic she was feeling as Mary leant across and grabbed her hand. Damian's attention had now shifted from Skylar's to Star's concern splashed across his face.

"Are you okay, Mummy? You've gone a

funny colour," Skylar said, her brow furrowing in the middle.

Giving a weak smile, Star stood up and said, "I think I need some air." She made a dash for the back door. Star left a set of concerned faces in her wake. Once outside she leant against the wall and doubled over, trying to catch her breath.

"Hey," Damian said, resting his hand on her back and rubbing soothing circles. "Is everything okay?"

Star straightened up, drawing a deep breath into her lungs. "Who was the woman in your apartment?" Damian looked confused. "The day you rang Lucas, there was a woman's voice in the background. You said you were in your apartment. Who was she?"

Clarity followed by something else, maybe guilt, appeared on Damian's face as he finally understood who she was talking about. "We probably need to talk about this ..."

"Oh God." Star bent double, so many emotions crashing into her at once. She was right; she *was* the other woman. He was with someone else and she didn't know.

"Star, what's going on?" Damian said,

bending down next to her.

"Who is she?"

Damian had the decency to look guilty. "She was my girlfriend,"

"And you didn't think you should tell me you have a girlfriend."

"*Had*, past tense. Star, walk with me." Damian took Star's hand, pulling her upright and heading away from the house. "Sabrina is no longer my girlfriend. She was there that day to collect all of her things."

"But you had a girlfriend and you slept with me?" Star's voice caught in her throat.

"No and yes. When I came back to run things for Dad, I had no idea you were going to explode your way back into my life. Yes, I'd moved on. Sabrina was on the verge of moving in when I came over here." Star's intake of breath made Damian stop and spin her towards him. Gripping her chin, he made her look into his eyes. "But it took five minutes in a room with you again even after seven years to realise, I didn't feel a fraction for her what I felt for you. When you and I got together, Sabrina and I were already over in my mind. I went back to the US because I felt I owed it to her to end things face to face.

When I saw you with Christian, I knew I wanted to fight for us – I couldn't just give you up again."

"But you wouldn't talk to me …"

"I'd already arranged my flight. I realised something was wrong when you blew me off." He tapped her nose. "You are a terrible liar by the way. I followed you and saw you meeting with Christian. I wasn't sure what he was up to, but before I threw my hat into the mix, I knew I needed to get my life in the States in order. Mum gave me a lecture about keeping people hanging, Sabrina had started ringing the house trying to get hold of me, so I'd already decided I needed to head back and set Sabrina straight."

"Why didn't you tell me about her?"

"Initially I was so shocked you were back in my life, I couldn't think of anything but you, and I couldn't tell you about her as I couldn't do anything about it at the time. Sabrina was on an assignment when I first came back, and we weren't in contact. When she came back and started contacting me, I'm not proud of myself, but I tried to ignore her … I didn't want to risk us for something I knew was over."

Star stared hard at Damian.

"I didn't realise you were going to be with

Dad that day. She'd showed up, and she wanted a clean break and didn't want to hold off collecting her things. We both realised we were in the relationship for the wrong reasons. She is far from heartbroken; I can promise you that. She's started dating a rock star, I believe," Damian chuckled to himself.

Star's jaw flew open. "Wait, Sabrina … Sabrina Croft? You were practically living with Sabrina Croft." Star sat heavily on a nearby wall, shock clear across her face. Sabrina Croft was one of the top fashion models and she had just begun dating Randy Howard, the lead singer of the heavy metal band, Rollercoaster.

Shock registered on Damian's face quickly followed by confusion, "Yes, but why does that matter?" he said.

"Only a man would say that!" Star snapped. "She's one of the world top models and she's beautiful! How do I compare to that?"

Damian laughed at Star's outburst and the filthy look she shot at him. Pulling her into his arms, he rested his chin on top of her head. "There is no comparison."

Star shoved away from him, before he reeled her back in.

"You are it for me Star Robert's. What we have is no comparison to any other relationship I've ever had. I should never have walked away seven years ago. I should have fought for you, but I myself was devastated, and I thought I was giving you what you wanted. It's what you do for the one you love." He kissed her neck, down into the crease of her shoulder. "I can't lose you again. I love you with all my heart."

Star reached up, encircling Damian's neck and burying her fingers into his hair, looking into his eyes, her own moist with emotion.

"Damian Hunt, you are and always have been 'it' for me, it was always you," she said, pulling his lips to hers and sealing their love with a searing kiss. Pulling away, Star looked deep into Damian's eyes, convinced what she saw was genuine. "We better head back to the house, I think I've worried your mum and dad, and we've abandoned Skylar with them."

Chapter Twenty

Star and Damian's relationship fell into an easy pattern over the next few weeks. They spent time together in the evenings and weekends. Damian even welcomed Christian into their fold, accepting him easily once he saw for himself Skylar's excitement and the love the man clearly had for Skylar. Damian also recognised that Christian was respectful of Star and her position in Skylar's life. He didn't undermine her authority, or overstep the mark, and that went a long way in cementing the men's relationship.

Lucas was starting to take a more active role in the day-to-day running of the office, although most of his time was still spent working from home. The Board was still causing issues behind the scenes, which had Damian firefighting when he really didn't need to. Although their relationship was not common knowledge, they were no longer hiding their comings and goings. Damian had made it clear that their relationship was not up for discussion, and Star's team was happy for her. Pam seemed to have let slip to a couple of people how they had dated at university, and that it was only the death of Star's sister that had led them to part ways. The rumour mill still ran but with a more positive spin, with many now understanding her strong bond with Lucas.

For three weeks life was idyllic, and then suddenly it wasn't. Some of the American clients were getting antsy that the head of the office was still out of the country and not dancing to their tune. Damian was fielding calls morning, noon, and even in the middle of the night. It soon became clear that he was not going to be able to stay away from the New York office for much longer, however much he wanted to.

"Come with me to New York," Damian said one night as they were curled up in his parents' snug. Skylar was upstairs in her newly decorated room. Mary had taken it on herself and had let

Skylar choose how she would like her bedroom to look when she came to stay.

"What do you mean?" Star said.

"You and Skylar – come to the US with me?"

Star was no longer sleepy, and sat upright, turning her body to face Damian's. "We can't," she said.

"Can't or won't?" Damian said, his voice taking on an edge Star hadn't heard before.

"Can't," she replied firmly. "Skylar's life is here. Her father is here. She's just found him, Damian, I can't rip her away from him."

Damian snorted, pulling away from Star. "No, but you'll forgo our happiness for a man who has had nothing to do with her for the past six years."

Star felt her temper rising. "This is not about Christian. This is about Skylar! Don't you think that little girl has been through enough?"

"Stop using her as a shield, Star! Yes, Skylar, had a rough start, and my heart breaks for her, but she's got an amazing life with you. You are her mummy – don't you deserve to be happy too?"

"I do," Star whispered. "But not at her

expense. Uprooting our life and moving to New York is not an option."

"Well, I can't stay here," Damian said falling back against the sofa. "I was hoping our relationship meant enough to you to come with me, but clearly I don't."

"That's not fair, Damian, and you know it!" Star snapped. "You came back here, you've joined our life, and now you want us to up sticks and move across the world because it suits you?"

"You know I run the New York office – I was always going to have to go back."

"Yes, and it's one of the reasons I have held back. I'm sorry, Damian, but I won't disrupt Skylar's life, especially now, I can't." Star got up and headed for the door, her stomach churning. "I'll sleep with Skylar tonight."

As she made her way down the corridor, a smash resounded behind her. Damian had thrown his glass against the wall of the snug.

Silent tears streamed down her face as she crawled into bed next to Skylar, already missing the warmth of Damian's arms. They had been doomed from the beginning. Watching her daughter sleep, she knew she was making the right decision, although the pain in her chest was acute. The day she'd agreed to raise Skylar, she'd promised her sister she would do her best for her, even if it meant giving her own happiness up. She'd done it once before; she would survive again. She was older and wiser now, and financially independent. She had a good job, great friends. Skylar would grow up to be balanced – she now had a male father figure in her life, her actual father who wanted nothing but the best for her and Skylar. Damian was a pipe dream, one Star had to let go of once and for all.

∞∞∞

Damian was gone by the time she awoke the following morning.

"He's gone back to the States," Mary said, disappointment clear on her face. The red rims around her eyes let Star know it had been far from an easy goodbye.

"Damian didn't say goodbye," Skylar said, her lips quivering as her eyes filled with tears.

Star ruffled her hair, trying to comfort the little girl. "He had emergency clients to see. He'll be back," Star said shooting Mary a look, not to contradict her. Her own heart was breaking, and it was all she could do to hold it together, but she couldn't see a way out of this predicament. She couldn't leave, and he had responsibilities there. There was no choice.

"We'll be out of your hair soon," Star told Mary, aware now that Damian had left that she was very much intruding.

"Don't rush," Mary said pulling herself together and smiling. "The house is going to be very empty. I've enjoyed the comings-and-goings."

But both Star and Mary knew it was coming to an end and it was never going to be the same again. With Damian gone, she and Skylar wouldn't be calling in and staying over. The fairy tale was at an end.

∞∞∞

Day-to-day life fell back into its usual pattern. Toby and Laura were happy to see them back. Star hadn't realised how much time she had actually been staying with Damian; her life had been one long dream, one that had ended up turning into a nightmare she wished she could wake up from. Together, Laura and Toby tried to distract her and help her move forwards. Christian was as attentive as always, although Skylar missed Damian and told Star so every night, sending love and kisses to Damian in America along with her kisses to her mummy in heaven. Christian had tried to question Star about Damian's departure, but she'd closed him down.

Over the next few weeks Star found herself caught up in a never-ending cycle of school run, work, all things Skylar, and repeat. The new project was taking off, which should have led to a feeling of satisfaction, but instead life itself held no interest for her, and she felt like she was going through the motions. Laura and Tobias tried to pull her out of her slump when Skylar was off with Christian, and to keep her friends happy, she went along, even though her heart wasn't in it.

"You've lost too much weight," her mum said, on one of her infrequent visits.

"Thank you, Mum. You look wonderful as always. The cruise must have been good."

"It was. Your father and I had the best time. Beautiful food and wine, and the sights, what can I say. Something you should try."

"I'll bear that in mind," Star said, wishing herself anywhere but here. She couldn't take her mum's criticism today; she didn't need her finding fault with everything she did.

"So what is this about Christian Dupree being back in the picture?" Daphne said, letting Star know this was not a social call. Her mum and dad were in the same social circles as the Duprees, so news had obviously spread that Christian had taken an interest in his daughter.

"Yes," Star said trying to cover up the sigh that was about to escape. "We met while working on a project. His company have asked Hunt and Hunt if we can create their new advertising project."

"Well, it's all very sudden," her mother sniffed. "I was talking to his mother at a function at the weekend – they are suddenly very interested in little Skylar."

Star's heart started to beat erratically. The last people she wanted around Skylar were Dupree Senior and his snobby wife. They had practically thrown Lily out on the street when she'd approached them.

"Well, Christian is proving himself to be a wonderful dad to Skylar," Star said covering up her discomfort. She'd need to speak to Christian about his parents.

"And so he should be – he is her father after all. Have you thought about giving him custody?" Daphne said, with no preamble.

Star couldn't hide the look of horror that crossed her face. "Skylar is my daughter!" she spat at her mother. "I will not be handing *my* daughter over to anyone. If that is what you think, then maybe you need to leave, Mother!"

"Don't be like that. I heard you split up with Damian Hunt again because you stayed here for Skylar."

"Wow!" Star said. "Gossip spreads fast in your circles. Damian and my relationship is nobody's business. Skylar is my daughter, and no one can take her away from me. You and the Duprees can stay out of her and my life. Christian and I have an arrangement that is working perfectly well."

Star's mother held up her hands, looking round the room before flicking some lint off her trouser suit. "Well, you never were one with any ambition. The Duprees could give Skylar everything. Instead, you have her living in shared accommodation with your university friends."

"I think it's time you left, Mum." Star stood up holding the living room door open for her mother who reluctantly made her way towards her.

"Think on what I've said. They're willing to compensate you for all you've done. Just think, you could move on with your life, have a family of your own, and stop ruining your own life for your sister's mistake."

"Skylar is my family, more than you will ever be. You might not have loved Lily and me the way we deserved – we were a means to an end for you, a way to trap Dad." The slap resounded through the hall. Star raised her hand to her face. "Get out, Mother, and don't bother coming back!"

Star watched as her mother flounced to her Jaguar F-Type and drove off. Star was glad Skylar was out with Christian, although she was going to find out from him what the hell was going on when they returned.

Toby entered the hallway with Laura.

"I take it you heard?" Star sighed, giving

way to the tears she had so valiantly held back.

"Couldn't really miss it," Toby said as Laura gently rubbed Star's red cheek. "The adoption is watertight, Star, as you know. The Duprees can go to hell."

They led Star back to the sitting room and sat down.

"But what if she's right? What if Skylar would be better off with them?"

"No way!" Laura said. "They are cold and uncaring. Toby had a long chat with Christian one afternoon, and he told Toby that his childhood was *cold and clinical* – those were his words. He said how happy he is his daughter is surrounded by so much love. He couldn't ask for anything better for her."

Star relaxed; she hadn't believed that this had come from Christian. Her mother's society friends, yes, she could see it. Her mother wanted to be accepted, as she was still on the outskirts, so having a granddaughter with one of the other families would give her brownie points. Well, Skylar wasn't going to be a part of her mother's games; Star and Lily had suffered enough at her hands growing up.

She would still speak to Christian when

he returned. They had a similar goal, to protect Skylar from their toxic parents.

∞∞∞

Christian returned with Skylar later that afternoon and must have realised something was amiss. Ushering Skylar inside, Star listened to her adventures with half an ear while making it clear to Christian that they needed to talk.

"What's happened?" Christian asked when Laura had managed to convince Skylar to help her make some cookies. "Don't say nothing because I'm getting to know you, Star, and something is bothering you."

"Let's go for a walk," Star said, grabbing her coat. "I don't want little ears listening."

Christian followed Star out of the house in silence. They walked to the nearby park, where Star dropped onto the nearest bench.

"I had a visit from my mother," Star said. "Seems like she's been talking to your parents."

A look that could only be described as horror passed over Christian's face. He was obviously aware of his parents' thoughts and

Star felt her defences rise.

"So, it's true then?"

"It depends on what you're asking?" Christian said, looking at his feet. "Are my parents suddenly interested in Skylar? The answer is yes. Am I letting them near her? Not a chance! I think you'd better start from the beginning. I didn't lie to you when I first came into Skylar's life, and nothing has changed, Star. I am more than grateful you are giving me the time to get to know my daughter, even though I know it has cost you."

It was the first time that Christian had acknowledged that he knew about Damian leaving and why. He placed a hand on her knee in comfort.

"My mother has said they are willing to compensate me if I hand over Skylar," Star said.

Christian's expression turned to thunder, a dark red spreading over his cheeks. "Don't worry, I'll handle it," he said. "Please forget you ever heard those words. They are the last people in the world I want raising my daughter." Christian rubbed her leg and then pulled her in for a hug. "I promise I'll deal with my father and mother."

Star leaned into Christian's warmth,

absorbing his comfort. He wasn't Damian, though, and the hole in her chest wasn't fixed by his closeness.

She nodded and stood up. "My mother is toxic," she said, "and I've kept her out of Skylar's life for a reason. I don't want to introduce anyone else to her who doesn't have her best interests at heart."

"I'm with you there. I'm no longer under their thumb. I promise you; Skylar is safe."

∞∞∞

A few days later, Star received a phone call from her father letting her know that he'd spoken to her mother and set her straight on a few things. Her mother had even come onto the phone briefly and apologised for her behaviour before her father had taken the phone away and told Star she had nothing to worry about, that he would deal with Mr and Mrs Dupree.

Star had never seen her father stand up to her mother, but maybe like her, he knew he needed to choose his battles. She felt a shift in their relationship; maybe they could grow something out of the ashes. They had never had a chance before – her mother had always commandeered his time when they were little when he got away from his other family. She had never wanted to share him with his daughters, and he had been only too happy to oblige, but there was definitely an ember and he seemed to want to fan it, asking her to meet him for coffee later in the week. Star had agreed, wanting to see where their relationship could go.

The office was chaos when Star arrived on the Monday morning. Skylar's class had been hosting assembly, so Star had promised her she would attend, which meant she was later into the office than usual.

Star called Mark over to her desk. "What's going on?"

"We have a company meeting on the top floor in half an hour – apparently there is some big announcement. I would have assumed you knew something about it?" he said, but with no malice.

"Nope, this is news to me," Star said, opening her computer and reading the email that had been sent company wide. Lucas was obviously in the building, as the invitation was from him and the rest of the board. Whatever it was they had to announce, it was obviously going to affect the whole company.

The office was alive with conspiracy theories by the time everyone had made their way upstairs. Lucas and the Board had positioned themselves on a platform at the end of the room. Everyone from the office was squashed into every corner. It looked as if the whole company, even those off-site, had returned for whatever was about to be announced.

"Thank you, everyone, for coming. We have an announcement to make, and felt that, to prevent rumours flying, it would be easier to have everyone together in one place," said Brian Fitzpatrick, the Chief Financial Officer and the most staid of all the Board members, speaking into the mic that had obviously been rigged up for the occasion. "I'm going to hand you over to Lucas Hunt, our CEO, who is going to make the announcement."

Lucas stood up, moving forwards, thanking his colleague and accepting the mic.

"Thank you for coming. As Brian said, we wanted to make this announcement with everyone present. As you know, this company has been my life for more years than I care to remember, and we are very much a family." Star's heart stuttered – surely Lucas wasn't going to announce what she thought he was going to announce. She held her breath as he continued: "My health has not been at its best recently. My heart surgery and recovery have taken their toll. I'm fighting fit, however, but this time away has made me re-evaluate things." The floor was silent as Lucas continued to speak. "As it stands, I am stepping down in my role of CEO." The place erupted. Lucas just stood silently waiting for the floor to die down again. "I'm not sure whether that was in celebration or commiseration," he said with a chuckle once he could be heard over the noise.

"Commiseration!" someone shouted from the back, before others joined in, ending with a round of applause for the man who had led the company to success.

Star watched as Lucas swallowed hard. She could see the mistiness in his eyes. She would miss her mentor and friend; the office was not going to be the same without him.

"I will be available for consults," he added,

"but I think my Mary deserves a round-the-world trip and some quality time with her workaholic husband." The floor erupted in applause again, and Star found herself wiping tears from her face. The future was changing.

Lucas held up his hands, calling for order. "I'd like to introduce my replacement as CEO of Hunt and Hunt – my son, Damian Hunt."

Star's heart stopped as she watched Damian appear from one of the side rooms and make his way to his father. Her cheeks flooded with colour and her palms grew clammy. She hadn't seen him for weeks, hadn't heard from him since he'd left, but he was here and taking over his father's position. What about New York? What about his position there?

Lucas returned to his seat as his son took centre stage. Damian's deep tones echoed round the room. "Thank you, everyone. I'm honoured to be here and want to thank the Board for making this transition as smooth as possible. My months working here made me realise that this is my home, and I'm proud to be working with you all in Hunt and Hunt London. We have some big projects in the pipeline, and this is going to be a mammoth year for all of us. I look forward to working with each and every one of you. Thank you."

Star found herself caught up in the swirl of people moving back to the exit and their desks. Her mind was all over the place, so she was shocked when she felt someone grab her arm and pull her sideways into one of the meeting rooms.

Spinning round, she looked up to find Damian staring down at her. "You came back," she murmured.

"I came back," he said. "I needed to sort out a few things, but I realised I couldn't live without you. You are my life, Star, and wherever you and Skylar are, I need to be there. I want to watch her grow up; I want to spend every night with you. I'm miserable without you."

Star felt the tears as they tracked their way down her cheeks, incapable of stopping them, not wanting to. They'd been hidden for too long. "How?"

"I had to go back. I'm sorry, but once I'd made up my mind, I needed to go and sort out the New York office. It was a mess when I got back, but that is something for another time. I didn't want to say anything to you, as I didn't know if I'd be able to keep my promise, but Dad deciding to retire, made the decision a lot easier and the Board was more than happy for me to step into his shoes." Damian smoothed her tears away with his thumb. "I love you, Star, you and Skylar. I want us to be a family."

Star felt her legs give out beneath her, the edges of her vision closing in. Damian was there in an instant, sweeping her up and settling her down in a nearby chair. Lucas entered and rushed over as soon as he saw Star, grabbing a bottle of water from the side table as he went.

"What have you done now?" Lucas said.

"Nothing!" Damian said, concern clear in his voice. "I only told her I wanted us to be a family and she fainted in my arms."

"I'm okay," Star said, smiling at them both. "I kind of skipped breakfast this morning, as Skylar had an assembly, and then with the meeting and everything, I haven't managed to grab anything."

"Take the girl home, or at least out to lunch," Lucas ordered Damian.

"My pleasure," Damian replied, scooping Star up into his arms and heading for the door.

Star smacked his shoulder gently, wiggling until he put her feet on the ground.

"I'm fine. Yes, I'd love to go to lunch, but I'm not having you carry me out of here like a damsel in distress. You can save that for our wedding night. I take it that was a proposal?"

Damian grinned, dropping to his knees in front of her. "Damn straight it was. Star Roberts, will you marry me?"

"A thousand times, yes. I'm never letting you go again," Star said, throwing herself at Damian, who caught her with ease.

Lucas huffed behind them, "Mary is going to be so mad she missed this!"

Chapter Twenty-one

Four Months Later

Star looked at herself in the mirror. Her dress fitted her like a glove, while her hair was loosely curled around her shoulders. Mary stood at her back, gently attaching her veil. Daphne Roberts stood slightly to her side, holding a beautiful diamond necklace in her hands. Star's relationship with her mother had improved over the past couple of months. The coffee Star had had with her father had been a turning point, and Daphne had softened, as if all she had ever needed was for Star's father to take control. And so, Daphne had mellowed overnight, even taking an interest in her granddaughter. There had been lots of tears that day, as her mother hadn't been as immune to Lily's loss as Star had thought. They had shared that pain, albeit seven years late.

Skylar quizzed her grandmother for more stories of Lily every time she saw her, which was now frequently.

Christian had held true to his promise and the Duprees went silently into the background. Christian had taken Skylar to see them after several discussions with both Damian and Star, and according to Skylar, they were wonderful. Star was not so sure she could ever forgive Mr Dupree for his treatment of her sister, but she held her own water whenever Skylar was around. Maybe time and age could mellow even the blackest of hearts. If only Lily had lived to see it.

Daphne fastened the necklace round Star's neck. "Something old," she said. "This belonged to your father's grandmother."

"Something old, done. Something new, my dress," Star said with a smile. "Something borrowed..." Her hand went to the tiara that was holding her hair in place; she'd borrowed it from Laura. "Something blue..." Star gave a shy smile, both mothers aware of the baby-blue underwear she was wearing under her wedding dress.

Skylar burst into the room, her father hot on her heals. "Mummy! You look like a princess. Doesn't she, Daddy."

"She does, angel. Damian is one lucky man," Christian said, kissing Star on the cheek. "Now, Skylar, you make sure you get Mummy to Damian okay – you are playing a very important role today. I've got to go and take my seat."

Skylar rolled her eyes at him. "Of course, Daddy. Hurry up, don't be late!" she said, and pushed him towards the door.

The photographer rushed in, taking some final photos of Star, Skylar, and the mums. This was a time for family. Star looked up at the heavens and sent a loving prayer to her sister before heading to the door, where her father waited to escort her to the love of her life. It was time to make an honest man out of Damian Hunt; this time, she wasn't letting him get away.

Emotion flooded Damian's face as he'd watched Skylar and Star approach him. They'd decided to get married at Lucas and Mary's home. The Manor was big enough and they had set up a marquee in the grounds. They had even arranged for yurts for any of the younger guests who wanted to stay over, while older guests were offered rooms in either the main house or the guest lodges. The house had been overrun with wedding planners and organisers for days, but Mary had taken everything in her stride and had loved the fact she could have a say in how things went. Laura, Toby, and baby Catherine were guests in the house. Laura had gone into labour a couple of days after Damian's return, and baby Catherine Lily Grant had come into the world six hours later. Toby was a goner from the first instant, and Skylar loved being a big cousin. Laura had decided that being a bridesmaid would have been too much with a four-month-old, but had arranged Star's hen party and had done all the things a maid-of-honour would have done.

Walking down the aisle towards Damian, Star's heart soared. She finally felt like she was coming home. It had been a rocky road to get here, but she knew they were stronger for it. When the priest had said for better or worse, they had both looked at each other and shared a smile. Their journey had been far from easy, but now they had each other, it could only get better.

Later, as they took to the floor for their

first dance, Star finally got a chance to look up at her husband and truly absorb the love that shone from his eyes.

"I love you, Mr Hunt," she whispered.

"I love you, Mrs Roberts-Hunt," Damian said, knowing Star loved the fact that she had taken his name, but had kept her own so that Skylar didn't feel like she'd lost something.

As the dance ended, Skylar joined them on the dancefloor, throwing her arms around both their legs. Damian bent down, scooping her into his arms.

"I'm so happy," she said, wrapping her arms around both their necks.

"I'm glad," Damian said, pulling his two favourite girls closer and smiling at her.

"No, *I'm* really happy," Skylar said more forcefully.

"Why's that?" Star asked, looking at her daughter.

Skylar looked at her, as though she were clearly missing the point. "Well, I have two mummies," she said. "Even if one is in heaven, and now I have two of the best daddies."

Skylar squeezed them both tight before squirming out of Damian and Star's arms and running back to Christian, who smiled, before turning his attention to his daughter. Star looked up to see Damian's eyes swim with emotion as he watched their daughter. Resting her hand on his cheek, she captured his gaze, radiating all her love before pulling his mouth to hers. They were a family at last, with their whole future ahead of them.

As their lips touched, a soft breeze brushed through the marquee. Star knew Lily was looking down on them all and smiling.

Afterword

Thank you for reading Star and Damian's story. If you would like to receive a free bonus scene of Star and Damian's first meeting from Damian's POV, then subscribe to my monthly newsletter at www.zoedod.com

If you have enjoyed this book, please leave a review on Amazon. Reviews help indie authors more than you know and encourage Amazon to recommend a book to more readers. It would be greatly appreciated.

Watch out for more in 2023 - both Andrew and Christian have stories coming.

If you want to hear more about my up and coming releases and free bonus material, please subscribe to my monthly newsletter.

About The Author

Zoe Dod

To sign up for Zoe's monthly newsletter; including deleted scenes, alternative POV's and new release information. Please subscribe on her website http://www.zoedod.com

You can also follow Zoe on
Instagram: @zoedod_author
Facebook: Zoe Dod - Author
TikTok: @zoedod_author

Zoe loves to hear from readers. If you would like to drop her an email, you can contact her at zoe@zoedod.com

Zoe lives in The New Forest, England with her husband, two teenagers, and her four rescue cats and dogs.

Before starting her writing career Zoe worked in

the City of London as a Development Manager, before retraining as a primary school teacher. She gave up her teaching career to spend more time with her family and then found a love for writing.

Aside from writing romance, Zoe loves reading, gardening, Zumba classes, and walking her dogs in the New Forest.

Acknowledgement

As someone who has read thousands of books in their lifetime, writing my own has been a dream come true (and a lot harder than I ever anticipated!). I would like to thank all those who have supported and helped me get this far, and made my debut novel possible.

Firstly, I want to thank my amazing husband, Steve. Your unwavering support has pushed me through; from discussing plotlines, to keeping me focused and positive when the pressure was building. Those dog walks through 'The Forest' helped to keep me on track. I couldn't have done this without you. Love you x

To my children: Thank you for listening to me witter on and on about my story. For telling me I'd get there in the end, taking up the slack and cooking dinner when I was trying to get a chapter finished. You are awesome, don't ever change.

To my family; my dad, sister and mother-in-law. You have always stood by me. You have supported and encouraged my dreams, it means more than words can say. Thank you from the bottom of my heart.

To my dear friend Dawn. You may be half a world away but you told me from the start I could do this. Your faith has helped push me through. The Masterclasses you bought for my birthday (to help get me started) and Elsa, so I had no excuses not to stay on track. Thank you, my angel x

To Karen, for all the love, laughter and support over the years. I got there! x

To Jo-Jo, you told me whatever I wrote, you would read. Well, I finished it, it's waiting for you. x

To my co-writers, especially George, who organises us all. You helped to keep me focused and got me over the finishing line. Talking to you ladies has kept me sane. I love you and the conversations we have. See you Wednesday!

To my editor Claire, whose positive comments and feedback gave me the strength and confidence to publish this. You have taught me a lot. Damian is for you. x

Finally, to you, the reader. Thank you for taking a chance on a new author. I hope you enjoyed reading Star and Damian's story as much as I enjoyed writing it.

Printed in Great Britain
by Amazon